CU00863873

FROM THE
SECRET NOOK
TO THE
MOUNTAIN LOG HOUSE

FROM THE
SECRET NOOK
TO THE
MOUNTAIN LOG HOUSE

LIVES FOREVER CHANGED

DOROTHY MURRAY

Library of Congress Control Number:		2020922292
ISBN:	Hardcover	978-1-6641-4180-3
	Softcover	978-1-6641-4181-0
	eBook	978-1-6641-4179-7

Print information available on the last page.

Rev. date: 11/19/2020

To order additional copies of this book, contact:
Xlibris
844-714-8691
www.Xlibris.com
Orders@Xlibris.com
818645

CONTENTS

I owe this to my son, Allan G. Murray, and my daughter, Andrea R. Murray, who gave their support, morally and technically, as I toiled hours to put my thoughts into words.

CHAPTER 1

It Started in The Nook

Savanna begged for mercy at the hands of her adamant kidnapper. A long period of struggle ensued in the secret nook. When he began to ascend the rugged terrain of Deadman's Mountain, holding her in his firm grip, Savanna perceived torture and her imminent death. Amidst her screams and constant struggles to free herself, her kidnapper forcibly pulled her up the rugged mountain path. Savanna wept profusely, knowing that each passing moment had been taking her farther away from her home, her parents, and her adorable siblings.

Most of all, each step she took up the mountain path, Savanna's hopes and dreams of an outlandish wedding with Harry Lovethon, the man of her dreams, had been slowly fading.

Savanna was quickly reminded of one of the golden rules laid down by her parents: "Never talk to strangers." The stranger could be a Red Viper approaching to kidnap his victim. Savanna was further reminded of Melvia's sound advice: "Whenever you hear a vehicle or the voice of someone on the quiet road, hide as securely as you can. Don't allow yourself to be seen." Savanna and her siblings had always followed the rules for their safety, but could it be that she was at a place she shouldn't have been? She'd perceived her little nook by the spring as the most secure place for hiding out with Bentley and subsequently with her soul mate, Harry.

Savanna was no stranger to the gigantic mountain of untrodden paths and its peak nudging the clouds. The mountain stood as a monolithic monument in the midst of the villages around its base. It was a mountain with legendary perceptions of frisky streams cascading over large rocks, crystal-clear springs flowing inside its large caves, and natural crystals forming and un-forming within its caves of spectacular rocks.

No one dared to venture up the mountain's rugged paths for fear of the imminent. The folk below were constantly alerted to the frightening sounds of boulders and rocks tumbling down the mountainside. The obvious cause of the avalanche were animals of the wild scampering across its rocky steep as they roamed around in their habitat. Without evidence of current human existence, the folk perceived the mountain as a place of caves containing bones of animals and prehistoric humans. Tales of the mountain and its likely human inhabitants continued to be legendary until Savanna's kidnapping. Her kidnapper was a testament to human existence on the mountain peak.

Day and night, the folk were constantly alerted to weird sounds up the mountainside. The thought of hauntings on the mountain further contributed to Savanna's mounting fears of what was amiss. As she was dragged up the mountain, Savanna had become broadsided by that which she feared the most: she was entering into the realm of a prehistoric human civilization and her unknown fate.

C H A P T E R   2

Bentley Skaffer

In the minds of the folk of Amerhurst, marriage was a most likely occurrence for the adolescents—and a surety for the young adults. It had therefore become a necessity for the young offspring of Isaack and Melvia Sevensen to learn the facts of life, facts about the birds and the bees. It was essential for the offspring to learn the facts about falling in love, about kissing frogs until they found the man and woman of their dreams. Savanna, the bright shining star of the couple, endeavored to kiss as many frogs until she found her soul mate.

Isaack and Melvia were faced with the tedious task of meeting eye to eye with their curious offspring. The generous grandparents had also played their role, instilling sound wisdom and giving advice that prepared the youngsters for the life ahead.

"Annetta," Grandmother Minerva said, her eyes as sharp as an eagle's, "why were you sitting by the edge of the woods, girl? The boys always hang out in the fields and on the banks of the spring, spying on young girls like you. I was once young, curious, and in love."

At Grandmother Minerva's warning, Annetta pouted as she retreated to her room.

The adolescent offspring were always held under the close scrutiny of Melvia and Isaack. Melvia's pursed lips had always done the job of alerting the youngsters whenever they got out of hand. A pursed lip and straight talk, however, could only be a deterrent to the offspring's naughty behavior if Melvia discovered their wrongdoings.

The Sevensen offspring were fully aware that they were destined for a life of marriage and becoming owners of their own estate. They therefore lived their young lives having the surety that a life of love and happiness was in their future. The young hopefuls faced each day having an ardent desire to meet and marry their soul mates.

Savanna had always been in a quest for answers to her many questions: "What will I really be when I grow up? Will I be married to the man of my dreams? Will I have offspring to care for like my parents?" She'd grown up in the shadows of her parents. She watched them live, love, and care for each other. Savanna watched her parents care for and nurture their offspring. There was a yearning in her heart to grow up and have a happy family, just like her parents.

Throughout her school days, Savanna stood out among her male peers as the charming and womanly schoolmate. Her constant radiant facial glow had always wowed the boys each time she walked by.

"Here she comes," one of her classmates often said to his peer.

Savanna's broad and charming smiles had often exposed her beautifully arranged teeth, which continually played a role in the configuration of her beauty. Savanna's girl peers thought she was beautiful and charming. They'd therefore sought out ways to adopt her characteristic traits as well as her beautiful and compelling smiles.

"Savanna," one of her peers said, "you're certainly beautiful and adorable."

At the comment of one peer, others drew near for closer scrutiny.

That Wednesday afternoon, when Savanna waited by Bentley's locker, at his request, there was no doubt that the young folk were in pursuit of love. They had an ardent desire to belong to each other forever.

Bentley Skaffer lived a short distance around the mountain. He'd always been fascinated by Savanna's radiant smiles and her charming looks. Whether they were in a classroom or in the schoolyard, Bentley had made every effort to be close to her. Savanna's looks had been charming him like a snake under its charmer's wand.

Bentley couldn't resist the addiction to be always in Savanna's presence. He therefore didn't miss the opportunity to sit close to her in the classes they shared together. His feelings for her had become much more than taking a quick glance each time she passed by. He'd become fascinated by her charming looks and had therefore waited for every opportunity to radiate his love toward her.

A golden opportunity finally came when Bentley thought of an excellent idea. Savanna was a day shy of her fifteenth birthday. Bentley hadn't perceived other contenders for her love. He therefore saw his opportunity to make the first move. Like a sly fox, he hung out beside Savanna's locker as he devised a plan of approaching her. Savanna didn't resent seeing Bentley hanging out beside her locker during and after school. She too had been in a quest to find a secret love with whom she could hang out.

On the eve of her birthday, in preparation for her walk home after school, Savanna noticed a note shoved in a crevice of her locker. The note immediately sparked her curiosity. She quickly retrieved the note and carefully opened it to read its contents. Her eyes popped wide open as she read the contents of the note. "Happy Birthday, Savanna! Signed, Bentley. XOXOXO."

Savanna promptly tore the paper on which the note was written. She secretly shoved it toward the bottom of a trash can nearby. Unbeknownst to Savanna, Bentley was secretly observing her actions. What had he been thinking? He'd just witnessed an act of rejection of his kind gesture of love. Bentley immediately rushed home, where he spent his night in turmoil.

Savanna ran all the way home but had pledged to keep Bentley's note a secret. Throughout the long night, she had restless moments, pondering Bentley's expressed love. Savanna waited for the next day, hoping to receive more secret notes from Bentley.

The next morning, upon arriving at school, Savanna noticed another note in a crevice of her locker, just as she'd anticipated. She carefully retrieved the note and eagerly read its contents: "Savanna, you're so beautiful. Happy Birthday. Sweet Fifteen!" It was just a finishing touch to the prior note Bentley had left and another attempt to win her friendship.

Savanna's heart had become overwhelmed with love and a yearning to be close to Bentley. She felt a deep desire for his love and therefore quickly responded to his notes.

In her prompt response, she wrote, "Dear Bentley, thanks for the good wishes on my birthday. I—" Savanna's thoughts went suddenly blank. She had a famine for words and therefore concluded with "Thank you, Bentley. Love, Savanna." She secretly shoved her folded note in a crevice of Bentley's locker before running off to class.

Savanna had no doubt that Bentley had kept the notes he'd left under close surveillance. She also had no doubt that he'd been secretly observing her placing her note in his locker.

It was her first recess of the day. Savanna hid herself from the view of Bentley as she watched him retrieve her note from his locker. He secretly unfolded the note and read its contents with heightened curiosity. Bentley knelt beside his locker before rising once more to his feet. His actions had given Savanna the assurance that her gesture of love had been accepted. She'd therefore remained confident that love had sparked between them.

Savanna's heart was aflame as she secretly observed Bentley's acceptance of her love note. She walked frantically around the school, displaying erratic behavior.

After school, Savanna arrived home in a joyful spirit. Did Melvia and Isaack and their remaining offspring have the slightest suspicion that Savanna was in love? As each day came and went, the entire household began to take note of her unusual behavior.

"What's going with Savanna?" Petror asked. At his young age, he'd also been hoping to find the girl of his dreams. He'd therefore interpreted Savanna's behavior as a young adolescent in love.

Savanna's remaining siblings maintained their silence as they observed her strange and unusual behavior.

Bentley continued to communicate with his new love by way of notes left in conspicuous places agreed on between them. In one of his notes to her, Bentley had specifically requested a meeting after school.

"Savanna, my love," the note read, "I can feel the earth move each time you walk by. Please wait by your locker after school today. XOXOXO. Bentley."

Savanna discreetly retrieved the note and carefully read its contents. She was definitely convinced that Bentley, in fact, had a crush on her. As the note suggested, she waited by her locker after the dismissal bell. As Savanna had hoped, Bentley showed up just in time. As he approached her, Savanna immediately noticed the coyness in his demeanor.

"Are you okay, Bentley?" Savanna asked in a low whisper. Her own bashfulness had been carefully concealed beneath her wide and cheerful smile.

Savanna had never felt love from one of the opposite sex. She'd therefore promptly returned Bentley's eye-piercing look with a charming smile. Meanwhile, her wide eyes continually surveyed the vicinity for any sign of her siblings or her peers who might be secretly observing her interaction with Bentley.

Bentley repeatedly took quick glances behind as if he'd anticipated rivalry of sorts from a secret contender. "I'm okay," Bentley said. He looked at Savanna as love sparkled in his large brown eyes.

Love quickly kindled between the young adolescents. Bentley had developed an addiction to his expression of love by the messages he repeatedly left for Savanna. He'd always wanted to meet her beside her locker after school, whatever the weather. Savanna had also become enchanted by Bentley's secret gestures of love. Love had begun to blossom as the young lovers commenced their brief meetings immediately after school and at venues around the vicinity.

To facilitate their frequent meetings, the new lovers built a nook by the bank of the spring. They made an enclosure of tree branches and withes, safely hidden beneath shrubs and the branches of small trees. The softly flowing streams of the spring drowned out the sound of their voices whenever they met in the nook. The secluded nook had securely hidden them from the view of whoever should venture in the vicinity.

Savanna had kept Bentley's last note containing instructions for their first meeting in the nook. After school on Friday, they quietly snuck across the field to get to their secret venue. Savanna was no stranger to the spring by the foot of the mountain. She and her siblings had often strolled among the thick tall grass to bathe in its crystal streams, certainly not near the little nook she and Bentley made beneath the tree branches.

It was their first meeting in the nook. Bentley's round face had become moistened by the perspiration of excitement. He'd never before gotten that close to a girl. As the perspiration oozed down his cheeks and soaked his brow, Bentley repeatedly wiped his wet and oily face with the palm of his hands.

Savanna's demeanor had suddenly changed. She sat on the leaf-covered ground as one who'd been aroused by a sudden surge of consciousness. Bentley's sharp piercing eyes were focused on the bank of the spring while his heart panted for the love and affection of his newfound friend. Bentley took deep breaths as he sat cuddled by Savanna's side. Savanna was enjoying every moment of their warm embrace.

"Savanna, you're beautiful. You're the apple of my eye," Bentley said with an assuring look of love in his eyes.

Savanna had been flabbergasted by Bentley's enticing words of love. "Bentley, you're a charming boy. My thoughts of you have taken my breath away," Savanna said. Her eyes had been slowly drowning in her own tears.

The young lovers continually exchanged looks of love. They shed tears of joy as they remained in each other's embrace.

"Savanna, each time we meet, the sun shines brighter," Bentley assured his sobbing friend. "We'll be in love forever."

The evening breeze gently rustled the leaves of the trees around the nook as the young lovers remained comfortably seated on the ground covered with dry leaves and withes. The young lovers had been enjoying the warmth of each other's embrace while they sat in the comfort of the nook. It suddenly crossed Savanna's mind that she'd missed her curfew.

With a sense of urgency, she rose to her feet. It was an unexpected interruption of what had been her most comforting moment.

"Sorry, Bentley," Savanna said. "I have to be home for dinner." She quickly brushed dry leaves from her skirt. Savanna quickly exited the nook and darted across the field.

Realizing that he too had missed his curfew, Bentley followed suit. He rushed along the quiet road leading to his home.

Savanna had developed a liking for the things of nature. In her quest to find strange creatures and exotic plants, she habitually spent her spare time exploring the farm and the edge of the field along the foot of the mountain. Her absence—and tardiness, therefore—hadn't raised suspicions among her household. Her frequent strolls were perceived as nature walks and a sentimental love affair with the outdoors. Lately, under the guise of exploring the outdoors, particularly by the edge of the woods at the foot of the mountain, she'd been meeting with Bentley Skaffer.

No one noticed each time Bentley snuck into the woods and entered the nook he'd made by the bank of the spring. Unbeknownst to his parents, he'd been meeting with the girl who lived a short distance around the mountain.

With each passing day, Savanna's love for Bentley began to reach new heights. The young lovers continually yearned to be in each other's presence. While school was out, they communicated by way of intriguing notes scribbled on the leaves of tree branches overhanging the nook. They'd scribbled notes to each other stating the day and the time they would meet in their secret nook.

The two lovers had begun to have strange awakenings each time they met in their secret hideout. Whenever Savanna tried to read the notes Bentley had written on the leaves, she noticed that parts of the leaves had been missing, along with parts of his notes. Likewise, Bentley realized that parts of the notes Savanna had left on the leaves had been torn off. The leaves were torn as if someone had deliberately removed certain words so that they were unable to read the messages left.

"Savanna, my lov—" A part of the leaf had been torn and removed, along with the remaining part of the sentence. Bentley had often read the notes in disgust.

"Who could have done this to our notes?" Bentley asked. He'd become puzzled and angered by the suspicious acts but knew not where to look for answers.

"We're in the woods, Bentley," Savanna said. "Creatures of the wild—grasshoppers, bats, or crickets—could have eaten parts of the leaves." In her young mind, she'd perceived insects eating away at the leaves to catch a meal.

Bentley nonetheless had a different perception. "Savanna," Bentley said, "the leaves are being carefully and intelligently torn so that only parts of our notes remain."

Bentley continued to ponder the torn leaves and the culprit who'd been deliberately destroying the notes. He'd pledged to find the culprit—whatever it took.

Each day came and left. Savanna ardently sought the love and embrace of Bentley. There hadn't been the slightest suspicion among Savanna's siblings that the boy they'd often seen loitering around her locker had a crush on her.

In the high season of her love and obsession with Bentley, Savanna had not informed Melvia and Isaack of the boy who'd been charming her in secret. The secret courtship had also been concealed from her siblings, to whom she'd been so closely attached.

Savanna's secret meetings with Bentley Skaffer began to raise suspicions among her school peers. News of her love affair quickly spread when their frequent meetings beside her locker became obvious. The boy who always wore the round yellow cap had been secretly observing the frequent exchange of notes the two had been leaving in each other's locker. It was a clear indication that there was a secret love affair between them.

A cloud of suspicion and ensuing rumors hung over the school environment. There'd been no end to the gossip that had quickly spread among Savanna's curious school peers. As the rumors spread, Bentley was quick to abandon his love affair that was no longer a secret.

He'd developed cold feet. Bentley immediately ceased leaving notes in Savanna's locker. He'd reneged on his last promise to meet her in the nook after school that Friday. He'd ignored the last note Savanna left in his locker, reminding him of their upcoming meeting in the nook.

Knowledge of Savanna's love affair with Bentley began to spark curiosity among her siblings of inquisitive minds. There'd been speculations and gossip beyond measure.

"There'll be a child bride in our household," Gorrana whispered among her curious siblings.

"Savanna has found her soul mate at fifteen," Arretha whispered in response.

"Will there be wedding bells? Will Savanna find herself locked in the loving arms of Bentley forever?" Petror said.

The siblings chuckled in unison. Savanna had made every effort to ignore the gossips.

The rumor soon reached Melvia and Isaack, who weren't too keen on hearing of Savanna's love affair at her tender age. The concerned couple, along with Savanna and her siblings, met in the big hall. They were united in one accord—to get to the bottom of the rumor.

Melvia eagerly waited to obtain the facts from her little angel. She therefore commenced the meeting by first permitting Savanna to speak. "Savanna," Melvia said, "tell us about Bentley Skaffer. Is your love affair just a rumor?"

Savanna looked bashfully around the hall. She'd been bombarded by the eye-piercing looks of Isaack and her curious siblings. All eyes met with eager curiosity as Savanna sat poised to speak.

"Bentley and I were madly in love," she said.

The hall was suddenly hushed. Everyone waited with curious expectation of hearing the ensuing details.

"Are you no longer in love?" Melvia asked.

The hall was once more hushed as all sat poised to hear further details of Savanna's love affair with Bentley.

"We're no longer together," Savanna said, "but I still love him." The trauma that resulted from their separation had kept the tears cascading down her face.

"Your love affair with Bentley is mere puppy love," Melvia said. "You're much too young to assume the responsibilities of genuine love and marriage. There's a world of opportunities, including your required education, which you must pursue."

Savanna wept as she pondered Melvia's sound advice and words of wisdom.

Isaack listened with keen interest until it was his turn to address the issue. "Savanna, you're still at an age of innocence," Isaack said. "Bentley is also just a young lad who lacks the ability to take on the responsibilities of caring for a family."

New tears flooded Savanna's eyes as Isaack spoke. Meanwhile, her siblings nodded in approval of Isaack's words of sound wisdom.

"It's okay to be childhood friends," Melvia said. "Once you become mature adolescents or attain adulthood, you can make decisions about marrying and raising a family."

"I believe we should meet with Bentley and his parents," Isaack said. "The young lad needs to know that it's okay to be in childhood friendship with a girl."

A ray of hope shone on Savanna's face as her parents gave their sound advice.

Melvia once more waited her turn to address Savanna and her remaining young offspring. "It's okay to be friends," Melvia reiterated, "without engaging in the 'birds and the bees' stuff."

Isaack and the remaining offspring nodded in unison.

As head of his household, Isaack felt he should speak the final word on the issue, and that, he proudly did. "We'll get together with Bentley and his parents for a friendly talk," Isaack said. With this statement, he duly rested his case.

The issue of friendship had become much clearer to their anxious offspring when Melvia and Isaack explained in detail love, marriage, and raising a family. The long meeting was finally adjourned. Savanna sobbed profusely as she left the hall. She'd been lamenting the fact that Bentley had shied away from their love affair.

The next school day, life had returned to normal for Bentley and Savanna. The gossip had not dissipated, but it certainly brought an end to the exchange of notes left in their locker. Although the sparkles of love had dissipated from Bentley's eyes, Savanna's radiant smiles and her sparkles of love continued to emanate toward him whenever they crossed paths.

Each day, as Savanna's young broken heart yearned for her lost love, tears persistently flowed down her cheeks. She'd become brokenhearted at her love affair that had ended so abruptly. Whether they would become soul mates in their later years, it would all be left to time.

When Savanna met Bentley Skaffer, she'd quickly perceived him as a promising childhood sweetheart. She had great expectations that their love affair would blossom and that marriage would ensue. Her youthfulness, however, had obscured her perception of love and belonging.

Nonetheless, she'd pledged to remain in pursuit of love and maintain that ardent yearning in her heart to belong. Savanna continued to perceive a future of love and marriage to the man of her dreams. She'd therefore remained hopeful that someday she would be a beautiful June bride.

The nook on the bank of the spring at the foot of the mountain had been left abandoned, while its existence remained a secret.

CHAPTER 3

The Young Savanna

Of the twelve babies born to Melvia and Isaack Sevensen, Savanna was the child who stood out, first and foremost. On that bright Wednesday afternoon when she was born, she was adored as the bright star of the Sevensen household. In the eyes of the young couple, Savanna emerged as a child displaying outstanding beauty and adorable charm.

Melvia and Isaack had given much significance to the birth of their seventh child. Throughout her toddler years, no other child born in the household attracted more attention. The couple's other newborns were just as adorable, but Savanna was remarkably unique. What made Savanna stand out among the rest? What was she going to become? These were questions raised in the minds of her proud parents as well as her grandparents of sound wisdom.

As she grew into adolescence, Savanna began to portray certain features of Melvia: high cheekbones and a firm and strong physique, though small in stature. She was just a notch below the average height and size of her girl siblings. Her beauty and charm were further enhanced when she gradually changed into her permanent set of teeth.

Time passed at a rapid pace. Savanna and her siblings followed on the heels of one another in age and size. Her taller and elder, as well as smaller and younger siblings always admired her height and stature.

Her short and petite figure had placed her among the younger siblings. Amidst kind and friendly gestures, her younger siblings had often made friendly comparisons.

"Savanna, I can look over your head while standing straight," Arretha said.

Savanna didn't resent the fact that she'd attained a mere average height.

Melvia and Isaack began to perceive a world of possibilities for their offspring, particularly Savanna. Her name had spoken volumes. At her tender age, Savanna's charisma had begun to shine forth. She'd become everything to everyone around her. Her siblings had persistently followed in her footsteps in their effort to adopt her charismatic qualities. The thought that her youth would fade as she grew older kept everyone adoring her beauty as each day emerged.

Young Savanna had always been in relentless pursuit of perfection. Hard work and a determination to succeed had predisposed her to an independent mind and self-motivation. As a young emerging Sevensen offspring, Savanna was a perfectionist who was not bent on outdoing others but on being the best at whatever she did. She had a strong determination to succeed in all her endeavors. While she continually strove forward, Savanna began to exhibit her charismatic characteristics among her siblings as well as her peers.

Melvia and Isaack had often pondered Savanna's talents and her eagerness to serve in a motherhood role in the household. In their perception, their adorable offspring had the ability for goodness and a capacity for greatness. As time passed, the couple waited to discover what the future held for their unusually talented offspring. They dared not imagine their household without her. The couple's remaining offspring couldn't imagine a day without their most influential sibling. She was perceived as a symbol of strength and courage. Her graceful charm and sharp wits had begun to fascinate the entire household.

Savanna had learned at an early age that life as a young girl on the Sevensen estate meant hard work. As a member of a large household, she'd taken on that which she perceived to be her responsibilities, assuming household chores and working alongside Melvia to care for and nurture her younger siblings, a motherhood role she eagerly assumed.

In the absence of Melvia and Isaack, Savanna led her siblings to assume the roles of big sisters and big brothers to one another. The young Sevensens understood that each had a role to play to maintain a well-structured household. They therefore didn't resent the fact that Savanna had been co-parenting with Melvia and Isaack. The couple welcomed the much-needed assistance attending to the needs of their younger offspring. The young offspring also had no objection to the fact that some of their instructions were taken from Savanna, their young motherly sibling.

"Gorrana, it's time for bed," Savanna often said.

Without further ado or resentment, Gorrana walked into her room, followed by her younger siblings.

Young Savanna had striven to work hard to see her siblings become successful achievers, but Isaack and Melvia held the beacon of hope for the bright future of their beautiful daughters as well as their fine sons. With Melvia's guidance and Isaack's straight talk, the youngsters strived to acquire sound wisdom that would direct their future paths.

The years swiftly came and left, taking away the youth of the couple's amazing offspring. They gradually entered the age of adolescence and moved on to adulthood. The offspring looked forward to achieving their goals as well as realizing their lifetime dreams—to get married and become owners of their estates.

As another new year appeared, the young Sevensens knew there was a life of love and good fortune ahead of them. They therefore remained in total readiness for their life ahead. Savanna was a budding youth and a picture of health. Her slender waist was put on full display each time she posed in her self-designed garments and nail-spiked high-heeled shoes, and like her elder siblings, each day, her heart yearned to find the man of her dreams.

Savanna spent her young life juggling her education in her quest to find a future career and preparing to meet her soul mate. She had an aptitude for writing amusing stories and had always been surrounded by her siblings of inquisitive minds. With her creative mind, she wrote intriguing stories for her siblings, young and old. Her short stories were instrumental in stimulating learning in the minds of her enthusiastic siblings.

At the end of a long day performing their chores, Isaack and Melvia took pleasure in joining the cheerful children to get in on the latest and most exciting stories written by Savanna. The big hall had become the venue for reading her stories. The household assembled in the hall as they waited for another session of fun and laughter. With her cheerful looks and a charming smile, Savanna waited to read her newest and most fascinating stories.

"It's time for a story!" her siblings often announced.

The curious siblings anxiously waited for another exciting session of storytelling with Savanna. Meanwhile, she'd kept busy dotting her *i*'s and crossing her *t*'s in preparation for her next story session. The moment for which everyone waited had finally arrived when Savanna stood poised to read her most recent story. All ears were perked up like those of a pack of hunting foxes when she commenced reading about the young lion that chased the big elephant, a giant of the jungle.

"The young lion chased the giant elephant and captured it at the bottom of the cliff. After the lion captured and killed the elephant, all the hungry lions of the jungle gathered to have a feast," Savanna read.

There were giggles all around the large hall, not only for the fact that the elephant was taken down by the young lion but because Savanna's story had staggered the imagination of her young and curious audience. The younger siblings pondered how a young lion could have chased down and captured a large elephant.

"How could this be?" Perry asked.

For such a fascinating story, no other sibling questioned the possibility of a small lion chasing and capturing a large elephant.

"And the elk ran off with the big old lion in its antlers," Savanna continued to read.

When she told the story of the elk running off with the big old lion in its antlers as the lion was too old to even try to catch the elk for a quick meal, the children became ecstatic. Isaack and Melvia took the excitement to a higher level when they commenced their loud laughter, adding to the children's high spirit.

Each thrilling story was instrumental in igniting the thoughts, minds, and senses of not only Savanna's household but also of the students she'd subsequently taught in the local school. With Savanna's great wits and charisma, the art of writing stories had not evaded her interest. She continued to write amusing and entertaining stories as long as she was challenged to write whatever entered her thoughts.

Just like Cecelia, her elder sibling, Savanna continually wrestled with her insatiable desire to succeed. She'd set out to become an accomplished teacher. At the same time, her heart yearned to become a beautiful wife to the husband of her dreams. Each passing day, Savanna continued to ride on the wings of hope that her dreams would become reality.

Like her elder siblings, Savanna stood poised to enter young adulthood. Throughout her tender adolescent years, her beautiful siblings as well as other fine young ladies of Amerhurst, perceived her as a female prodigy and a symbol of beauty and elegance.

Now a young schoolteacher, Savanna worked hard to juggle a teaching career and mentor her siblings, at the same time maintaining high hopes that she would someday become a beautiful June bride.

CHAPTER 4

The Barn Dances

Isaack and Melvia could not ignore the swift passing of time. Another of the couple's fine offspring had just entered the age of adulthood. The couple had been forced to face the reality that there were no toddlers and young children remaining in their household. Over several years, they endured the painful process of watching their adorable offspring rapidly growing up. They'd become broadsided by one of the realities of life: their once cuddly newborns had grown up. Melvia had been gradually freed from her young life of devotion to the constant care of her toddlers. For her and Isaack, their child-rearing era had ended.

The couple soon realized that time had also been taking its toll on their youthfulness. After her many years of devotion to caring for and nurturing her offspring, Melvia realized that she needed much care and nurturing from Isaack. He'd given her the assurance that he was always there for her. Melvia reciprocated with her assurance of love and care for him. With the toddlers off their laps, the couple's life of romance was quickly rejuvenating. They could once more rekindle their love for each other. Melvia maintained close bonding with her offspring but realized that it was equally important to maintain her matrimonial bonding with Isaack.

The local barn dances continued during their child-rearing years while they were preoccupied with attending to their ever-extending family. Years had passed since the couple attended their last barn dance. The fun and excitement they'd had at previous barn dances had lingered in their memory. On the other side of the mountain, the Meldissens had always extended an invitation to the folk of neighboring estates to attend their frequent barn dances. How Melvia and Isaack wished they were in attendance!

As opportunities once more began to knock at their door, the couple felt that it was time to step out into the evening air for a time of fun and amusement. They'd once more resumed their life of pleasure. Melvia revisited the adorable pairs of dancing shoes, her elegant dresses, and the fine complementary jewelry stacked away in her wardrobe. Surprisingly, her elegant dresses were still a perfect fit. Child-rearing did not alter her adorable figure. Isaack's Sunday-best garments had remained in his wardrobe while he toiled to maintain his household.

Melvia had been clinging desperately to her youthful looks. Her beauty and charm had also remained intact. She'd always complied with the beauty tips given by her adorable and youthful girls. The flames of love had been vibrantly ignited between Melvia and Isaack as they clung desperately to their revived existence. As Melvia revisited her wardrobe of elegant outfits, she displayed her glamor and poise before Isaack, jogging his memory of their good times.

"Isaack, do you recall our most wonderful day?" Melvia said as she paraded around the room in her elegant wedding dress.

In admiration of Melvia's adorable charm, Isaack smiled from cheek to cheek. "Melvia, let's pretend it was our wedding day." Isaack promptly planted his best kiss on Melvia's lips.

The couple had been reliving the beginning of their lives as man and wife. Child-rearing had put a long hold on their evening pleasures, but their former days of fun and excitement had once more entered into the limelight.

The couple began making preparations for their first barn dance. They were fully aware they'd lost their dance steps and therefore began to brush up on every movement. Melvia had still maintained her dance techniques, but to be assured that she was ready for the dance floor, she'd resumed practicing her steps with Isaack. It was doubtful whether Isaack still had his elaborate dance moves—the ability to swing, step, and turn with his partner. He'd been careful not to step onto the dance floor, dancing as one having two left feet. He was also careful not to embarrass Melvia, particularly on their first night out. Isaack had gotten off to a good start, practicing his steps in preparation for the first dance.

The beautiful flower garden was the venue where the couple spent time practicing and perfecting every dance step. Melvia had often been busy carrying out her daily chores. Nonetheless, Isaack stepped out into the garden to perfect his dancing skills. He practiced his dance steps by holding onto a branch heavily laden with brilliant flowers. Isaack practiced his elegant moves, perceiving the branch as his partner in the dance. His younger offspring had always been amusingly entertained as they admired their father making careful steps, left and right, and turning around, holding onto the branch.

The evening of the couple's first big event had finally arrived. Melvia was certain to look her best for the occasion. For promenading and dancing with Isaack, she'd set aside the shoes with heels designed for that occasion. Savanna carefully scrutinized Melvia's elegant dresses, particularly the ones she'd proudly designed and made for her. She further instructed Melvia on girding her waist to coordinate with her beautiful spike-heeled shoes.

Savanna and her siblings, who'd had a flair for fine jewelry, chose earrings that coordinated well with Melvia's adorable garments. It was unfortunate that Melvia would be forced to remove the clip-on earrings when her earlobes developed painful blisters. In preparation for her evening out, Savanna and the older girls gave a modern touch to Melvia's hairstyle. The eager offspring braided her hair in the most contemporary style.

The proud Isaack, dressed to the T, stood in front of the long thick mirror in the entrance to the large family room. He closely admired his physique as well as his noble looks. He turned in every direction to admire his spiffy gray suit, complemented by his fancy shoes. To complement their evening attire, Melvia cut the best and brightest rose from the garden. She carefully placed it in Isaack's lapel. The older Sevensen boys gave the finishing touches to their father's meticulously designed suit. They'd also given him the assurance of his noble appearance.

Under the close scrutiny of their cheering offspring, the couple stepped out into the crisp evening air, displaying their elegance and charm.

"How do we look, Sav?" Melvia asked Savanna, knowing well she was the designer and the one most likely to give her honest opinion.

"You and Dad look fabulous and in love," Savanna said.

Her siblings added the finishing comments to Savanna's assuring opinion.

"You're the lord and the lady of Amerhurst," Petror added as the couple politely bowed.

The offspring watched Isaack and Melvia step onto the quiet road. The couple climbed gently into their horse-drawn carriage and departed. They were on their way to an evening of fine entertainment. What a perfect image the couple had been displaying before their youngsters, who were poised to become lords and ladies of their estates!

Melvia and Isaack were proud parents of their glamorous young ladies and fine gentlemen. The couple had therefore made every effort to see them attain their goals. Adolescence and young adulthood were crucial stages in the young lives of the Sevensen offspring. At their early age of adulthood, it was time to anticipate meeting their future wives and husbands and making wedding plans.

With a household of young and promising offspring, Melvia and Isaack had laid the groundwork, educating them on the facts of life, the "birds and the bees" stuff. Their offspring were further educated on the likely act of kissing frogs until they found their soul mates. Savanna had remained assured that her big day would come. She'd therefore continued to hope and dream about her tomorrows.

Time was swiftly passing by. Seasons came and went while the fine young Sevensen ladies and gentlemen remained on high alert for signs of love from the young folk on other estates. To facilitate their interaction with hopefuls from far and near, Savanna and her siblings organized dances in the big barn. Melvia and Isaack happily welcomed the barn dances and other entertainment events, with the hope that wedding bells would begin to peal for their offspring. The young folk were certain to brush up on their good mannerisms and quickly rid themselves of those that weren't proper. They'd pledged to put Melvia and Isaack's good grooming and pruning on full display at all times.

Barn dances gave the folk of Amerhurst an opportunity to meet new friends and to get up close and personal, with the hope that frequent interaction and socialization would spark attraction. The barn dances were the venues for meeting and mingling with many hopefuls, with the hope that someday wedding bells would peal for all. In preparation for the first barn dance, the fine young Sevensen ladies and gentlemen stood poised to show off their glamor as they put their finest creations on display.

The young ladies displayed beauty and adorable charm in their elegant dresses, designer jewelry, and fine shoes. The young Sevensen girls had not only become great fashion designers. They were also early adopters of the newest and finest fashions they'd created. Savanna guided her siblings in elegant fashion designs that enabled them to become models walking on their own runways. There were garments made from the finest cotton, linen, and silk from faraway countries, taffeta and well sought-after fine laces used to meticulously design elegant dresses.

The young men were quite conscious of their charming looks. They therefore displayed their elegant evening wear, suits with trousers seams as thin as a blade. Young men who hadn't learned the skill of tailoring their own garments, engaged tailors of Amerhurst to make their fine suits. Petror had kept busy tailoring fine men's wear for the occasion. In preparation to be scrutinized by the elegant young ladies, the young men strived to look their best and put their good upbringing on full display.

The young Sevensen ladies showed off their bulky curls, neatly placed on their forehead. Large thick curls flowed gracefully on their shoulders, landing neatly on the napes of their necks. The beautiful ladies placed much emphasis on their hair. A fluffy head of hair was

coveted by each of the fine young ladies. They sincerely felt that their
beauty was embedded in the hair on their heads. The hair therefore had
become the focal point on every adorned young lady.

The adorable clip-on earrings complemented the ladies' elegant
evening wear. The earrings, however, had always become a menace to
the young ladies' earlobes. The gorgeously designed earrings had ceased
to be complementary to the ladies' garments when they were forced to
remove them during the dance. The fine earrings inflicted blistering
bubbles on the ladies' earlobes. The ladies who'd insisted on wearing
their earrings throughout the event were forced to cope with swollen
and blistered earlobes.

It was the eve of the first Saturday evening barn dance on the
Sevensen estate. The atmosphere had become charged with anxiety.
Melvia and Isaack as well as the entire household busied themselves to
prepare the venue. Folk who'd been talented in preparing savory meals
got together to prepare the menu for the occasion. There were roasts,
barbeques, bakes, and foods cultivated in the Sevensens' as well as the
neighboring gardens. Other exotic items for the menu were purchased
in Bragerston. In preparation for the festivities, the gas lanterns were
polished to maintain their brilliant glow around the venue. The shades
of the lamps located in every room of the Sevensen house and in the
big barn, were cleaned and their oil replenished.

The day of the dance finally arrived. After a day of brilliant
sunshine, the golden sun gradually sank over the horizon. Evening
shadows began to fall, setting the atmosphere for an evening of great
entertainment. The Saturday evening atmosphere around the Sevensen
estate had begun to teem with activities. Skillful musicians fine-tuned
their instruments in preparation for the commencement of the dance.
Isaack and Melvia remained behind the scene, adding the finishing
touches to the menu. They soon retreated, leaving the young folk to
dine and mingle.

Under the early dusk, the young guests began to arrive. Elegant
ladies and fine gentlemen stepped out into the evening air that was
charged with hope, love, and great expectation. The offspring from
wealthy estates arrived in their glitzy carriages. Automobiles from the

wealthiest estates appeared among the carriages. Many beautiful ladies and charming young men arrived on horseback. Ladies of neighboring places, who hadn't been privileged to be transported, made every effort to gain ground as they walked to the venue in their spike-heeled shoes. The ladies' anxiety and effort were at times, impeded by shoes with heels that were a bit too tall for the short walk to the dance venue.

The hopeful Sevensen young ladies made their way to the dance. Their elegance and adorable charm were on full display as they streamed into the venue. Likewise, the fine Sevensen gentlemen stepped out into the crisp evening air, having great expectations to meet the elegant ladies of their dreams.

Adorable ladies were adorned in their most beautiful attire, each having a touch of elegance. With their slender waistlines and long beautiful legs, partially covered by knee-length skirts, the meticulously adorned ladies made their way into the dance venue. They arrived with the expectation of meeting and mingling with fine gentlemen.

In the big barn house, Savanna and her siblings prepared for the arrival of the guests. Victoria was delegated the duty of greeting the young guests, a responsibility she'd delightfully accepted. She politely welcomed each guest, pointing them in the direction of the dance floor;

"Hello and welcome to the dance! Go that way, miss. Walk this way, sir." Victoria didn't miss out on the opportunity to scrutinize the ladies' elegant dresses and their adorable shoes.

The atmosphere had become charged with ecstasy as arriving folk made themselves comfortable. They waited in hope and with anxious anticipation. The hopeful young ladies as well as the fine gentlemen placed themselves in conspicuous locations where they were sure to attract the most attention.

Elegance, beauty, and charm were on full display as Savanna and her siblings paraded around the venue. Young lovers who'd already met their soul mates paraded past the elated crowd as if they were setting the stage for what lay ahead for the many hopeful ladies and gentlemen. The young flamboyant bachelors flaunted their flare as they walked ostentatiously by the promising young ladies.

Cecelia stepped out into the pleasant evening air, adorned in her blue elegant taffeta dress. Her garment was meticulously designed by her, with the assistance of Savanna. Cecelia was the most eligible bachelorette of the Sevensen household. She'd been anticipating leaving Amerhurst to attend nursing school. Nonetheless, Cecelia had striven to look her best for the barn dance. By a stroke of good luck, she could meet her prospective soul mate during the dance.

In the suspenseful atmosphere, the guests conversed incessantly. There were secret glances and exchange of smiles between young hopefuls who'd attended the dance to try their luck at love. School sweethearts and secret lovers had the opportunity to hang out together, taking advantage of the opportunity to get up close and personal with one another. The atmosphere was charged with gossip as secret lovers were spotted exchanging smiles and the occasional bashful kiss.

Savanna wished Bentley was a bit more mature at the time she met him. Had they not separated, Bentley would have been her date. She reminisced on the secret nook at the foot of the mountain where they'd often met for a time of warm embraces and frequent kisses.

The well-anticipated interactions between the fine gentlemen and the beautiful ladies took on momentum. The young folk put their good parental upbringing on display in an effort to leave a lasting impression on their prospective partners. Throughout the event, there were frequent winks and smiles from passersby or from the flamboyant gentleman seated alone by the side of the dance floor.

The most eventful night advanced. Young gentlemen were quick to demonstrate how well they could care for the beautiful ladies they'd chosen for the night. They proudly put their good mannerisms and sound etiquette on display, serving their partners refreshing cocktails, tea, and the general meal on the night's menu. The young Sevensens paraded among the guests in a spirit of kind hospitality. Their glamor and good parental upbringing were on full display before the scrutinizing guests.

Thrilling episodes of events kept the guests entertained. To spice up the event, talented young ladies and gentlemen stepped on-stage to perform, at the same time putting their elegance and charm on display, not to ignore the fact that they were advertising their availability. The men had become overnight impromptu actors, as did the ladies. Savanna didn't miss her opportunity to shine. She proudly made her debut by reading one of her short stories to the cheerful audience.

Young folk mingled during the dance, knowing quite well that it was their opportunity to shine. When the band commenced playing waltz music, young lovers got close and comfortable with each other. In the pre-midnight hour, the waltz music gave the folk an opportunity to once more get up close for a soft embrace before the event crawled to an end. Savanna and her siblings as well as other young hopefuls who hadn't been successful in attracting a mate, left with bittersweet tears, but they remained hopeful that love would spark each time they would attend future barn dances.

Subsequent barn dances kept the flames of hope alive. Love continued to spark among the young hopefuls. Rumors and gossip had been continually stirred up, while wedding bells pealed for another lucky young couple. Savanna and her siblings remained hopeful that soon, they would be among the lucky ones for whom wedding bells would peal.

C H A P T E R 5

Victoria's Wedding

Savanna sat on a wooden bench beneath the branches of the tree by the side of her home. From the comfort of the bench, she watched the brilliant rays of the midday sun beaming down from the mountain peak. In that serene atmosphere, she replenished her thoughts with dreams of someday being married to the man of her dreams.

At their offspring's tender age, Melvia and Isaack had taught them some hard facts of life, facts about growing up and entering young adulthood. There would be a time when they would become wives and husbands. The beautiful girls would be kissing frogs until they found the man of their dreams. Likewise, the boys would be among the frogs kissed until they found the lady their heart desires. There would be a time to be the beautiful June bride and the handsome bridegroom. Time would appear to move slowly while their young minds became impatient and restless. The couple encouraged their offspring to be patient as that special day would come for all.

The small stone church at the foot of the mountain stood within close proximity to the Sevensen home. The church had become a revolving door to young couples taking their vows of marriage within its walls. Hopeful adolescents and young adults anxiously waited for the moment when they would walk the aisle to take their marriage vows.

It wasn't long before Melvia and Isaack realized that their first offspring would be walking down the aisle. The household had been making preparations for Victoria's wedding. When Victoria officially introduced Aldbright to Melvia and Isaack, her siblings were reminded of the encouraging words of their parents; hence, patience had become a virtue for the hopefuls.

Victoria met her soul mate, Aldbright Scoullion, during their early teen years. The young lovers had become inseparable. As love sparked between them, the barn dances offered further opportunities to get up close and bonded. They gradually solidified their friendship and were assured that they'd found their soul mate. Their decision had been signed, sealed, and delivered when Aldbright made his marriage proposal on the tranquility bench by the side of the pond.

Victoria had been quite certain she was ready to wed Aldbright, but her siblings as well as her peers felt she was still too young for marriage.

"Victoria, you should not be bonded at such an early age," Arretha said.

Victoria, however, begged to disagree. She was quite certain her ship had come ashore. Melvia and Isaack had remained indecisive of Victoria and Aldbright's marriage proposal. At nineteen, Victoria was still one of "Mom's little angels" who hadn't known much about what it entails being a married woman, except the facts of life she'd received from Melvia and Isaack and her grandparents of sound wisdom.

As they were faced with an upcoming wedding, Melvia and Isaack scheduled a series of meetings with Marton and Josceline Scoullion, Aldbright's parents. Victoria was a young lady of adorable beauty and graceful charm. The Sevensens nonetheless had their doubts about whether she would be readily accepted as the girl suited to marry the Scoullions' son.

Traditionally, a proposed marriage could only be finalized after the families of the bride-to-be and the groom-to-be, held a series of heated debates. As the marriage would unite the families, those who would become in-laws, ensuing debates ascertained that there were no opposing views. Melvia and Isaack had no intent on objecting to the marriage. The series of meetings were designed to be a test of strengths and decisiveness of the young future couple as well as the future in-laws. The first meeting gradually took on momentum in the Sevensens' big hall. The curious Sevensen offspring waited at conspicuous listening posts around the venue.

Being head of his household, Marton made the opening statement. "Mr. and Mrs. Sevensen, I have no doubt that Aldbright and Victoria will make a good couple," Marton said in strong defense of his son's choice. "Seems to me and Josceline that it will be a marriage of true affection." Marton felt confident about the Sevensen family and therefore looked forward to joining union with them.

Josceline further sealed Marton's acceptance of the marriage proposal. "I wouldn't stand in the way of the young folk getting married," Josceline said. "They're old enough to make decisions about love and marriage and their lives ahead. I strongly believe that Aldbright, at twenty-one, is quite capable of caring for a wife and the children who will follow," Josceline further acclaimed.

Marton further sealed his approval with a vigorous nod and a smile. Melvia and Isaack were quite certain that Victoria had made a sound decision when she accepted Aldbright's offer of marriage. Nonetheless, Melvia spoke with that wait-and-see attitude.

"If the young folk err in their decision, they must subsequently face the consequences," Melvia said. "Before the wedding date is set, the young folk will solidify their wishes to be married or have a change of heart."

Isaack begged to disagree. "Melvia, young folk never change their minds," Isaack said assuredly. "They often have a mindset once they make their decision. If the young folk do change their minds, it's often much too late."

At Victoria's tender age of nineteen, Melvia as well as her remaining offspring maintained their strong belief that she was much too young for marriage. Isaack, however, appeared nonchalant about the young folk's decision. Melvia felt that she'd given her point of view. She therefore promptly gestured to Isaack to give his independent opinion on the future couple's marriage proposal.

"If the young folk can live happily together, they've made their decision to get married," Isaack said. "Victoria is quite capable of deciding her own destiny."

Melvia and Isaack continued their ifs and buts about the marriage proposal.

"Victoria is still Dad's and Mom's little angel," Melvia said. Tears slowly trickled from her eyes.

Isaack promptly refuted Melvia's comments. "At nineteen, Victoria is not a child to be cradled. She's a young lady about to be married. Let her be, Melvia," Isaack said in a state of increased anxiety. "It's much too late to be casting doubts about the young folk's proposed marriage."

Josceline and Marton listened keenly as they waited for another opportunity to further voice their opinion.

"Victoria's wonderful future husband will certainly teach her more of the facts of married life," Josceline said in defense of Isaack's statements and on behalf of her son, Aldbright.

"We must not ignore the fact that at twenty-one, Aldbright is himself just a young fellow," Melvia said, cunningly gesturing to Isaack.

The Scoullions gestured in agreement as the next round of the debate commenced. They, however, continued to express their assertiveness about the marriage.

During the rounds of heated debates among the future in-laws, Victoria sat cuddled by Aldbright's side. The future couple joyously smiled, nodding in approval and shaking their heads in disapproval of their parents' sometimes whimsical comments. The meeting had moved well into overtime amidst continued heated debates. There'd been a meeting of the minds of the soon-to-be in-laws. Marton and Josceline had no doubt that Victoria and Aldbright would make a good married couple. They therefore continued to vouch for the marriage.

"I think we should continue to counsel the young folk. With sound advice, they will decide whether they wish to go ahead with the marriage," Josceline said, and Marton once more nodded.

Scheduled meetings between Melvia and Isaack and the Scoullions continued even after Aldbright and Victoria had set a date for their wedding. By the end of their final meeting, the families parted with the consensus that there would be an upcoming wedding for which they must make preparations. News of the announcement of Victoria's wedding date triggered excitement among her siblings. They were poised to witness the first wedding in the Sevensen household. Aldbright would also be the first of Marton and Josceline's offspring to be married.

The day of the wedding was gradually drawing closer. The Scoullions and the Sevensens were occupied with the intricacies of planning for the occasion. Melvia and Isaack lived each day in an exhilarating spirit—their first offspring was soon to be married.

The anxious families perfected their skills at baking a perfect wedding cake, fit for a queen and a king. Armed with the skills they'd acquired in their school's home economics class, Savanna and her siblings carefully prepared the icing and the beautiful designs to create the best dressed wedding cake. The remaining items on the menu were tested and perfected by folk who had the professional touch catering for weddings.

Josceline and Melvia, mothers of the bride and the bridegroom-to-be, meticulously arranged the beautiful bridal bouquets. The flowers were freshly cut from their gardens. Flowers of a wide variety were designed to coordinate with the bridesmaids' colorful dresses and the bride's and bridegroom's elegant wedding garments.

On the morning of Victoria and Aldbright's big day, the air was pleasantly toasted with fragrances from the radiant June flowers of every color, shape, and size. The summer breeze from the gigantic mountain towering above continually rustled the flowers and leaves of the surrounding trees, setting the atmosphere for the wedding festivities.

On that festive occasion, the chirping birds in their beautiful plumage, frolicked among the branches of the trees, as if they were poised to contribute to the joyous festivities. The spring at the foot of the mountain could be heard as its flowing streams constantly glided over stones and pebbles along its path. It was the kind of day when the sun cast its brilliant rays across Amerhurst, making every heart cheerful on that blissful wedding day in June.

A village wedding was perceived as a family affair. A cordial invitation was therefore extended to everyone in the community to attend the wedding of Victoria and Aldbright. The folk joyously joined in the festivities, decorating their homes and laying adorable flowers along the wedding route.

Victoria awoke at the crack of dawn to the joyful reality that her wedding day had finally arrived. She'd been joyously serenaded by Cecelia's melodious voice cheerfully greeting the day of new beginnings. She sang wedding songs, which further stirred Victoria's awareness of the fact that it was her wedding day.

"Get her to the church. It's her wedding day." Cecelia sang her melodies as she joined the household in preparation for the wedding festivities.

The horse-drawn carriage that would escort the bride to the church, had been beautifully decorated by Victoria's siblings the day prior. The horses were brushed, fed, and well rested for their long day ahead. Meanwhile, at the Scoullions' home, Aldbright, the bridegroom, had been stricken with anxiety. He'd remained poised to take his marriage vow with his adorable bride.

On the day of the wedding, it was considered bad luck for the bride and the bridegroom to see each other before the marriage ceremony. The future couple therefore remained in hiding from each other. Aldbright made his way to the church, escorted by his proud father. Marton and Josceline had given their finishing touches and last words of best wishes to their son.

The church was located in close proximity to the Sevensen home. The carriage escorting the bridegroom therefore traveled along a hidden path, shielded by the shadow of the gigantic mountain. Under the brilliant Saturday midday sun, the wedding bell pealed and could be heard from miles away. The cheerful folk began to appear from every direction to congregate in the church sanctuary for the joyous occasion.

The proud mothers of the bride and the bridegroom, adorned in their elegantly designed attire, proudly made their way into the sanctuary. Their remaining beautiful and hopeful offspring walked close by their side. They were joined by other relatives of the bride and the bridegroom. Groups of prestigious dignitaries from wealthy estates around the great mountain, gracefully took their reserved seats in the front pews. Folk from all neighboring places waited in great anticipation to witness the union of Victoria and Aldbright. Most of all, they sat poised to witness the first wedding of the two households.

In Amerhurst, a wedding was the most exciting and entertaining event. In a quiet community where life was low-key, and entertainment opportunities scarce, a wedding ignited the curiosity of the folk as well as created excitement for all. A wedding offered the folk the opportunity to adorn themselves in their most elegant attire. The hopefuls put their individual beauty and charming looks on full display.

The adorably dressed bride and her bridegroom jogged the memories of those who'd once walked the aisle on their big day. A new wedding also brought hope to those whose hearts yearned for their big day to arrive. The bride's and her bridegroom's wedding attire therefore remained under the close scrutiny of all marriage hopefuls.

Without much fanfare, the adorable bridesmaids and the maid of honor had duly taken their place in the sanctuary. They'd quietly taken their positions around the bridegroom as he waited in solemn reverence for his adorable bride to appear. Marton Scoullion, the proud father of the bridegroom, sat by the side of his son, both sharing anxious moments.

In the modest church sanctuary, the atmosphere was charged with great anticipation as the audience waited for the arrival of the bride. All anxiously waited to behold the bride in her magnificent splendor as she walked up the aisle to join her waiting bridegroom. During that blissful moment, Savanna dreamed dreams of walking up the aisle with the man of her dreams.

Amidst the still quietness, soft intermittent whispers could be heard. Folk who had not seen one another for some time, exchanged pleasant smiles and nods that served as their gestures of saying hello. The occasional giggle resonated among the young folk who could not endure a moment of silence.

On that solemn occasion, under the constant peal of the wedding bell, Isaack and Melvia anxiously waited to witness their first offspring walk up the aisle on her wedding day. In a similar fashion, Marton and

Josceline, along with their remaining offspring, waited to see Aldbright walk down the aisle with his beautiful wife.

As father of the bride, Isaack stood poised to escort his beautiful daughter up the aisle. It was Victoria's day to shine in the midst of the elegant ladies. It was also Isaack's day to put his best foot forward, walking by the side of his adorable daughter.

Back at the Sevensen home, Victoria had long waited until the way was clear. She was on her way to the church in her elaborately decorated carriage. The carriage had duly arrived at the entrance of the church. Victoria stood poised and ready for her wedding march.

Suddenly, the sound of the organ rang out in the sanctuary. Its sound echoed for miles, signaling that the way was clear for the bride to alight from her carriage and make her triumphant entry into the sanctuary. At the commencement of the wedding march, the organist pulled out all the stops as she commenced playing "Here Comes the Bride."

Amidst silence and total reverence, Victoria entered the sanctuary. As the wedding march progressed, heads turned, necks craned, and eyes popped wide open. The anxious audience waited to get a first glimpse of the beautiful bride, adorned in her elegant white wedding dress, complemented by her elaborately designed bouquet.

Isaack stepped in strides by the side of his adorable daughter as they made their way up the aisle. Melvia and Josceline watched the proceeding with tearful eyes. Their first little angels stood poised to leave the nest in which they'd been securely kept all of their young lives. With tearful eyes and the occasional sob, Savanna and her siblings stood to observe the spectacle. The marriage hopefuls craned their necks as they scrutinized the bride's and her bridegroom's elegant wedding garments.

Marton, father of the bridegroom, stood poised to relinquish his noble son, Aldbright, to his arriving elegant bride. Tears continued to flow profusely down the cheeks of Melvia and Josceline, mothers of the soon-to-be couple. The fathers observed the proceeding with broken hearts but with subdued tears.

The solemn march up the aisle ended. Victoria gently took her place by the side of her bridegroom. Aldbright, the proud bridegroom, turned reverently to acknowledge the arrival of his adorable bride as she was relinquished by her proud father, Isaack. Victoria had reached her climatic moment when she proudly stood by the side of her beloved bridegroom.

In a rather short and prompt ceremony, the Reverend Christopher Beckharry delivered his most rhetoric sermon of sound wisdom and marital advice. The bride and her bridegroom duly took their marriage vows. They sincerely pledged their commitment to love and cherish each other. The newlyweds had made their brief stop into the vestry for the signing of the marriage register.

At the end of the most solemn ceremony, they commenced their triumphant walk down the aisle. The newlyweds basked in the ambience of their most ecstatic moment. Victoria's cheeks were radiant with glee as she walked down the aisle as Mrs. Victoria Scoullion. Happiness had been welling up in her heart. Her proud husband, Aldbright, stepped in bold strides by the side of his wife as the couple paraded past the cheering audience. The newlyweds took a brief look at the faces of their parents, a silent gesture of bidding their goodbyes.

Wedding photos of a number of vital poses were taken during the proceeding. These were considered good enough to enable the newlyweds to view themselves during the marriage ceremony, particularly during their most ecstatic moment of tying the knot. As the newlyweds exited the church, the remaining Sevensen offspring greeted them with welcoming arms, amidst hugs and kisses.

"Congratulations, Victoria!" they shouted in a gleeful spirit.

"Good cheers, Victoria. I hope to be married someday too," Savanna said as new tears flooded her eyes. She did not hesitate to reveal the yearning in her heart to be married.

In the same fashion, Josceline and Marton, along with their remaining two cheerful offspring, waited at the exit of the sanctuary. The couple greeted their newly married son and extended a red-carpet welcome to their adorable daughter-in-law. Victoria and Aldbright, along with their elegant bridal party, walked the path toward the waiting carriages that would escort them to the wedding venue. As the newlyweds proudly paraded through the cheering crowd, they were kept under the close scrutiny of the young marriage hopefuls.

The newlyweds climbed onto their waiting carriage that would escort them to the reception venue at the Scoullions' home. They paraded along the beautiful scenic route lined with brilliant flowers. Carriages escorting the bridesmaids and the maid of honor joined the procession. The newlyweds' proud parents, along with their remaining elated offspring, brought up the rear, riding in their carriages. Wealthy dignitaries drove their automobiles along the procession path. Other folk joined the procession, escorted by carriages.

Beneath the brilliant afternoon sun, the sounds of carriages and footsteps, like marching soldiers, could be heard as the wedding procession slowly progressed. The procession finally made its way through the gate of the Scoullions' estate and toward the large barn that had been elegantly laid out for the wedding reception. It was quite fitting for the wedding reception to be held in a farm setting where the animals of burden played such a contributing role. The horses escorted the bride and the bridegroom to the church and subsequently to the reception venue in the barn.

Beneath the most brilliant blue sky, the guests took their places in the barn setting. The newlyweds quietly took their place in preparation for the commencement of the reception. Proud dignitaries and other cheerful guests converged on the Scoullions' estate for an evening of entertainment, celebrating the union of two young lovers.

The Sevensen offspring were posted at conspicuous locations where they took in the spectacle of the family's first wedding. Savanna yearned deep in her heart to be the next beautiful bride of the household—as soon as she could meet her soul mate.

At the wedding reception, the new in-laws took the customary step forward to officially introduce themselves as part of the combined family. They pledged to provide guidance to the newlyweds in matters pertaining to marriage and raising a family. The guests were having their time of pleasure, adoring the newlyweds amidst sharing pleasant thoughts and dining on several courses of meals.

The live band commenced playing a gentle ballroom waltz. Victoria and Aldbright made their debut onto the dance floor. It was time to commence their traditional first steps into a bright future as man and wife. Throughout the entire evening, families and guests joined the newlyweds as they danced joyfully beneath the starlit sky. The young guests mingled incessantly with guests of other estates, with the hope that, wedding bells would someday, chime for them.

The evening of wedding festivities gradually drew to a close as the guests began to disperse. After a full day of ecstasy, the newlyweds were escorted in their carriage to their matrimonial home. As *honeymoon* was not a part of the folk's vocabulary, the couple's home was the venue for their honeymoon and the place where they commenced their lives as a married couple.

In the Sevensen household, the marriage festivities had finally ground to a halt. A cloud of great expectation and anxiety hung over the remaining offspring. As the days, weeks, and months came and went, anxious hearts and minds were teeming with hopes of marriage. The big question lingered in the minds of the young Sevensens: "Who will be the next bride or bridegroom?"

Victoria's wedding was merely a prelude to the many others Isaack and Melvia anticipated. The boys worked alongside Isaack, hoping to someday, get married and become owners of their estates as well as the heads of their own families. The girls remained hopeful that their dreams would come true.

Savanna entertained visions of being the next June bride to walk down the aisle of the small stone church, but she wasn't the next Sevensen offspring in line for marriage. Cecelia had also been an older hopeful. She'd been waiting for her big day, but it appeared that her career had taken precedence over getting married and raising a family. Who then would be the next bride or bridegroom? This question lingered in crevices of the minds of the Sevensen offspring.

CHAPTER 6

Cecelia Left Home

Life in Amerhurst had returned to normal after the blissful moments aroused by Victoria and Aldbright's wedding. Hopes and dreams were once more revived as the remaining Sevensen offspring resumed their daily routines. Isaack and Melvia were deeply saddened by the departure of Kladius, the first of their offspring. He'd left home for the first time to reside in the UK. The couple endured the heartache of seeing their young adult son leave home. It was a double whammy when Victoria bowed out to assume her married life.

Cecelia and her younger sibling, Savanna, had been playing a dominant role in the Sevensen household. Being the eldest girl, Cecelia was regarded by her siblings as a role model. She'd also been perceived as a tomboy each time she perched in the trees while the gentle breeze swayed their branches. And just like a songbird, from the branches of the trees, she sang melodious songs to her attentive household. Cecelia's influence on the lives of her siblings had proven that there's always a sunny side to life and a bright side to every adverse situation.

As the eldest girl of the household, Cecelia maintained a strong fascination for studying diligently to achieve her goal. There hadn't been a doubt in Melvia's and Isaack's minds that she'd placed marriage on the back burner. On the strength of the education she'd acquired, Cecelia secured a teaching job in the local school. She later felt that teaching was not the lifetime career she wished to pursue. She'd therefore turned her interest elsewhere.

Cecelia imagined the culture shock her elder sibling Kladius encountered when he arrived in the UK. She'd therefore sworn not to put herself in that frightening situation, leaving her homeland and arriving in a strange world—most frightful of all to live among total strangers. Her quest for a wider scope of knowledge as well as a new career, had therefore directed her interest to the town where she felt there was a world of opportunities.

Cecelia had been quite certain that the nursing school in the distant town of Berrimore could help her aspire toward her new career goal. She therefore promptly submitted her letter of intent. She'd been mindful of the fact that a career in nursing would require her to leave Amerhurst for a job in the town. Not long after submitting her application, Cecelia's dream of pursuing a new career had come true.

On a Saturday morning in the month of August, just as the first birds began to make their debut, a sturdy elderly man rode his bicycle into Amerhurst. There was a loud knock on the Sevensens' wooden gate. Rex and Spicer, being protective of their territory, quickly ran to the gate in a barking frenzy. The frightened man immediately fled the scene.

The commotion created by the loud barking dogs alerted Isaack. He quickly ran toward the gate to investigate the cause of the dogs' anxiety. Isaack arrived at the gate in the nick of time to see the man riding away from the scene. Without further hesitation, he called out to the fleeing man.

"Hello, sir!" Isaack yelled.

The man, feeling a sense of safety, turned his bicycle around, riding cautiously back toward the gate. "Good morning, sir," the man greeted Isaack. His early morning ride from the town of Bragerston had left his cheeks damp and oily. His face portrayed an enquiring demeanor, a suggestion of uncertainty as to whether he'd stopped at the right house.

The presence of a stranger at his gate, and at the crack of dawn, raised suspicions in Isaack's mind. "Good morning to you, sir," Isaack said. "How can I help?"

The man reached his long sturdy hand into a red bag suspended from his shoulder. He pulled out a light gray envelope and commenced reading the name. "I have a telegram for Miss Cecelia Sevensen. Is this where she lives?" The man stood poised to return the envelope to his bag.

Isaack had been reluctant to admit that the gentleman had stopped at the right gate. The thought of a telegram sent chills along his spine and down to his toes. Although the man had specifically asked for Cecelia, Isaack's thoughts immediately reflected on Kladius in the UK.

"Yes," Isaack said, his hands tightly pressed against his chest. He'd hesitantly admitted that Cecelia, in fact, resided at his home.

In Amerhurst and beyond, a telegram denoted sad news—news of death. Isaack therefore stood poised to commence his period of somber grief. While his thoughts were on the imminent, Isaack quickly recalled Cecelia's letter to the nursing school. He slowly regained his composure and hesitantly accepted the envelope. Isaack securely guarded Rex and Spicer until the man turned his bicycle around and rode off into the misty dawn.

The messenger had scarcely left the scene when Isaack rushed into the house, holding the telegram. The scuffle by Rex and Spicer had awakened the household and put everyone on high alert. To be awakened by a stranger in the early dawn was quite an unusual occurrence for the Sevensens.

"Wake up, Cecelia!" Isaack said. "A telegram was delivered for you."

Cecelia rushed from her room. "What is it, Dad?" she asked. Her voice had been groggy from a night of sound sleep.

"There's a telegram for you," Isaack said in a much louder tone.

Cecelia rushed into the big hall, repeatedly wiping the Friday night sleep from her eyes. "A telegram!" Cecelia shouted.

Isaack handed her the envelope as she entered the hall.

"Thanks, Dad," Cecelia said. Her eyes appeared twice their normal size. She ripped the envelope in which the telegram was enclosed and commenced reading its contents. "Dear Miss Cecelia Sevensen . . ." Cecelia commenced reading the telegram in silence but had become overwhelmed by its contents. She yelled in great elation and in a resounding voice, "Listen, everyone! Listen to this! I'm going to nursing school in Berrimore!"

Her siblings quickly gathered in the big hall. Smiles shrouded a few sleepy and saggy faces. There were mixed emotions as Cecelia stood poised to read the contents of the telegram.

At the sound of the commotion, Melvia and Savanna made a mad rush from the kitchen, where they were occupied preparing breakfast. The word *telegram* had not rested well in Melvia's mind. She'd been mindful of what a telegram entailed and had therefore entered the hall with mixed emotions. Isaack met her at the door and quickly briefed her on the subject of the telegram. Melvia and Isaack joined the curious offspring in the hall as Cecelia read aloud the contents of her telegram.

Dear Miss Cecelia Sevensen,

We're pleased to inform you that you've been accepted to be trained at the Melvorn School of Nursing. At the completion of your training, you'll be assigned to your position as a resident nurse at the KHC Hospital. Upon the completion of your internship, you'll be assigned as a nurse at the same location.

You will commence training on September 15. Please be present at the school no later than August 25.

Kindly respond by way of a telegram no later than August 20 to accept or decline this offer.

Signed,
Dr. Charhaton Ainsberth
Recruitment Division
Melvorn School of Nursing

After reading the telegram, Cecelia danced gleefully around the hall. Isaack and Melvia watched with tearful eyes. There were audible sounds as their remaining offspring wept profusely at the thought that Cecelia was about to leave home. They'd been mindful of Kladius's departure to the UK. Victoria's marriage had created another gap when she left home. Cecelia's departure, they felt, would leave another gap in the fabric of the tightly knit family.

The young siblings had slowly begun to realize that life in a household of many offspring meant growing up and moving out. The thought of Cecelia leaving home was a bittersweet pill for Melvia and Isaack to swallow. The couple had been delighted that Cecelia was accepted to study in the town but had also been mindful of the ensuing painful separation.

That early morning event had brought a turning point in Cecelia's life. She'd immediately commenced making preparations to leave for the nursing school in the town of Berrimore. Her first major task was to accept the offer by way of a telegram. She must also meet the August 20 deadline, the critical date to respond. Later that same morning, Cecelia had promptly replied to the telegram. She'd gladly accepted the offer to study at the Melvorn School of Nursing.

The next Monday morning, at the crack of dawn, Cecelia and Savanna were on their way to Bragerston, where the telegram would be sent off to Berrimore. Savanna had begun to feel the pains of separation from Cecelia, her mentor and confidant. She therefore couldn't hide the tears of grief that cascaded down her cheeks.

"Sav, keep your eyes and your mind open to see and perceive the bright future ahead of you," Cecelia said. Cecelia tried to console her younger sibling but had begun to perceive the pains she too had been enduring as she prepared to leave home. "Continue to strive for the best that's within your reach. As you pursue your career as a fine teacher, prepare yourself to be the most beautiful wife to the man of your dreams. I hope to be at your wedding to participate in the joyous festivities."

Cecelia was overcome by grief as she spoke. A fountain of tears continuously flooded her eyes. The thought of leaving home for the first time had gripped her heart. As Cecelia made her way back to Amerhurst on the local bus, Savanna sat snuggled by her side.

The entire household was grief-stricken when Kladius had left home for his foreign destination. As Victoria resided within close proximity to Amerhurst, the tears were lessened when she had left home. Cecelia was a symbol of love and cheerfulness to her siblings as well as to Melvia and Isaack. The thought of her leaving home had therefore ignited added grief and unrelenting tears.

A state of sadness and bitter tears had been the order of the days leading up to Cecelia's departure. Melvia cried to see her third child making preparations to leave home. Isaack expressed his grief the way a father could, silence and a heavy heart ruling his every day. Amidst her own tears and a grieving heart, Savanna attempted to cheer the hearts of her remaining siblings as tears were being shed everywhere.

As Cecelia prepared to embark on the long journey to Berrimore, her last few days had been critical. A new career path and her strong determination to succeed prompted her to relinquish her teaching position. Amidst her mad rush, Cecelia was the only one who could have expressed her overwhelming excitement. She'd commenced assembling her personal items in preparation to embark on the long journey to reach her distant destination—not to ignore the sadness of leaving home and severing ties with Melvia and Isaack, her closely knit siblings, her grandparents, and the teachers and students of her school. She'd also been leaving other close acquaintances who'd been dear to her heart.

August 24 had quickly made its appearance. The sun had begun to dry the thick dew on the ground as Cecelia gathered her luggage and commenced bidding her goodbyes. It was a tearful departure when she bade her many goodbyes amidst hugs and kisses. Savanna hadn't imagined the impact Cecelia's departure would have on her emotions. She'd been weeping incessantly. Amidst her cascading tears, she didn't hesitate to remind Cecelia of her promise to return for her wedding.

"See you at my wedding, Cecelia," Savanna said. "Will you return home for my wedding?"

"I'll most certainly be at your wedding, Sav. I promise," Cecelia said.

The big door of the bus quickly closed, separating her from Savanna. Savanna began to shed new tears as the bus took on momentum and quickly disappeared in the distance. It was a day that would remain indelibly on the minds of her entire household. At Cecelia's departure, Melvia and Isaack, along with their remaining offspring, wept as though she'd passed away. In the minds of Cecelia's siblings, she was the big sister who'd brought so much joy to their young hearts. Most of all, she was sadly missed by Savanna, who'd developed a special bond with her elder sibling.

Meanwhile, new tears flooded Cecelia's eyes as the bus took her farther away from her home. She was leaving the nest for the first time to settle in a faraway town. As the local bus commenced its journey to Bragerston, Cecelia felt and endured the pains of severing close ties with her household—and the home she'd known all of her young life. With a grieving heart and firm determination, she was on her way to commence a new career. The local bus arrived in Bragerston Town, a fair distance from Amerhurst. From Bragerston, Cecelia boarded the train to embark on her long journey to the town of Berrimore.

At Cecelia's departure, Savanna assumed her role as the dominant offspring of the household. She boldly took up the beacon, endeavoring to be the guiding light for her remaining siblings. There'd been no doubt that her mind continued to be plagued by her quest to find the man of her dreams.

CHAPTER 7

Harry Lovethon

There was no telling the impact Cecelia's departure had had on the life of young Savanna. She felt as if the good life had ceased for her, but she'd been constantly reminded of her younger siblings' reliance on her for mentoring as they faced their future, and like her siblings, Savanna had been constantly reminded of her own future that lay ahead. She must pursue her career as a young and promising teacher in her local school.

As each day passed, Savanna remained hopeful of becoming a beautiful June bride just like Victoria. The persistent sound of wedding bells chimed in her ears. She perceived a future with her wonderful husband and a household of beautiful offspring.

Amidst her quiet moments of hope and wild imagination, Savanna continued to pursue her career as a teacher and a mentor to her fine siblings. She'd remained devoted to working alongside Melvia, caring for and nurturing her younger siblings. Melvia continued to marvel at Savanna's generosity in caring for the young offspring. She strongly believed Savanna's commitment to serving in the household had predisposed her to becoming a devoted future wife and a caring mother of her own offspring.

On a bright and sunny Monday morning in September, Harry Lovethon joined the staff of Amerhurst Villa School. He felt he'd landed a teaching job in a prestigious environment. Savanna immediately met face-to-face with the flamboyant young gentleman who'd joined the staff of her school. There was no doubt that she envisioned meeting the man of her dreams.

As a new teacher of the school, Harry established a good rapport with the staff as well as the welcoming folk of Amerhurst. His good nature had quickly won him the respects of the folk. It had been their greatest delight to have a fine gentleman teacher of prestige among them.

Upon Harry's arrival, Amerhurst had come alive in more ways than one. The hopeful young ladies began to brush up on their good etiquette at home and among their peers. Charming young ladies had become contenders for the handsome gentleman who'd moved into their community. Each day, knowledge of Harry's presence reached the ears of the young folk around the mountain. In the eyes of every eligible young lady, Harry was Prince Charming. He was regarded as a most mannerly and eligible bachelor. Harry's presence had begun to ignite sparks of love in the eyes of the hopeful young ladies.

Harry had become the handsome guy all the young ladies would die for. The young ladies adored his poise, his statuesque figure, and his graceful charm. He'd always smiled, giving freedom to his facial muscles while, at the same time, allowing his charming looks to radiate. The young contending ladies had become captivated by Harry's comely smile, which always compelled their reciprocity. The beautiful ladies of Amerhurst and beyond had a yearning to be loved by the tall and handsome young bachelor.

Who was Harry Lovethon? Who would he choose? Had he an interest in these contending ladies? These were the big questions among the hopeful young ladies and their parents. There hadn't been much known about Harry Lovethon. He'd been known only as the fine teacher of Amerhurst. Beautiful ladies, adorned in their elegantly designed garments, paraded along the road passing by the house Harry rented in Amerhurst as if they were on a hot date with Mr. Invisible.

The competition among the beautifully adorned ladies had become more intense as each day came and went.

Savanna and her beautiful girl siblings had not joined the group of contenders. They'd held their hopes high nonetheless. By chance, Harry would regard them among his group of possible choices. Savanna, also being a teacher of Amerhurst Villa School, felt she had a better chance at meeting Harry. She had more privileges and opportunities than the ladies who'd set themselves up to charm and tantalize the handsome young bachelor.

Harry went about his active teaching duties, but he intentionally and persistently placed himself in paths where he was certain to cast a wink at Savanna. She'd always found herself in the paths of his tantalizing glances. Savanna had always been forced to reciprocate with a glance and a smile. There was the occasional exchange of hellos whenever they passed each other in the hallway of the school.

When Harry first came face-to-face with Savanna in the lunchroom, she'd become the subject of his focus and admiration. He'd cunningly chosen his seat at the table where she habitually sat for lunch. Savanna felt the assurance that she'd grown up a long way from the Bentley era. She'd fully understood the concepts of two young adults falling in love. She therefore spent each day hoping that love would spark between her and Harry.

Days turned into weeks and months since Harry had joined the staff of the villa school. Several months passed before he finally got up close and personal with the young lady he'd been tantalizing with his secret winks and smiles. Their contacts had surpassed the occasional hello. While they sat at the table for lunch, Harry finally opened up for a dialogue.

"Hello, Savanna," Harry said, his face portraying that usual charming smile.

For a brief moment, Savanna sat without uttering a syllable. She politely emptied her mouth of the bite she'd taken from her sandwich. When she responded, the words came out clumsily from her lips. "Hello, Harry." She turned her face slightly to avoid his eye-piercing stare.

"You're an excellent teacher," Harry said. "For how long have you been a teacher?"

Savanna could no longer avoid his eyes as they charmed her with looks of admiration. She was held captive by Harry's constant stare as he waited for her response. "Just a bit shy of a year and a half," Savanna said, insinuating that she was still an adolescent.

The question session continued amidst discrete amiable glances of love toward each other. They'd become conscious of others seated around the table and had therefore kept their glances to a minimum. When the big bell pealed across the schoolyard, it was time to return to retrieve their eager students.

"It's time to go, Savanna," Harry said. "I'll see you after school."

They promptly parted in separate directions to receive their pupils. The children had eagerly lined up by the main entrance of the school. Throughout the afternoon, Savanna pondered that which had transpired between her and Harry.

As he'd promised, shortly after the last bell and while the children were on their way home, Harry promptly waited for Savanna by the exit door. He quickly resumed his fact-finding conversation on their short walk home. Savanna had always dressed like a typical farm girl—a simple blouse, a long pleated skirt, and thick shoes. Harry appeared always as the flaunty country gentleman. During the course of the evening and prior to bedtime, Savanna had much to share with Melvia and Isaack and her curious siblings—she'd met someone very special.

Harry and Savanna's subsequent walks home together after school had culminated into a more serious relationship. There was no telling what had been stirring in Harry's heart as he dreamed about the beautiful young lady he had met at school.

When Harry finally asked Savanna out on a date, the stars in the sky shone their brightest. Deep within her heart, Savanna knew she'd found love, but she felt that it was much too early to triumph in her victory. In the town of Bragerston, Savanna basked in the sunshine of their glorious togetherness as she walked by Harry's side along the busy streets.

Savanna reflected on her days with Bentley. When Bentley had planted a kiss on her lips while they walked along the edge of the woods, it was her first kiss. In her young heart, it was genuine love. Since she had severed ties with Bentley, Savanna continually shed tears of grief at the bittersweet memories she'd left behind. She remained hopeful that her love for Harry would bring fading memories of her first love. At her young age of nineteen, soon to be twenty, Savanna perceived genuine love in Harry's heart. She therefore had no doubt that their love would culminate in marriage.

As their love continued to spark, Harry never ceased meeting Savanna for their frequent strolls after school and on Sunday afternoons, when he returned from visiting his parents. Harry's frequent meetings with Savanna further solidified their love and friendship.

The young lovers had been planning their meetings away from the view of the folk of inquisitive minds, folk who might be monitoring their movements and their courtship. Harry had also been mindful of the beautiful, vigilant ladies who'd been following on his heels. What better venue to make their formal introduction and exchange smiles, hugs, and kisses than in the secluded nook, the hideout where Savanna had met frequently with Bentley? Savanna had thoroughly checked out the abandoned little nook. She mended the broken sides to ensure its continued privacy.

After a long night of restlessness, Harry welcomed the morning he'd planned to meet with Savanna for their Wednesday morning stroll. School was out for the day, giving the lovers the free time to meet and to further solidify their love and friendship.

Savanna had often taken her solitary strolls in the meadow and by the edge of the woods along the foot of the mountain, a place the village folk regarded with fear and misgivings. She'd spent countless hours wandering alone around the farm and taking short walks along the quiet road passing through Amerhurst. Since she met Harry, she'd been privileged to take her usual strolls with him. Whenever she ventured near the foot of the mountain, she felt a sense of security, knowing that Harry was by her side.

The young lovers made their frequent promenade along the foot of the mountain. They listened to the sound of the spring as its fast-flowing streams glided over ivory stones and pebbles beneath its surface. They strolled through the field while the birds in their sanctuary continually chanted their melodious songs. The morning dew was still on the ground as Savanna strolled among the wet grass and shrubs, holding Harry's hairy hand firmly. Dew from the thick shrubs had quickly drenched their shoes and saturated their feet as they made their way to the nook.

They'd finally reached the nook, safely hidden beneath thick shrubs, withes, and overhanging tree branches. Savanna led the way to the entrance, beckoning to Harry as he followed close behind.

"Come in," Savanna whispered. "Welcome to my secret world."

Harry cautiously walked into the nook. He was careful not to be overwhelmed by harmful creatures hidden beneath the tons of trash.

"Have a seat, Harry," Savanna said. She promptly took her seat on the ground, in the mound of dry leaves Bentley had piled into the nook.

Without further ado, Harry took his seat by her side. Savanna sat cuddled by Harry's side in the comfort of the nook. It was certainly not the best hideout for Harry, but he sat with his ears perked up for any sound of creatures of the wild that might venture into the nook.

"This place is like a lover's cove," Harry said.

He slowly planted a kiss on Savanna's cheek. This was Harry's first kiss since meeting Savanna. She was immediately brought to tears as she reflected on her first kiss, which she'd received from Bentley. While their hearts panted only for closeness to each other, they repeatedly exchanged looks of love amidst a warm embrace. In Savanna's eyes, Harry appeared intriguingly handsome. His neatly cut hair appeared to always receive his constant tender loving care.

Savanna sincerely expressed her appreciation for Harry's presence in her secret hideout. "Thanks for joining me in my quiet nook, Harry. It has not been occupied for quite some time."

Harry looked into Savanna's eyes, which held a brilliant glow. His heart was set aflame with delight as he regarded her enchanting beauty. He'd become mesmerized by Savanna's looks of innocence as he planted another kiss on her brightly glowing cheeks. "You're the apple of my eye, Savanna," Harry said. "Your cheeks glow like the brilliant flowers in the month of June."

They remained in the nook for a time of caring and exchanging their thoughts, Harry showering her with words of love and adoration. Savanna's heart yearned even more for the handsome gentleman she'd adored over the many months since he joined the staff of her school.

"Your charming looks have set my heart ablaze, Harry," Savanna said. "When you first appeared in school, my heart had such a yearning to be close to you."

Harry planted another gentle kiss on Savanna's lips, an attestation of his genuine love for her.

The streams of the spring constantly flowed softly by. The young lovers continued to exchange kind words amidst looks of love within the quiet nook. It was a heartbreaking moment when they left the nook for the short journey back home. Savanna wished she could have remained in Harry's warm embrace forever. The midday sun had dried up the dew-drenched path as the young lovers made their way back to their respective homes.

Harry expressed his love and adoration of the secret nook. "Savanna, it was certainly my pleasure spending the morning in your nook," Harry said.

"It was a pleasure having you in my little hideout, Harry," Savanna said.

They parted with pleasant smiles and a warm embrace. Harry watched as Savanna walked through the large wooden gate leading to her home.

Savanna's early morning meeting in the nook with Harry was the commencement of many subsequent meetings in the venue. Upon Harry's return from his weekend visits with his parents, he'd scheduled every Sunday evening to meet with Savanna in the nook.

Harry's life of teaching and meeting with Savanna began to spark gossip among the teachers as well as the folk of Amerhurst. There'd been no doubt that Harry had made his final choice among the ladies contending for his love. The contending ladies had therefore quickly abandoned their display of glamor and reflective charm.

At the news of Harry's choice of Savanna, Melvia and Isaack and their remaining cheerful offspring welcomed him with wide-open arms. In the hearts of the Sevensens, Savanna had attracted the son of noble parentage. Harry was therefore cordially invited to the Sevensen home, where he'd quickly become a part of the family.

Under the warm glow of the Friday afternoon sun, Addriana and Henry Lovethon, Harry's parents, rode into Amerhurst to visit their son. Harry had invited Savanna to meet up for a stroll, under the guise of introducing her to his parents. While Savanna waited at Harry's gate, he proudly stepped from his house, his parents following close by his side.

Harry promptly stepped toward Savanna to make his introduction. "Mom, meet Savanna."

Addriana stood poised to speak—but not before Harry moved Savanna forward to be introduced to his father.

"Dad," Harry said, "this is Savanna."

Henry's eyes quickly met Addriana's.

"I'm delighted to meet you, Savanna," Addriana said with a warm and welcoming handshake.

Henry seconded the welcome with a firm handshake. "I'm most delighted to meet you, Savanna," Henry said. "You're an adorable young lady." Henry's praise was seconded by Addriana's nod of approval.

"Thank you, Mr. and Mrs. Lovethon," Savanna said in her acceptance of the compliments showered on her by her potential in-laws.

The couple was duly introduced to Savanna, the name that had become a household word in their home. Harry had been carefully observing the interaction between Savanna and his parents. He'd hoped to detect any negative vibes, vibes that might signal the rejection of the beautiful Amerhurst lady he'd chosen.

Harry's impromptu introduction had placed Savanna on full display before his elated parents. Addriana and Henry's eyes had become glued to the charming young lady. There hadn't been a doubt that Henry had dissonant thoughts about the beautiful lady he'd been privileged to meet. Addriana had reservations about the young lady Harry had chosen, but she'd remained tight-lipped, not wanting to express her thoughts prematurely.

The brief introductory session ended when Harry excused Savanna for her departure. She promptly excused herself from the couple but not before gesturing her wishes to see them again in the near future. Under the golden rays of the evening sun, Savanna walked along the quiet road back to her home, which was a short distance away. She'd remained under the close scrutiny of Harry's parents until she disappeared around the bend.

In her heart, Savanna felt she hadn't gained the acceptance of Harry's parents. However, she strongly believed that it was much too early to seal her conclusion. Savanna arrived home in a state of restlessness and uncertainty. She promptly informed Melvia and Isaack and her curious siblings of her meeting with Harry's parents.

C H A P T E R   8

Savanna's Wedding

It was a sunny Sunday afternoon when Harry met with Savanna in their secret venue. He'd just finished his appetizing dinner with the Sevensens after his early return from visiting his parents. On this particular Sunday, he'd returned home early for more reasons than one.

Savanna's heart was ablaze with wild expectations as she was joined by Harry in the nook. They'd taken their usual place on the leaf-covered ground for another pleasurable moment together. Savanna was pleasantly surprised when Harry handed her a bouquet of wildflowers he'd gathered along the way.

"Thank you, Harry," Savanna said, her face sparkling with delight. "These are the most adorable flowers. I watched you gathering them as we walked in the field."

"It's my pleasure, my angel," Harry said.

Under the brilliant Sunday evening sun, Savanna sat by Harry's side in the nook. She always had an ardent desire to be close to him. The young lovers exchanged words of love and a warm embrace in the secluded nook.

Savanna sincerely loved Harry. There'd been secret love and passion kindling in her heart. Each day, she looked forward to their meeting in the nook or whenever they strolled along the quiet road. In her heart, she had the assurance that she'd found her soul mate, the man with whom she wished to spend the rest of her life. Savanna had no doubt that Harry felt the same way about her.

The young lovers sat in the ambience of the evening shadows the Sunday sunset cast around the nook. The sound of the streams in the spring contributed to the serene atmosphere. There'd been rustling sounds among the shrubs and fallen leaves around the nook—sounds, Savanna perceived, were made by animals and creatures of the wild. A period of silence ensued as if Harry had a famine for words of love.

He suddenly broke his silence with the question that jolted Savanna's heart: "Savanna, my adorable lady, will you marry me?"

Savanna sat dumbfounded. Tears trickled down her cheeks as she collapsed into Harry's arms. "Harry," Savanna said with sincerity, "I love you very much. I'll certainly marry you."

She remained breathless as tears of joy flowed from her eyes. Harry felt the effects of her pain of love and began to wipe his tearing eyes. He'd been greatly elated at the thought that Savanna had similar feelings in her heart—she loved him too.

As she remained in Harry's warm embrace, Savanna had the assurance that her ship, which had been sailing the wide ocean, had finally come ashore. She'd found the man of her dreams. She had no doubt that Harry felt the same way, that he'd found the lady of his dreams.

Savanna perceived from Harry's commitment and sincerity that he was not merely compensating his insatiable appetite for romance with a beautiful young lady. Harry had been showing his genuine love and affection for her. As their love blossomed, Savanna felt that Harry portrayed a shepherd's heart, the heart that would lead and guide their future lives.

In the comfort of the nook, Savanna remained in Harry's warm embrace. In her heart, she had no desire to live in her world with anyone else but Harry. Likewise, Harry had given her his seal of approval. His world would be empty without her in it.

Savanna had quickly lapsed back into her dream world. Rays of hope shone around her as she imagined being a beautiful bride and the wife of her handsome soul mate, Harry. Savanna's heart yearned for her big day, which she was quite certain would come soon.

Amidst tears of joy and kisses, the young lovers left the nook to take the good tidings to Melvia and Isaack. Savanna's siblings had been poised to welcome the news of Harry's proposal. Momentarily, Harry's parents, Addriana and Henry, would receive the good news of his proposal to the beautiful lady Savanna.

Savanna's heart was overwhelmed with joy. Her eyes sparkled with love as she rushed home to share the good news of Harry's proposal. When she arrived home with a broad smile and with an exhilarating spirit, her siblings knew she'd come home bearing good news.

"Mom," Savanna said in a most elated mood, "meet my future husband. Harry has just asked me to marry him."

Melvia and her remaining offspring stood speechless. They once more adored the handsome gentleman standing in the hall. The atmosphere had been stirred by the news of Harry's marriage proposal. Harry proudly stepped forward to formally introduce himself to his future in-laws.

"Hello, Mrs. Sevensen," Harry said as he extended a firm and official handshake to Melvia.

"I'm most delighted to hear the good news, Harry," Melvia said as her face glowed with delight.

One by one, Harry shook the hands of Melvia's remaining offspring, who'd gathered around Savanna with cheerful smiles. Isaack entered the hall, just in time to get in on the excitement.

At his appearance, Savanna yelled with a gleeful voice, "Dad, meet Harry, my future husband!"

Isaack stood without emotion. He'd remained poised, waiting to obtain further details of the marriage proposal.

"Harry has just asked me to marry him," Savanna said in a gleeful spirit.

Harry stepped toward Isaack, who'd immediately taken his place by the side of his daughter. "Hello, Mr. Sevensen," Harry said, reaching out in anticipation of Isaack's cordial welcome.

Isaack promptly extended his firm welcoming handshake. In Harry's mind, he'd been officially greeted by Isaack and Melvia as their future son-in-law. "I'm delighted to welcome you as a future member of my family, Harry," Isaack said assuredly.

As she stood by Isaack's side, Savanna's face glowed with a cheerful smile and a look of assurance that she'd finally found love. Harry had been officially accepted as a future member of the Sevensen family. He'd therefore endeavored to leave his best and lasting impression, and he knew just how to do it. The rapport he'd established with his teaching peers at the villa school, and with the folk of Amerhurst, gained him acceptance by all who'd met him. The folk formed their good opinion of the noble gentleman who'd become a resident of their community.

Melvia and Isaack had first met Harry at a parent-teacher meeting. The couple immediately perceived him as a fine gentleman of noble heritage. They'd therefore taken great pleasure in accepting the fine gentleman they felt was fit for one of their beautiful daughters.

Nothing could have changed or altered Melvia's opinion of Harry. She'd therefore gladly spread her red carpet to welcome him as a future member of the Sevensen family. Isaack, meanwhile, doubted whether an early marriage was good for the young folk. He had reluctantly endorsed Victoria's marriage at age nineteen. Savanna had passed her nineteenth birthday, but she was not yet twenty. Isaack therefore felt she was a bit too young for marriage.

Harry had officially introduced himself as Savanna's future husband. This had quickly stirred up mixed emotions among the Sevensens. To Melvia and Isaack, another of their little angels was about to leave home. Meanwhile, the offspring joined their merry hearts to cheer and congratulate Savanna on meeting her handsome prince. Hope was further ignited in the hearts of the remaining offspring that they too would find love.

With news of the marriage proposal behind them, Harry was cordially welcomed to the Sevensen home, where he received overwhelming hospitality. Like the waves of the wide ocean that never ceased from returning to the shore, Harry continually visited the Sevensen home just to be close to Savanna, his future bride. Savanna and her siblings continually looked forward to having Harry return for the barn dances and other entertainment events.

Getting acquainted with her future in-laws, Savanna felt, was the beginning of her life of marriage. She'd therefore become eager to be formally introduced to Harry's parents. With the marriage proposal now official, it was also time for Melvia and Isaack to be introduced to their future in-laws. The couple had been waiting for this day with eager curiosity. The families scheduled a series of meetings in which they would hold heated debates designed to accept or reject the proposed marriage.

Under the warm glow of the Saturday midday sun, Melvia and Isaack, accompanied by their curious offspring, traveled several miles to the Lovethon estate. The families gathered in the home of the Lovethons around their large round table. The curious offspring of both households joined the session. The ultimate motive was to form an opinion on their future extended family.

Upon learning of Harry's proposal, Melvia and her remaining offspring immediately arrived at the consensus that he would be the best gentleman to marry Savanna—should Harry's parents give their consent to the marriage. In Melvia's mind, the marriage should be sooner than later. Isaack, in the meantime, had remained indecisive about the marriage. In his opinion, Savanna was a bit too young for marriage. Meanwhile, there hadn't been a doubt that he'd welcomed the handsome gentleman.

In preparation for their first debate with the Lovethons, before Harry and Savanna set a date for the wedding, Melvia and Isaack sat, well-rehearsed for the debate. The offspring kept their mannerisms in close check as they waited in silence to observe the proceeding. The stage had been set for the first heated debate that would determine the young adults' suitability as well as their preparedness for marriage. It was also a time of judgment as to whether there would be compatibility between the extended families.

At the commencement of the debate, the Lovethons expressed doubts as to whether they should release their noble son to wed a girl he'd scarcely known, beautiful as she appeared.

"The big question shared by Henry and me is whether the young folk genuinely love each other. Harry has never had an obsession with a young lady as he has had with Savanna. He speaks her name even while he sleeps," Addriana said. "I strongly recommend that further marriage plans be put on hold while the young folk rethink their decision." Addriana sat poised, waiting for Henry's gesture of agreement.

He instead gestured for her to continue.

"Are the young folk acting too quickly? At twenty-one, Harry is still at a tender age where he's incapable of making firm and binding decisions."

Henry listened with keen intent while he gestured for Addriana to continue expressing her doubts about the marriage.

"Will they seek divorce down the road?" Addriana said. She adamantly expressed her doubts with the intent to ignite fear in the hearts of the future couple.

Henry nodded in approval of Addriana being the dominant speaker of the session. Little did Addriana realize that she'd placed her own character under the microscope.

Melvia's thoughts quickly reflected on Savanna's devotion to household responsibilities. She therefore commenced her argument for the marriage based on Savanna's capabilities. "At the tender age of nineteen, soon to be twenty, Savanna is mature and quite capable of making binding decisions," Melvia said as her offspring listened in silence. "We have no doubt that Harry is the young man to take the hand of our daughter. Savanna is a well-disciplined young lady that a gentleman like Harry seeks. She has proven that she can care for her household." Melvia further reaffirmed her position as she vouched for the marriage the best way she could.

Henry's eyes once more collided with Addriana's while Melvia maintained her affirmation about the proposed marriage.

Melvia carefully voiced her concerns. "Does Harry have his estate prepared for his future wife? Is he capable of caring for his future wife and the children to follow?"

Isaack listened to the ifs and buts of the future couple's proposed marriage, but he'd remained on the fence with his opinion. "The young folk are intelligent beings who can make their own decision as to whether or not they should marry," Isaack said.

Addriana promptly objected to Isaack's laid-back attitude. She had her reservations about Harry getting married at such a young age. "Your daughter appears to be the fine young lady that a noble gentleman like my son seeks," Addriana said. "However, it's my opinion—and I'm quite certain it has been Henry's—that the young folk should think seriously about their marriage proposal. Should the marriage end in divorce, my family will be left in an embarrassing dilemma. Harry's chance of finding another wife will be greatly diminished."

The debate continued as Addriana and Henry held on to their firm reservations about their son's proposed marriage to Savanna.

Throughout the meeting, Savanna's eyes were preoccupied, observing the consistent winks and reading the lips of her siblings. She'd clearly interpreted their message as "We love him, Savanna." She wished her siblings had the final word on her marriage proposal. Meanwhile, Harry had not been given the opportunity to speak. He'd therefore remained in unwavering hope that his marriage would proceed. Harry remained overwhelmed by his passionate love for Savanna. The teardrops that continually fell from his eyes were no doubt tears of genuine love.

At the adjournment of the meeting, Addriana and Henry remained doubtful with regard to whether their son had made the right choice. The families had therefore scheduled a series of future meetings. They were bent on ironing out their differences and putting all doubts to rest before a date was set for the wedding. Harry remained adamant while the families debated in the hope of arriving at a mutual decision.

Despite mounting uncertainties between the families, Savanna had been making secret visits to Bragerston. She scrutinized wedding dresses, shoes, and fine jewelry in anticipation of her big wedding day. An adorable pair of white shoes displayed in the window of a small designer boutique caught her keen eye. Savanna imagined her feet adorned in the beautiful sparkling white shoes on her wedding day.

The marriage debate had moved into round two. A second meeting was scheduled, this time in the Sevensen home. As the couple awaited the arrival of Harry's parents, Melvia sat in anxious fear. In her heart, she prayed that Harry would become part of the Sevensen family.

"Isaack, I'm afraid Savanna will miss this great opportunity to become the wife of this fine gentleman," Melvia whispered in Isaack's ear.

Isaack remained nonchalant about the whole situation. He sat at the table as one having no care or concern about the proposed marriage. "I believe we should let time determine the outcome of this marriage proposal," Isaack said in a subdued tone. "If Harry doesn't marry Savanna, every hoe has its stick in the forest. She will someday find her husband."

Melvia begged to disagree. She felt that Harry was the man to marry Savanna. Isaack, nonetheless, could not be swayed from his sitting-on-the-fence attitude.

Henry and Addriana finally arrived under the sweltering heat of the Saturday midday sun. They were occupied with fanning their brows and wiping the perspiration that flowed heavily down their cheeks. It was questionable whether the couple had been crying buckets beneath a constant flow of perspiration. In preparation for the commencement of the meeting, the Lovethons had duly taken their place at the table in the Sevensens' large hall. Savanna had secured her place among her siblings, while Harry took his position on the right side of his father.

At the commencement of the meeting, the stage was set for both families to voice further concerns about the proposed marriage. Moments passed as neither family voice their concerns. Suspense had become the order of the moment. There hadn't been a doubt that the Lovethons should be the first to speak. They'd left the prior meeting having reservations as to whether their son should marry Savanna.

Addriana therefore cleared her groggy throat as she began to speak. "Be it known that, having second thoughts, and further discussing the issue of Harry's proposed marriage, Henry and I have reached our final consensus." Addriana promptly paused for a deep breath. She kept her gaze around the hall, raising fear and suspicion among the anxious folk.

Melvia held firmly onto Isaack's hand while she waited in sustained agony. Savanna observed the cascading tears of her siblings as they cried on one another's shoulders. Melvia and her vigilant offspring had no doubt been expecting the worse. Isaack observed the proceeding, unperturbed by whatever would be the outcome. Harry maintained a subdued emotion as he sat by his father's side. There were no gestures or nudging by Henry as he too waited for Addriana to continue where she'd left off speaking.

The hall was once more brought to silence when Addriana resumed her opening speech. "Further discussions held by myself, Henry, and my son Harry have led us to arrive at a final consensus. Henry and I have determined that Harry is quite capable of making decisions that will govern his future. He's therefore ready to proceed with his marriage to the beautiful young lady he's chosen."

The atmosphere became permeated with giggles and whispers among those who'd made their pledge to give due respects while the meeting was in progress. Addriana had cleared the air with her brief unexpected announcement to the Sevensen family.

After a moment of expressed exhilaration, it was Henry's turn to speak. As he'd always been the secondary speaker, Henry added the finishing touches to Addriana's brief announcement. "Mr. and Mrs. Sevensen, I'm convinced that Harry will be an excellent husband and a generous provider for his beautiful wife, Savanna," Henry said amidst still silence. "Addriana and I therefore have no objection to the young folk joining in marriage."

A moment of stillness and suppressed cheers ensued before Henry continued to speak.

"Further to concerns raised with regard to Harry's ability to provide for his future wife, a large estate has been allotted to our son Harry," Henry proudly announced.

Harry proudly took his place by Savanna's side as the elated future couple exchanged a warm embrace.

"Mr. and Mrs. Sevensen, Addriana and I are pleased to present to you our son Harry Lovethon, to be wedded to your beautiful daughter Savanna."

With Henry's exhilarating words, the elated couple cheerfully shook hands with Isaack and Melvia. It was a decision that had been signed, sealed, and delivered in the most agreeable manner. Cheers and laughter filled the hall as the families embraced in love. The Sevensens had long held their silence before they had another opportunity to address the session.

Melvia commenced her short speech of acceptance as she looked toward Savanna and Harry. "Mr. and Mrs. Lovethon, I thank you for the honor of releasing your fine son Harry to marry our daughter Savanna," Melvia said. Tears cascaded from her eyes as she silently nudged Isaack to speak in response to the Lovethons' offer.

Isaack had once more been given the opportunity to speak the last word. As the proud father of the soon-to-be bride, he stepped toward the center of the hall. At his swift gesture, Savanna stepped forward, holding the hand of her soon-to-be husband.

Isaack smiled cheerfully as he addressed the session. "Mr. and Mrs. Lovethon, on behalf of Melvia and myself, I proudly offer to your son Harry our beautiful daughter Savanna to be his wedded wife."

The hall was instantly permeated with sounds of laughter, amidst smiles and all the formalities of a festive occasion. Isaack's brief statement had solidified Harry's proposal to wed Savanna. In Isaack's view, Harry and Savanna had been left alone to make their own decision to marry.

The meeting was promptly and joyfully adjourned. There was no doubt that all had arrived at the consensus that the marriage was a go. Harry's parents showered the future couple with hugs and smiles. Harry and Savanna kissed their parents, a sign of gratitude that they'd arrived at a consensus for their marriage to proceed. In a similar fashion, Harry's siblings, Garfeld and Katharene, delightfully greeted Savanna and her joyful siblings. Savanna's siblings continually showered her with hugs and kisses.

With the marriage now fully approved, there were no further scheduled debates. Harry and Savanna therefore resumed their frequent meetings in the secret nook. The next critical event was to set their wedding date. The next Sunday afternoon, when Harry had returned from visiting his parents, he duly met with Savanna in the nook.

"My beautiful lady," Harry said as he showered her with love and kisses, "soon, we'll be together for life."

Savanna was immediately overcome with joyful tears, which she continually wiped with a handkerchief she had retrieved from her bosom. "Harry, my love," Savanna said amidst her flowing tears, "I cannot wait for us to begin our life of happiness. We must set a date for our wedding."

Harry knew the wedding date was contingent upon many factors. He'd therefore left the ball in Savanna's court. "What date will be best for both of us, Savanna?" Harry asked.

After moments of contemplation and debates, both agreed on November 15 as the date of their wedding as both felt that it was appropriate. At the end of the harvest season, an abundance of food and other provisions would be in the storehouse. Brilliant flowers and bulky roses would still be in the garden. A kaleidoscope of colors had always been the setting for the beginning of the autumn season. The trees from the top of the mountain to the plains below would commence displaying their brown, green, red, and yellow foliage to complement the season and hence create a perfect farm setting for the autumn wedding.

At the end of their short meeting in the nook, Savanna rushed home with the news of her wedding date. Her siblings gathered in the big hall to celebrate the occasion. They'd pledged to participate in whichever way they could during the wedding preparations.

Isaack and Melvia were occupied with giving last-minute advice on love and marriage to their soon-to-be-married young daughter. Likewise, Addriana had taken every step to mentor and groom her son on becoming a married man, with some assistance from Henry. Cecelia was no doubt making preparations to return home for the wedding, as she'd promised. Cecelia stood poised to furnish her younger sibling with sound advice on matters of joggling her teaching career and being the best wife to her noble and flamboyant husband.

Serious wedding plans had been taking on momentum. Melvia and Isaack had frequent meetings with Harry's parents as they drafted every minute detail of the wedding. Savanna and her siblings tirelessly ran errands to town. They sought out the most adorable designer jewelry. More times than one, Savanna revisited the wedding gowns she'd earmarked. She purchased the adorable shoes, so beautifully displayed in the window of the designer shoe store. They were a perfect fit for her feet. In preparation for her wedding day, Savanna brushed up on her smiles. She practiced a variety of steps in her elegant designer shoes, and for the most lavish wedding ever in Amerhurst, Isaack and Melvia had spent a fortune.

Addriana, in the meantime, took on the difficult task of finding a designer for Harry's lavish wedding outfit. It was her duty to ensure that her offspring portrayed the wealth and prestige representative of his noble heritage. By the same token, Melvia and Isaack did their utmost, endeavoring to adorn their beautiful daughter to reflect the Sevensens' wealth and prestige.

As parents of the future bride and bridegroom, the couples selected their priceless wedding garments for the occasion. They had a duty to present themselves as the most noble citizens of Amerhurst. The offspring of both couples designed their garments from priceless fabric purchased in the town. Their fine garments were complemented by elegant shoes and delicately crafted jewelry. The offspring flaunted their flair for elegance as they rehearsed for their role in the most lavish wedding to be held in Amerhurst.

Isaack purchased a new carriage to escort the bride to the distant church and subsequently to take the newlyweds along the scenic route to the reception on the Lovethon estates. Meanwhile, to accommodate what had been perceived as the wedding of the century, the Lovethons' landmark church had received a significant makeover. For the upcoming wedding, skilled workmen gave the finishing touches to the Lovethons' big barn, the venue for the reception. Meanwhile, Harry had been delightfully overwhelmed by his big day ahead. He too was a young adult looking forward to a new life of marriage with his beautiful wife, Savanna. Harry therefore relied on his parents, particularly Addriana, to groom him on his mannerisms and wedding etiquette.

In anticipation of their new lives as a prestigious married couple, Savanna and Harry practiced to get up close and comfortable with each other. As their wedding day drew closer, they met more frequently, promenading along the quiet road and meeting in the secret nook. Under the midday sun and the golden sunset, the young lovers sat on the bench of tranquility by the side of the pond. The soothing breeze fanned the waves across the emerald-green surface of the pond. Pure white lilies suspended from long green stems around the edge of the pond had always kept their hearts cheerful. For a time of closeness and tranquility, the quiet nook had become the future couple's regular venue. In the confines of the nook, they dreamed dreams of a married life of genuine love and happiness. Savanna perceived her big mansion, a lavish lifestyle with her soul mate, and her adorable offspring.

The wedding day was drawing closer. The young lovers tirelessly attended to the final details of their upcoming big day. Both families were occupied, adding the finishing touches in preparation for the grand finale.

CHAPTER 9

On That Somber Autumn Sunday

It was a bleak and cloudy October day in Amerhurst. Wherever the sun had been along its traveled path, thick gray clouds obscured the brilliant rays it normally spread from the mountain peak down to the plains. A melancholy mood had been the order of the entire day.

The folk had succumbed to the autumn blues after a long season of summertime cheerfulness. No one welcomed the autumn season of dark clouds, the occasional threat of rain, gusty winds, and a dreary sky. Dark clouds and thundering sounds up the mountain peak had brought the Sunday outdoor activities to a grinding halt. The Sevensen household waited for the sun to burst forth from behind the obscuring clouds. They wished to carry on with the usual outdoor pleasures, but the day went on without a speck of sunlight—just a dreary and soupy sky.

It was a family tradition to attend the only church in Amerhurst. It was also a Sunday tradition where the youngsters prepared the meals and served the older folk first, their way of showing respect to the elderly. The dinner session had ended. The young folk cleaned up after the big meal. In the Sevensen household, it was time to make preparations for the upcoming Monday activities.

On that somber Sunday afternoon, at the end of the dinner session, Savanna's siblings left home on their independent errands. Melvia and the future in-laws were making last-minute preparations for the wedding, which was a matter of weeks away. Isaack was allowed much-needed rest after his week of hard work around the farm.

Victoria was with her husband, enjoying her married life. Cecelia had left for her new life in the distant town, but she was soon to return home for the wedding. Kladius was no doubt enjoying his life in the UK. He was not expected to attend the wedding; however, Savanna anticipated his good wishes by way of a beautiful card, just as he'd sent for Victoria when she got married. Savanna had been slowly weaning her siblings, who'd clung to her like stamps on a letter. She'd been spending most of her leisure time with her soon-to-be husband, Harry.

Under a dark and dreary sky, Savanna was on her way to the nook. Harry had left Amerhurst for the weekend but had promised to meet her in the nook as soon as he returned that Sunday afternoon. Harry would never forget to join his soon-to-be bride in their secret meeting place. To ensure that he didn't forget, Savanna shoved a note beneath a rock beside her gate, the place where they habitually left secret notes to each other. She was quite certain that Harry would check for any note she might have left before he ventured out to the nook.

On her way to the nook, Savanna sat briefly on the tranquility bench by the edge of the pond. From that focal point, she enjoyed the sights and sounds in the atmosphere. She'd always been intrigued by the ripples glittering on the surface of the pond beneath the brilliant sunlight. On that day, although the surface of the pond had been constantly stirred by the soft, gentle breeze, there was an absence of the usual glittering ripples. The sun had not cast its rays over Amerhurst. As her journey progressed, Savanna walked along a bed of late-harvest berries. She stopped briefly to gather a bunch that she felt would be a good treat while she sat with Harry in the nook.

Savanna had become an avid lover of the intriguing things of nature, particularly the large plain stretched out with its tall trees and shrubs. She quickly noticed the trees as they hung limp, their branches swaying momentarily at the behest of the gentle evening breeze. She spent some time admiring the bright autumn flowers along her traveled path.

The birds chirped their melodious songs as they frolicked among the branches of the surrounding trees. With the lack of sunlight, there remained an absence of the cheerfulness that had always been in the air. Savanna followed the path leading through the cornfield. The dry brown corn leaves hung limp beneath the dreary autumn sky. The long summer sun had robbed the corn foliage of the rich forest-green coverings they'd proudly displayed during the spring season.

The remaining corns in the field had long passed their time of harvesting. Isaack's farm had produced corn in abundance. His hard labor of planting was rewarded by a bumper crop, too much to reap before the autumn season set in. Savanna adored the dry golden corns that hung limp on each stem, each neatly wrapped in its protective husk while exposing rows of golden grains. Like the adorable golden dry corns, Savanna thought, she too would soon be adored and cherished by the one for whom she would be waiting in the nook.

The sound of the spring at the foot of the mountain had become more audible as she approached the nook. Savanna snuck quietly inside the nook. She took her usual place on the ground covered with withes and dry leaves. Her young heart panted for a time of caressing by her handsome soul mate while they were solaced by the calm serenity of the flowing streams.

In the quiet nook, Savanna waited, hoping Harry would arrive momentarily, but her patience was wearing thin. She hoped he would arrive before the dusk began to overshadow the vicinity. Minutes turned into an hour since she'd been waiting for Harry to arrive. While she waited, she took advantage of every passing moment to imagine her new life ahead. Savanna perceived the love and care she would continually offer to the man soon to be her husband and soul mate. As Harry's wedded wife, Savanna anticipated her household of adorable offspring.

Savanna's anxious heart yearned to have her Prince Charming by her side. The bleak October weather, coupled with Harry's tardiness, plunged her into a melancholy mood. She wished that Harry had arrived on time for their arranged meeting. He would certainly offer her solace in her moment of gloom.

Her wait for Harry seemed like it was taking forever. On Sunday evenings, he'd always returned home on time. His tardiness had no doubt left Savanna to ponder whether some unexpected mishap had occurred. Harry was definitely due back in Amerhurst on that Sunday afternoon. This was the time he normally spent preparing school work for Monday morning. His Sunday afternoon return was therefore a certainty. With added assurance, Savanna continued to wait in the quiet nook. As the long wait persisted, she commenced reading an old edition of a magazine she'd brought along.

The atmosphere was still and quiet when Savanna suddenly had that creepy feeling that she was not alone. A short distance from the nook, she was immediately alerted to a slight rustle among the dry leaves. Her first reaction was to remain still. Peradventure whoever or whatever was invading the vicinity would not notice the nook. Audible footsteps and a sudden commotion could be heard among the tree branches and shrubs covering the area around the nook.

Were those the footsteps of Harry? Savanna wondered. It was certainly out of character for Harry to have approached the nook in such an erratic manner and with intimidating intentions. Savanna thought it could have been one of those days when Rex and Spicer came running toward the nook and wagging their tails as they greeted her. She therefore continued to leaf through the pages of the magazine while her ears remained perked up.

The rustling sounds among the lower branches of the trees gradually got closer to the nook. Savanna once more insinuated that animals in the wild may have climbed down from the cleft of the mountain rocks to have a drink in the spring. However, as she looked toward the entrance of the nook, her eyes beheld much more than she'd anticipated.

The fast-approaching monstrous image had plunged her into a daze. Savanna remained in the nook in a state of shock. Amidst fear and trembling, she quickly closed her eyes to avoid beholding that which had entered the nook.

Savanna momentarily built up enough courage to behold the imminent. To her great astonishment, she found herself face-to-face with a monstrous creature. His eye-piercing stares had left her motionless.

Savanna immediately froze and collapsed in her seat of leaves and withes. It was like the hold of death as the creature held firmly to her wrist.

With her strong will and stern determination, Savanna lunged forward at the monster. A fierce fight ensued as she commenced fending off her attacker. *He'll never take me away*, she thought, struggling fiercely to free herself from the monster's strong hold.

She'd mustered up the courage to make a mad dash through the woods and escape the imminent, but the monster had become overwhelming. The monster firmly clutched her hands with eagle-like fingers, long enough to delve a deadly wound to her wrists, should she attempt to resist his strong hold. Savanna immediately lapsed into a state of shock, but she continued to fend off her attacker.

"Let me go!" she screamed and wrestled to free herself from the strong grip the monster had placed on her wrists, but he held on steadfastly.

Amidst Savanna's persistent trembling, the creature raised her upright into a sitting position. Except for the sound of rustling leaves on the surrounding trees and the quiet streams flowing in the spring, there was a stillness in the atmosphere. Savanna sat cold and motionless. The monster reached out with his claw-like fingers and clutched her right shoulder. She attempted to scream, but her voice didn't resonate beyond the confines of the nook. She'd been silenced by fear. Savanna remained seated on the ground. She'd been overwhelmed by fear and uncertainty.

For the first time, a growling voice spoke into her ears. "Be not afraid. I won't harm you."

These words were meaningless to his victim, on whose shoulder he'd placed a deadly hold. The monster attempted to place her in a standing position, but Savanna's feet were like jelly. She repeatedly slumped back to the leaf-covered ground.

A gruff voice once more sounded in the nook. "Please don't make things difficult, madam. Stand on your feet." With his strong arms, he placed Savanna once more on her feet and held her firmly to prevent a further collapse. "Remain standing," the monster repeatedly coaxed her.

Savanna had become breathless and frightened at the sight of the overpowering, monstrous being. She wished that Harry would come to her rescue, but he didn't arrive. She was therefore alone and helpless in the hands of her attacker.

When the monstrous creature clutched her firmly around her waist, Savanna knew she had no chance of escaping. She attempted to free herself from the strong hold of one who'd been overpowering, but her efforts failed. Savanna once more built up the courage to speak; peradventure she could make her escape by some cunning means.

"Who're you?" she said with a tremor in her voice. "Please let me go."

Without the creature responding, a pair of eagle-like eyes peered straight at her face and traveled down her slim body. Amidst fear and trembling, Savanna's wobbly knees gave way, casting her to the ground with a loud thud. It appeared she'd been taking her last breath when she began to moan as one in distress.

Her monstrous captor once more began to speak. "Be still, madam." This time, he'd spoken in a much softer tone while he raised her to her feet. "I won't hurt you," he once more assured her.

Savanna had refused to be solaced by one who posed a serious threat to her safety. "Leave me alone! Go away, please!"

Savanna made her desperate plea, but the monster was in no way perturbed by her appeal and her struggle to escape. A crippling fear had now taken hold of her. The overpowering hold by the monster's strong hands, coupled with the radiance emanating from his bloodshot eyes, had rendered her motionless.

With great courage, Savanna secretly scrutinized the tall rough figure that had taken control of her physical being. Long matted hair flowing from his head obscured her view of the monster's facial features. Thick eyebrows crowned his round eagle-like eyes as they landed piercing looks up and down her body. A straight nose protruded from bundles of thick long matted hair extending from his head. The monster's large sturdy arms were barely visible from the thick hair covering his skin. Savanna wondered whether the monster was of human origin or he was a creature of the wild.

The monster stared fiercely around the interior of the nook as if he were contemplating his next move. Savanna remembered the smart advice she'd received from Melvia and Isaack: "Whatever it takes, fight for your life." She therefore made a last-ditch effort to put up a fight with the monster. As the struggle ensued, Savanna once more attempted to escape the monster's strong hold. When it seemed all had failed, she pleaded for immunity.

"Please let me go! I must go home to my parents!" Savanna screamed incessantly.

Her screams and struggles, however, had not deterred her determined captor, who'd maintained his firm hold around her waist. She soon realized that her loud voice hadn't been a deterrent to one who had firm intentions.

"I can't let go of you, madam," the monster said while he maintained a firmer hold. "I now have you." His eyes were focused toward the exit of the nook.

Savanna had become suspicious of the monster's intentions. She once more struggled to gain her release, but all attempts at making an escape had failed. The monster had taken control of her.

"Please come with me, madam," he said. This time, he'd spoken in a much firmer tone.

Savanna's persistent resistance and intense struggle to gain her release had become futile. The monster forcefully led her out of the nook and commenced swift strides along the bank of the spring. Like a leopard carrying its young, he quickly crossed the shallow waters of the spring. The monster commenced swift strides toward the grove of trees by the foot of the mountain.

Savanna's effort to free herself from the adamant monster had become futile. Her thoughts were immediately on Melvia and Isaack as well as her siblings, who didn't know her whereabouts. She'd remained hopeful that Harry would return home to provide details of their planned meeting in the nook.

Feeling confident that he had his victim, the monster held his face like a flint. After taking a series of deep breaths, he commenced his climb up the side of the mountain, maintaining a firm grip on his victim's wrist. Savanna looked up the side of the rugged and treacherous mountain and immediately perceived her destiny. She screamed and yelled with whatever sounds could have resonated from her faltering voice.

"No! Please let me go! I must go back to my parents and my siblings!" Her thoughts were immediately on Harry and her wedding day, which was fast approaching. "Harry!" she cried. "I love you!" Savanna quickly reconnected with reality. She realized that Harry was not present to hear her pleading or to come to her rescue. Savanna once more begged for her release. "Please do not take me away." Her unrelenting pleas, however, had fallen on the deaf ears of her captor.

The big monster turned his focus toward the mountain peak and commenced his steep ascent, maintaining a strong hold on the frail hand of his victim. Savanna's constant struggles with her captor had left her weak and defenseless. She therefore followed his lead up the mountain path. Great fear gripped her heart as she resumed her persistent pleas for her release.

"Please let me go!" Savanna cried once more.

Her captor was in no way perturbed by her cries or persistent pleading. He therefore continued to ascend the mountain, holding his precious prize. Savanna's heart pounded against her chest as fresh tears flowed from her eyes. Her captor swiftly gained ground as he ascended the rugged mountain terrain. Savanna soon realized that the climb was taking her farther away from her home and from Amerhurst. Distance became a factor in her expectation that someone would come to her rescue. Her constant fountain of tears finally touched the heart of her determined captor.

"Why are you crying, madam?" he asked. "I'm not hurting you."

Should Savanna take him at his word, or was it just a tactic to lure her farther up the mountain? She'd refused to be swayed by his false assurance that he'd meant her no harm. Savanna looked up at the huge figure standing beside her. She felt that only time would determine her fate. Savanna was fully aware that persistent resistance could jeopardize her safety. She therefore followed her captor like a silent lamb being led to its slaughter.

The climb up the mountain was becoming more treacherous. Savanna continued to ponder her fate in the hands of a total stranger and kidnapper. Fear had taken hold of her pounding heart. She perceived that there was no other place her captor could be taking her than in the deep mountain forest—to her imminent death. It was the beginning of an ordeal she felt would have no pleasant ending.

Under the somber evening sky, her captor ascended the rugged mountainside. It appeared he'd been following imaginable paths leading to his destination—or wherever he was heading. There were no picturesque routes or exquisite sceneries but rugged winding paths known only by him.

A thin ray of hope remained that there was a slim chance at escaping down the mountain. However, Savanna soon realized that it was a futile effort, attempting an escape. There hadn't been a trodden path left behind. It was like leaving drops of water along a path in a thick rainforest. There hadn't been traces of footprints or signs of a trodden path made by creatures of the wild or by humankind. Had there been trodden paths, they were obscured beneath thick shrubs, impeding tree branches, and rocks of various sizes that obstructed a thoroughfare.

Her captor's trail had therefore left no traces behind them as he made his way up the mountain, lugging his prey along. He walked as one following a rugged terrain of invisible paths. The path traveled had been further impeded by large rocks, stubborn shrubs, and branches of the forest trees. Nonetheless, her captor seemed to know the mountain quite well. He therefore made his way up its path with minimum effort.

The strength her captor exerted suggested that no rescuer could have freed his victim from his strong hold. Savanna was fully aware that any attempt at making an escape could have dire consequences. She therefore placed her life in the hands of providence. Whatever was her captor's intent, she felt that only time would reveal it and hence, determine her fate.

Like a stubborn animal resisting the leading of its master, Savanna once more resisted her captor's pulling and lugging as he made his ascent. When she'd stubbornly resisted his lead, he reached out with his strong arm and clutched her by the waist. It was like the hold of death as he forcibly carried her up the mountain. Savanna cried tears of agony as the climb progressed.

Dusk was fast approaching. The sound of the gently flowing streams in the spring gradually faded in the distant valley. Savanna took quick glances behind her as she perceived her home gradually disappearing in the distance. As her home disappeared in the distance behind her, so did Harry and those she greatly cherished. All her hopes and dreams of a happy marriage faded by the minute.

Savanna reflected on the nook and her long wait for Harry to arrive. There was the possibility that Harry had arrived at the nook but much too late to save her. For certain, he would be concerned about her absence and the nook that had been left in disarray. Harry would certainly be faced with the unexplained. What would he think? What would he tell her worried parents and her siblings? Savanna's muscles and limbs had become weakened by her captor's overpowering hold. Nonetheless, she made a last-ditch effort to gain her release.

"Please, sir!" Savanna cried. "I can't go with you. I must go home to my family and my siblings, who're searching for me. And Harry. Oh, Harry! He's the love of my life."

At her mention of Harry, her captor gave her that consuming stare while placing a firmer grip around her waist. He promptly responded in a rather consuming voice, "Come with me, madam. I can't let you go back to your home." He repeatedly looked in the direction from which they'd come while making his ascent with firmer determination. "Please tell me your name, madam," her captor demanded. His voice was fading from exhaustion.

Savanna firmly believed that her cooperation could win her release. She therefore complied with her captor's demand. "My name is . . . Savanna." Her voice trembled as that of one who'd been traumatized from fear.

"Where do you live?" The sound of his growling voice echoed down in the valley below.

"I live in that house down on the plain." She pointed down the mountain in the direction from which they'd come. Savanna felt it was an odd question to ask since her house was the only one in the vicinity at the foot of the mountain. Nonetheless, she provided the information he sought.

Through an act of bravery, Savanna boldly reciprocated by asking questions of her captor. She was determined to pry into his life for whatever he was willing to disclose. "I've never seen you in Amerhurst or anywhere else. What's your name?" Savanna inquired of the stranger, who hesitated before responding.

"I can't tell you my name, madam," he said. "It's not for you to know at this time."

Savanna trembled at the sound of his gruff voice. She immediately thought of the golden rule laid down by Isaack and Melvia and her concerned grandparents: "Never talk to strangers or provide information to them." Savanna found herself in a precarious situation where rules had to be broken. In her situation, she'd become overwhelmed by a stranger who stood to take her life if she refused to cooperate.

Savanna also felt she might have given too much information that could jeopardize her family's safety, particularly her siblings. By volunteering too much information, she feared her captor could lurk in the woods and snatch another victim—one of her siblings. Having these thoughts and perceptions, she pledged to refrain from providing further details about her place of origin.

A myriad of thoughts flooded Savanna's mind as she kept a close watch on the movements of her captor. Was he alone? Had he been waiting for his accomplice or having thoughts about what to do with his victim? Savanna looked at the face of the one who'd been painstakingly lugging her up the mountain. She couldn't have ignored his teeth, which appeared stained for lack of proper dental hygiene. Whether he was charming, handsome, or ugly, there was nothing left to her imagination, for the bundles of hair that obscured his facial features. His high cheeks and adorable lips, however, were telltales of the face beneath the obscuring hair.

As the opportunity arose, Savanna discreetly scrutinized her captor for any form of identity she could capture. Should she escape with her life, she would have sketchy details to give to the town authorities. Savanna was quickly reminded that a dead man tells no tales. It was therefore futile to make further attempts at procuring details on her captor's identity. Nonetheless, her eyes were discreetly scrutinizing every minute detail she felt she could capture.

When it appeared that all efforts had failed to gain her release, Savanna commenced weeping persistently. New tears continually cascaded down her cheeks. With the front of his tattered and tarnished shirt, her captor wiped the tears from her face. Upon closer scrutiny of his ragged shirt, Savanna noticed dark wood stains. Dark wood stains had also changed the color of his tattered trousers. She was quickly overcome by the smell of black soot that had drastically changed the color of her captor's clothing. There was no telling that the outdoors had taken its toll on his torn and tarnished shoes.

Her captor continued to take painstaking strides up the mountain, lugging his victim along. The climb progressed as Savanna's resistance, coupled with impeding rocks and thorns, made the journey more treacherous. She watched thick sweat oozing from beneath her captor's thick facial hair. Nonetheless, he persevered, challenging the steep mountainside.

Further resistance as well as her chance at gaining her release had become futile. Savanna felt there was no other tactic she could apply that would have changed the mind of her adamant captor. She therefore followed his lead while maintaining her silence. Exhaustion, coupled with excruciating pains, had taken their toll on her joints and muscles. At that juncture, it had become obvious that she was approaching the imminent.

In Amerhurst, the folk had often told tales of the legendary caves on Deadman's Mountain. Savanna reflected on the tales of human and animal bones in the caves of the mountain. The caves were said to have once been the burial places of ancient folk who had made the mountain their sanctuary. Legend also had it that Deadman's Mountain had derived its name from the rituals and sacrifices of the ancient mountain folk. As the climb progressed, Savanna imagined hers being included in one of the legendary caves of human bones.

Savanna perceived the deep and dark caves where her voice would not be heard—should she be taken into their interior. Never in her wildest dreams had she thought she would be climbing the mountain full of fearful legends and caveats. The mountain was known as the place of untraversed territories. There were places unknown to the residents below and where no human feet dared to tread. There were places where no feet in the villages below had trodden—until she became broadsided by the reality of climbing up its paths to her unknown fate.

Despite her many failed attempts at gaining her release, Savanna had refused to give in. She therefore attempted once more to scream her loudest. She soon realized that her voice did not resonate. Her captor had taken her deep into the woods where, if ever her voice had resonated, it would not be heard. Besides, there were constant sounds of mountain creatures in their habitat. The sound of her voice would have blended with the sounds of the creatures of the wild, thus making it difficult for anyone to identify a human voice. Savanna was promptly reminded of her pledge to silence. She therefore followed, in compliance with her captor's demands.

Dusk gradually engulfed the mountain and the plains below. Savanna's shivering feet failed to support her now frail body. She fell clumsily to the ground among protruding rocks and thorns beneath the forest trees. Her captor quickly raised her to her feet and gently placed her on his shoulder. Like a giant exerting his mighty strength, he continued his strides up the mountain.

Savanna's thoughts were preoccupied, sifting through a myriad of possibilities of her fate on the mountain. She'd heard horror stories of girls who were kidnapped and had never been found. Cecelia and Kladius had often told her and her other siblings about movies in which girls were kidnapped and held as slaves until they were finally found. They also told of beautiful girls who were kidnapped and kept as lovers by mean old men.

The climb progressed up the dark and rugged mountain terrain. Savanna's fate rested solely in the hands of her captor. Was he taking her to her imminent death? Was he one of the Red Vipers? These were questions for which there were no immediate answers.

CHAPTER 10

Wedged Among Tall Rocks

Dusk gradually settled on the mountain. The entire vicinity was dark and frightful. Savanna had suddenly found herself out of her comfort zone. The path had become steeper, thus creating havoc as the ascent progressed. As she remained on her captor's shoulder, suspense became the order of every moment.

The soupy clouds that had darkened the sky throughout the entire day had completely dissipated, but the moon was not present in that part of the universe. With the absence of moonlight, the night sky was spectacularly lit by stars of varying sizes and brilliant twinkling lights. As far as her eyes could see from her vantage point beneath the forest trees, the sky was spectacular. Despite their glow, the brightness of the stars in the universe was not sufficient to brighten the mountain path, crowded with tall trees, shrubs, and rocks of varying sizes. The sounds of a myriad of creatures of the wild were everywhere, thus contributing to the spookiness of the mountain wilderness.

Just when a greater fear began to take hold of Savanna's heart, the long journey ended among large rocks and thick clusters of tall trees and shrubs. Her captor began to make sharp ascents among a series of large rocks. He maintained a firm grip on his weeping victim, whom he continued to carry on his shoulder. Like a chicken without its head, he began to walk in circles around sharp bends and between narrow rocks. His series of erratic turns abruptly ended between two tall rocks.

As she approached her captor's apparent destination, Savanna was immediately stricken by mounting fears and ardent curiosity. Her heart was gripped by a strong feeling that she'd been moving closer to the imminent. Savanna kept her close scrutiny of the objects that stood in the darkness, although she was unable to determine their size, shape, and color. She'd been closely scrutinizing the vicinity when her eyes stumbled upon a rugged structure camouflaged among rocks and tall trees. At the sight of the structure, she began to tremble in her captor's arms.

With a great sense of relief, he carefully placed her on her feet. She immediately lost her footing and landed on the rocky ground. No sooner had her captor placed her on her feet than he collapsed on the rocky ground. Savanna watched in awe as he commenced gasping from exhaustion. Great fear struck her heart as she pondered the welfare of her captor. Should he die from exhaustion, she feared she would be left alone in the mountain wilderness.

The faint sound of the flowing streams in the spring could be heard in the distant valley. Creatures of the wild could be heard quietly signaling to one another in preparation for their night of rest. Savanna had creeping feelings as she awaited her fate in the presence of her captor, who, at that point, remained sprawled on the ground.

He suddenly appeared to have replenished his strength when he slowly rose to his feet. He raised Savanna to her feet and commenced careful strides between the rocks, holding firmly to her wrist. While maintaining a firm hold on his victim, he slowly opened a door in the dark space between the large rocks. Savanna struggled fiercely as she resisted entering the house, but her captor aggressively shoved and pushed her through the narrow wooden door leading into the house. He promptly barred the door through which they'd entered.

Neither spoke as Savanna was dragged into the dark, gloomy atmosphere inside the house. No sooner had they entered the house than her captor quickly disappeared into the still black space. It was a daunting moment as Savanna stood in the still darkness while she awaited her fate. She felt she was taking her last few breaths and therefore began to whisper words of comfort to her trembling heart. Savanna softly whispered a prayer for Melvia and Isaack and for her siblings. She said a prayer for her grandparents as she called them by their names. Most of all, Savanna prayed for Harry. Should she not survive the night, she had been privileged to speak the names of her loved ones in the last moments of her existence.

Savanna remained in the still dark space, pondering the whereabouts of her captor. It wasn't long before she had noticed a small flickering glow appear in the still darkness. He'd returned, holding a candle he carefully placed on a log table in one corner of the space where she stood. From the faint glow of the flame, Savanna scrutinized the small space. She quickly noticed two wooden benches positioned in opposite directions.

When her captor slowly approached her in the semi-dark space, it was much more than Savanna could have borne. She immediately lapsed into a state of convulsion and crumpled to the hard log floor. To further add to her agony, her captor slowly raised her to her feet. He led her further into the hall and carefully placed her on one of the log benches that stood along a wall of logs. Savanna was relieved to finally rest her aching feet as well as her sore and aching body. She was nonetheless, quickly reminded that she had been awaiting her unknown fate.

Savanna lay reclined on the bench as one in a deep sleep. She was immediately overcome by fatigue and constant fear. Her ears were perked up for any sudden sound or movement in the remaining dark areas of the house. Meanwhile, like a hunting lion that had just taken down its prey, her captor sat slumped on the log bench opposite the bench on which he'd placed her. He continued to gasp for air after a long and grueling journey carrying his victim up the rugged mountain terrain.

Each terrifying moment left Savanna drowning in her tears, wondering what her captor's next move would be. Had there been other victims in the house? Was her captor acting alone? Savanna's mind brewed over many questions, but she relied on time to bring forth the answers. She remained slumped on the hard log bench but kept her captor under close surveillance. Whatever fate awaited her, she uttered a silent prayer that it would be over before the dawn. This would bring an end to her fears and agony.

When it appeared that her silent captor was falling into a deep sleep, he slowly rose to his feet. Like a lion waking from its restful sleep, he uttered an audible, ugly yawn. His growling voice echoed across the hall, taking Savanna's fears to its climax. She promptly sat upright on the bench as she anticipated the inevitable. The dim glow of the candle revealed her captor's broad shoulders and an enormous physique. Savanna candidly observed him as he stood like a tired, snarling animal waiting to consume its prey. He'd exhibited signs of anger and annoyance that were obvious signs of fatigue. Her captor once more sat on his bench as one who'd received replenished strength. As Savanna had least expected, he began to speak.

"Madam, please tell me your name." His resounding voice echoed in the atmosphere of the hall.

Savanna was immediately overcome by vigorous trembling. She looked candidly into the piercing eyes of her intimidating captor while clinging firmly to the bench on which she was seated. Seconds of silence ensued before Savanna built up the courage to communicate with her terrifying captor.

"My name is . . . Savanna," she said.

Her captor sat in silence as if he were scheduling his next action. It was an act of sheer bravery when Savanna mustered up the courage to reciprocate by asking for her captor's name. She felt she had a right to know the name of the monstrous creature that had captured and carried her up the mountain. Savanna had refused to be a coward in the midst of danger.

"Please, sir, tell me your name," Savanna said with tremors in her voice. She could faintly see the bloodshot eyes of her captor and further feared his unpredictable reaction.

"My name is . . . Tom."

His voice thundered across the hall while he stared at the face of his trembling victim. With his eagle-like eyes peering beneath thick eyebrows, he tossed sharp glances around the hall. Savanna sat in great fear while she pondered her captor's next action.

Tom once more began to speak with his trembling victim, this time in a much softer tone. "Madam, you must stay here with me," he said.

Savanna felt her heart skip a beat as she became broadsided by the grim reality that she would never go back home. "Please, sir," Savanna cried, "let me go back home! My parents are searching for me."

Tom remained in the comfort of the wooden bench, unperturbed by Savanna's incessant pleading. He'd been joyously amusing himself as he made repeated eye-piercing stares at the new tears flowing down her face. Savanna had become leery in the presence of her captor. Most of all, she was terrified by the dead silence in the strange house. In her heart, there was that constant yearning to go back home. Savanna therefore continued to beg for her release.

"Please, sir, take me back home," she pleaded once more.

As their eyes met, she noticed an awfully weird smile as her captor's eyes sparkled and his stained teeth were exposed beneath thick facial hair.

"Madam, please call me Tom," he said, "I cannot take you back home. You must stay here with me." With those words uttered, he rose to his feet and slowly made his exit through the main door by which they'd entered the house.

Savanna's heart was stricken with added fear as she watched Tom exit the house. She remained in the semi-dark hall to ponder her fate in the strange environment. From the still silence around the house, Savanna imagined that darkness had fully engulfed the mountain.

Shortly after leaving the house, Tom reentered, holding an object in his hands. The atmosphere was immediately charged with the spicy aroma of cooked meat. While holding the aromatic object, he made swift strides through a narrow doorway leading into a pitch-black space. It was the black space from which he'd earlier appeared holding the pale candle.

Not long after he'd left the hall, a voice echoed back from his new location in the semi-dark house—"Come this way, madam."

There was silence once more as he waited for her to appear. Savanna tried to control her movements as shivers ran down her spine. She slowly built up courage and proceeded cautiously toward the area where Tom's voice was heard. Savanna entered a much smaller space where she noticed a wooden table surrounded by four wooden blocks. The space was lit by the small glow of a candle resting on the table. Tom was seated on one of the blocks around the table. He promptly beckoned for her to join him.

"Take a seat, madam," Tom said in a much calmer tone.

Savanna cautiously took her seat on the block opposite where Tom was seated. Both sat around the table beneath the glow of the candle set into a small stone.

"Madam, please eat," Tom said. "You must be hungry."

Savanna carefully scrutinized the aromatic object placed on a metal plate. It was half of a smoked bird wrapped in edible green leaves. Savanna had no appetite for food or thirst for drink. The excessive fear that had welled up within her had drowned out all feelings of hunger and thirst. Her hunger and thirst had refused to be compensated when her life was being weighed in the balance. Nonetheless, she felt she must eat to replenish her strength.

Savanna had never seen meat prepared in that manner, but to appease Tom, she worked up an appetite and cautiously ate the unsavory meat, along with the leafy green covering. She discreetly winced at the taste of the bird and the roasted leaf. Meanwhile, Tom devoured his portion ravenously. He promptly returned to the first area of the house. Whatever was the next item on his agenda had remained anyone's guess, but Savanna had not ceased from expecting the inevitable.

Savanna had remained seated at the table in the second hall when a voice echoed in the semi-dark space—"Madam, please return to your seat."

Savanna promptly made her way back to the first hall, in obeisance to Tom's command. She once more took her place on the log bench, where she waited for further instructions. Tom reverted to his reclining position on his bench, still reeling from exhaustion. The silence in the atmosphere became unbearably loud as neither spoke. Savanna therefore remained hopeful that Tom would spark up further conversation. She waited in hope that every precious moment would unveil his true intent.

Tom had kept her confined to the first area of the house, but Savanna entertained thoughts that there might be other victims detained in hidden dungeons. She could hear the early night breeze rustling the leaves of the surrounding trees. Except for nocturnal creatures scurrying among the nearby tree branches, there was not a sound or a stir by any human.

Savanna had remained in total silence as she sat on the bench in front of her rugged captor. Her thoughts had remained preoccupied. She wondered what the night would bring and whether she would see tomorrow. As each moment passed, her hope remained dangling in the silence of the log house. Amidst the silence, she remained calm, surrounded by a stagnant atmosphere of suspicion. Savanna remained in silence while she anticipated Tom's next action. His eyes surveyed the hall as often as he blinked.

As if he'd awakened to a new level of consciousness, Tom unexpectedly rose to his feet and began to speak once more. "Madam, please come with me."

At his regimented command, Savanna fell to the hardwood floor in a state of panic. Tom made a bad situation worse when he quickly went to her aid. He slowly lifted her up, only to see her slump back on the floor. When she once more crumpled to the floor, Tom painstakingly sat her down on the bench. Perspiration oozed down Savanna's face. Innumerable goose bumps popped up on her arms. She slowly regained her composure and remained in a state of sustained calm. Savanna was constantly reminded that there was no easy way out of her dilemma.

Tom's heavy feet pounded the floor as he made giant steps across the hall. He made his way toward the second hall where he'd served the roasted bird. Fear once more struck Savanna's heart like a bolt of lightning.

"This way, madam," he said.

Despite Savanna's state of fear and panic, Tom continued to demand her cooperation. With a display of great courage, Savanna hesitantly followed his lead. With each step she made, shivers could be felt whirling down her spine. Tom walked her through the area where they'd eaten the smoked bird. There'd been no further introduction required in that section of the house. He therefore commenced leading the way to another area of the crude structure. Savanna followed at a distance, watching her every step and anticipating the worse. The thick and rugged slabs on the floor had not left a smooth surface for her trembling feet.

Tom's voice once more resounded in the quiet atmosphere. "Come, madam. I'll show you."

He struck a match and lit another candle that was set into a small stone. With the tiny glow from the candle, he trudged slowly across the hall and opened the door to a small room. Savanna followed as she peered cautiously into the semi-dark room. Tom pointed toward a small wooden bed in one corner of the room. At the sight of the bed and the semi-dark room, their eyes quickly collided, but no one spoke. Savanna suddenly had the shivers. She almost hit the ground when Tom held her in an upright position.

"You will sleep in this bed, madam," he said.

In the semi-dark atmosphere, Savanna scrutinized the contents of the room. She was overcome by fearful thoughts about falling asleep amidst the unknown—should she be fortunate to fall asleep. Without further dialogue, Tom led the way into a slightly larger room. As Savanna stepped into the room, she felt chills traveling down her entire body. Beneath the glow of the candle, she noticed a double-sized bed made of logs and covered with layers of linen. Tom did not give an introduction of the room. Instead, he walked promptly toward another area of the house.

"Please follow me, madam," he said in a soft tone.

Still guided by the flickering glow of the candle, Tom entered another compartment, a room much smaller than the second one she'd seen. Savanna followed cautiously as he entered the room. She carefully scrutinized the small bed that stood in disarray in one corner of the room. The bed was lined with the skin of animals. Tom's eyes had scrutinized every area of the room before he finally commenced his introduction.

"This is my room, madam," he said.

Savanna's eyes surveyed the room as shivers traveled down her spine. Under quick scrutiny, Savanna noticed miscellaneous items strewn around, as if there'd been an earlier scuffle. Tom remained standing in the center of the room. His eyes were focused on her as he pondered his next action. At that juncture, Savanna began to tremble. Their eyes immediately met in direct focus. Both stared in silence as if neither knew what to do next.

Savanna quickly turned and exited the room, leaving Tom standing as one in a state of unexplained delirium. She immediately returned to the first hall and perceived making her escape in the direction she'd entered the house. However, in the middle of a mountain jungle and under the cover of pitch darkness, Savanna perceived the impossible.

Moments elapsed before Tom exited his room. He also returned to the hall, where he found Savanna standing close to the exit door. Once again, he beckoned for her to follow. Savanna remained poised to make her escape, wherever her frail legs could take her, but she was fully aware that there was no place to run. She therefore cautiously complied with Tom's request to follow him on the remaining tour of the house. There hadn't been much introduction required when a fireplace was seen in one corner of a space lined with black soot. There was a small glow from an ember still burning in the fireplace. The flickering flame from a small candle resting on a wooden table, shone faint light around the soot-lined area.

Tom walked across the gravel floor of the area and exited through a shabby wooden door. Savanna was overcome by fear but followed cautiously. The guided tour continued on the exterior of the house and in pitch darkness. Tom, however, continued as one who wasn't able to differentiate light and darkness. He promptly turned around and reentered the house. Savanna stood in the spooky darkness, pondering her fate in a strange and eerie environment. She was immediately surrounded by fierce flying insects swishing around in the dark somber night air.

Tom returned promptly, holding the candle he'd left behind. The small flame cast a faint glow around the immediate vicinity, showing a narrow path for Savanna to follow his lead. The path led them around a dark corner that was like a cavern. The stench that greeted her nose was a telltale of what was around the corner. It further aroused Savanna's awareness of Tom's need for a place of release whenever nature came knocking.

Tom walked closer to the cavern—his mountain outhouse. Savanna followed but remained at a distance. Tom carefully surveyed the area before turning back in the direction he'd come. Savanna had been carefully scrutinizing the strange outhouse when she suddenly realized how badly she needed to use the facility. She made her impulsive response to the call of nature before rushing toward the entrance of the house.

On the opposite section of the outhouse, Savanna heard the sound of a quiet stream. She'd stopped promptly to investigate the source of the water when Tom's candle cast its glow on a crystal stream flowing gently in the hollow section of a rock. Savanna had no questions but began to wash her dark and leaf-stained hands in the flowing stream.

Tom promptly escorted her back into the house before barring the door. Savanna had that too-close-for-comfort feeling when he led the way back into the first hall. She immediately slumped back onto the hardwood bench and once more succumbed to fear and fatigue. Most of all, her heart was revisited by that constant yearning to go back home.

Tom let out a laborious sigh before slumping into his usual place on the bench across from her. Chronic fatigue appeared to have prevented further communication as he lay on the bench in the eerie atmosphere. Savanna pondered Tom's silence and what was welling up in his heart. She regarded him with fear and caution and wondered whether his silence was a prelude to that which she felt was the imminent.

Like a voice coming out of the abyss of silence, Tom began to speak. "Madam, you may go to sleep," he said.

Savanna breathed out a silent sigh of relief to be absent from Tom's immediate presence. She promptly stood to her feet and walked toward her designated room but not before making a proper departure. "Good night, Tom," Savanna said as she exited the hall.

She heard his faint voice as if he'd been overcome by fatigue— "Good night, madam."

On that note, the atmosphere once more returned to silence. By the tiny glow of the candle in the second hall, Savanna carefully made her way to the entrance of her designated room. She remained in a state of fear and uncertainty as she cautiously opened the small door and stepped into the room. Whatever fate awaited her in the dead of night was left to time and to her imagination. Fear and much grief welled up in the pit of her stomach as she realized that her life rested in the hands of Tom.

Savanna was thankful as she realized that Tom communicated in English, although it appeared that English was not his mother tongue. He appeared to be well versed in the English language nonetheless. Occasionally, a word or two of the language of his mother tongue slipped from his lips, leaving Savanna to think that he'd been speaking gibberish. Savanna could not identify the language of his mother tongue. She had no knowledge of the other languages of the world. Nonetheless, Tom's knowledge of the English language had given her the confidence that they could communicate without faltering.

It was anyone's guess, whether Savanna would fall asleep in the midst of her dilemma. As she fearfully waited for much-needed sleep to arrive, she had reflections on her journey up the steep mountainside. She recalled that the sun had hidden its brilliant glow behind thick clouds for the entire day. Savanna perceived that it was the end of that day and another sunset before her longest and darkest night in captivity.

Savanna began to scrutinize the room under the glow of the candle Tom had left on a small log table beside her bed. Her movement in the semi-dark space was left to her keen senses and perception. A careful scrutiny of the small room revealed items that raised unanswered questions. There were sleeping accessories that appeared to have been placed on the bed for quite some time. A beautiful pair of pink and gold slippers had been conspicuously placed on the floor beside the bed. Savanna wondered whether the room had been prepared for another expected guest. She'd been preparing for a time of much-needed sleep but maintained a creeping feeling that Tom could strike without warning.

Savanna was continually reminded of her strength and courage. However, she realized how defenseless she was in the confines of the house with one of monstrous strength. While she remained behind the heavy wooden doors of the log house, she had a sense of security from the dangers that lurked without, but Savanna perceived impending dangers within. Amidst fatigue and a rising climate of fear and suspicion, she was forced to recline for the night. She reluctantly changed into the night accessories left in the room. Like a heavy log, she fell on the hard bed.

The silence was a golden moment for her to reminisce on the joyous life she'd had back home. Should she not escape with her life, Savanna felt she'd had a joyous short existence on earth, particularly among her siblings. Although she'd escaped from Tom's immediate presence, she was constantly aware of impending dangers that lurked around her in the semi-dark log house. Savanna became even more traumatized as she realized she was held captive by a kidnapper—a total stranger. He'd spared her life up the mountain, but it was anyone's guess as to what dangers awaited her in the house and beyond its wooden walls.

From the little comfort she'd been enjoying on the small bed, Savanna's eyes surveyed the room for whatever she could see and perceive. There were many unanswered questions about the room. Had Tom been expecting her or another guest to arrive at the house? Was there another woman living in the house with Tom? If so, who was she, and where could she be? Savanna pondered these questions for which the answers were not forthcoming. As she lay awake, her mind was at work attempting to unravel the mysteries of the log house and its occupant. Most of all, her thoughts were preoccupied with planning a way of escape from her ordeal.

As she'd perceived, the night was dark and alive with the sounds of creatures of the wild. The shrieks and howls of the nocturnal creatures could be heard in the outdoors as they prowled about for whatever they could capture. The desperate cries of unsuspecting creatures could be heard as they were captured by ferocious nocturnal predators.

Like the unsuspecting creatures on the outside, Savanna feared she too might become prey to her captor and whoever else might be lurking on the inside. With Tom holding vigil in the house, Savanna became vulnerable to horrifying incidents while she slept. She further feared that there were accomplices lurking on the outside to snatch her in the dead of night.

In the stillness of the night, Savanna's heart beat quietly. She'd been having her ample dose of solitude, being held in confinement in an isolated mountain log house. Savanna's heart yearned for the family to which she'd been so tightly attached. As the night progressed, she continually struggled to come to grips with her dilemma.

In the silence of the small room, Savanna reflected on her household and the exhilarating life to which she was accustomed. Melvia's voice habitually resounded in the distance as she sang to express her happy and pleasurable married life, a pleasant and caring husband, and many wonderful offspring. Animals continually made their presence known around the farm by their bleating sounds. Her household looked to the gigantic mountain towering above the village. It was the source of abundance of rain that kept the plains below lush, green, and thriving. It supplied the spring in the valley with crystal waters flowing over ivory stones and pebbles.

While she waited for much-coveted sleep to appear, Savanna's ears remained perked up like those of a keen watchdog. She was alerted to every movement in the house and never took any sound for granted. In the still silence, she heard a brief stir in the hall, followed by a rusty, grumbling voice. Savanna immediately rose to her feet. Had someone entered the house? She wondered. In her heart, she thought that that which she feared had begun to materialize—Tom's accomplices entering the house. The brief stir was followed by still silence. It was Tom who'd stumbled in the dark hall on his way to his room. Savanna cautiously lay back on her bed. As each moment passed, suspense lingered amidst mounting fears.

The tiny flame from the candle in her room flickered until it suddenly died. The room was left in a state of utter darkness. Savanna's inner vision began to create light—colorful images in the darkness. A myriad of mesmerizing colors began to play hide-and-seek with her vision. Her preoccupation with the colorful scenes brought to her mind a sense of serenity.

Savanna lay restlessly on the rugged bed lined with hard wood and the skin of animals. As if she'd had a sudden awakening to reality, her troubled mind went back home. She perceived the frenzy among her entire household as they realized that she did not return home from wherever she'd wandered off to. More troubling was the fact that no one knew her whereabouts or where to concentrate their search to find her. Should Harry turn up at the nook, he might see the rubble left behind, but items strewn about in the nook would not provide much clue to her whereabouts. For certain, her parents as well as her worried siblings would think that she'd been captured by the Red Vipers.

Savanna wondered whether she was Tom's first kidnapped victim. There hadn't been previous incidences of attempted kidnapping or sightings of unusual activities in Amerhurst. Had Tom been one of the Red Vipers, no one in Amerhurst or elsewhere had ever reported sightings of him. In the pitch-black room, Savanna's thoughts remained focused on her home and the frenzy among her folk. She soon realized that sleep chooses its victims. She therefore hoped that amidst her fears, she would be among those chosen victims.

CHAPTER 11

A Household in Turmoil

Back in Amerhurst, it was a long and turbulent Sunday evening when the Sevensen household realized that Savanna had not come home. Great fear and an air of confusion gripped the hearts of the entire household. Night fell, spreading darkness around the vicinity. Concerns grew as the mystery deepened. Melvia and Isaack, along with their worried offspring, felt it was out of character for Savanna not to return home, particularly on a dark night. She'd always been certain to be home on a Sunday evening to prepare for school the next day.

When Harry had failed to arrive by the local bus passing on the outskirts of Amerhurst, as he always did, the Sevensen household was further thrown into chaos. On a Sunday afternoon, the local bus had always been Harry's customary means of travel from his parents' home, back to his rented house in Amerhurst. Harry had always been certain to arrive on Sunday evening to prepare for school on Monday. Upon his return, he'd always received a cordial invitation to dine with the Sevensens, just to be close to Savanna. Harry's failure to return home had not left a doubt in anyone's mind that Savanna had left Amerhurst to be with him. Melvia and Isaack, along with their remaining offspring, had therefore restrained their tears. They strongly believed that the future couple would arrive home with some convoluted explanation for their absence.

Under the early dusk, the household gathered around the dinner table in the big hall. The grandparents joined the session to quell the tide of grief that had stricken the household. Grandmother Minerva prepared pastries and hot tea that was meant to calm the troubled minds of those who'd remained panic-stricken. Gwenna, one of the younger offspring, placed the dessert plates, teacups, and linen napkins at each place setting on the table. The household sat prepared for a session of sound reasoning and discussion, this time of a much different nature. Savanna's siblings immediately began to theorize, hoping that someone would come up with a clue leading to the whereabouts of their favorite sibling.

"Sav has eloped with her soul mate, Harry," Arretha said. "There's no other place she could be."

"This is a possibility," Petror said. "Victoria was on the verge of eloping with Aldbright when she felt her wedding day had been taking forever to arrive."

Florence waited patiently for her opportunity to speak. "There's no way that Aldbright's parents would have tolerated his act of eloping. Besides, Aldbright had stood to lose his fortune if he'd eloped with Victoria," Florence said.

Melvia sobbed profusely. She repeatedly rested her head on Isaack's shoulder while her offspring formulated their theories about Savanna.

"Savanna just wanted to be married quickly," Gorrana said. "The process of courtship, proposal, engagement, making wedding plans, the marriage ceremony . . . This process takes too long for two persons in ardent love."

The remaining offspring nodded in understanding of Gorrana's reasoning.

Isaack entertained similar thoughts and therefore held to his belief that Savanna would return home soon. "If Savanna and Harry decided to elope, it will be a matter of time before they emerge as man and wife," Isaack said.

Just as Arretha and Gorrana had presumed, Isaack strongly believed the lovers had eloped. Melvia's remaining offspring were not all in agreement with the thought.

Melvia could not be solaced by Arretha's theory that Savanna had eloped. She therefore continued to shed tears of grief and sadness. "Isaack," Melvia said, "Savanna is a beautiful young lady who would never leave Amerhurst without informing the household. She has never been out with Harry at this time of the night."

Melvia desperately tried to restrain her flowing tears. Melvia had spent a handsome fortune on Savanna's wedding dress. She therefore would not dare to think that Savanna had eloped.

"Isaack, we could have afforded the cost of Savanna's wedding," Melvia said. "As a matter of fact, we've fully paid for the wedding. Henry and Addriana have also laid down their fortune to prepare for Harry's wedding. We'd also fully approved of Savanna's choice of Harry as her future husband." Melvia spoke in great length and sincerity. Nonetheless, she had failed to convince Isaack and the frightened offspring that Savanna's disappearance should not be taken lightly.

"Let the young folk be, Melvia," Isaack said. On that note, Isaack rested his case.

The couple had also spent a mint on their offspring's elegant outfits.

"We've paid a high price for our wedding outfits," Auwen said. "What will we do with them if there's no wedding?" Auwen spoke on behalf of himself and his siblings who'd also spent a fortune on elegant garments and meticulously designed shoes, not to ignore the young ladies' designer jewelry. No one had an answer for Auwen's thought-provoking question.

As the offspring theorized about Savanna's disappearance, Petror came up with his theory, which no one could ignore. "There's a possibility that Savanna had been captured and taken away by the Red Vipers," Petror said.

At Petror's mention of the Red Vipers, Melvia sobbed profusely. Great fear welled up in her heart at the thought that Savanna could have been taken by a Viper. Legend had it that evil ruffians known as Red Vipers, habitually lurked along quiet roads to kidnap children as well as vulnerable adults. Legend further had it that the Red Vipers fed their victims potions before taking off with them to places unknown.

Petror, along with some of his siblings, strongly believed that Savanna had been captured by the Red Vipers. His mention of the Red Vipers had finally brought the household to tears. They were constantly solaced by Grandma Minerva, who'd also been sobbing uncontrollably. Melvia had always warned her offspring about talking to strangers, although not many strangers ventured through Amerhurst. If they did, she'd warn her offspring that strangers having evil intentions do not often make their presence known. They often snuck up on their victims before snatching them away.

The disappearance of Savanna triggered thoughts that she'd been kidnapped by the Red Vipers. While no one had seen or heard any strange occurrences in Amerhurst on that quiet Sunday afternoon, there remained the possibility that Savanna had been kidnapped by the Vipers. This was a possibility worth exploring, but Isaack and others of his offspring maintained their belief that Savanna had eloped with Harry. Despite a strong belief that Savanna had eloped with her future husband, an air of sadness and tearful moments hung over the Sevensen home.

Darkness slowly overshadowed Amerhurst and beyond. Under the early night sky, Isaack and Melvia remained surrounded by the elderly as well as their remaining grieving offspring. The household remained in the big hall to console one another in their time of grief.

"I knew there would have been some incidence involving Savanna," Isaack said. "Harry has been mad about her lately, particularly since their marriage proposal."

"Dad, do you think Savanna found another secret lover with whom she could have eloped?" Annetta asked. "I couldn't imagine her running off to get married without telling us, her siblings."

At Annetta's new assumption, the atmosphere in the hall became calm and quiet. No one in the household had knowledge of or had ever seen Savanna engaged in a conversation with anyone other than Harry. Annetta's theory was therefore rejected.

When Auwen brought forth his theory, everyone began to have second thoughts. "I looked into Savanna's room and noticed that she'd left all her belongings behind," Auwen said. "Do lovers leave their belongings behind when they elope?"

"They'll do anything to get away quickly," Isaack said.

Melvia wiped her eyes once more with the linen napkin placed inside her cup.

Arretha came up with another theory that appeared quite authentic. "I once read in one of Cecelia's magazines about the runaway bride," Arretha said.

The silence was quickly broken as the entire household was overcome by a fit of laughter.

"She didn't love her future husband as she thought she did and therefore ran away on the eve of their wedding." Arretha had drastically changed the eerie atmosphere when her tale ignited laughter among the grieving folk.

The consensus among the household was that, no one in Amerhurst and beyond had ever eloped, but there's always a first time for every incident. If Savanna had been kidnapped, she would also have been the first in Amerhurst. With Arretha's new theory in their thoughts, Melvia reverted to her belief that Savanna may have been kidnapped by the Red Vipers.

As the household grieved, the folk continually wiped their tearing eyes with the white linen napkins placed on the table. The grieving grandparents were too heavy-hearted to speak. They therefore continued to sob profusely. Melvia and Isaack had their concerns about the old folk's weak hearts. They were aware that the family couldn't deal with the added casualties if their parents collapsed from heart failure.

Meanwhile, Grandfather Samuel, who'd maintained sound wisdom, had also held back his grief. "I think we should wait for the details of Savanna's absence," Grandfather Samuel said. "The young lady may have taken off to be with Harry."

With Grandfather Samuel having the last say, the session ended just as it had begun. Everyone left the table of cold tea and uneaten pastries as the household continued to ponder the whereabouts of Savanna. Mounting concerns about Savanna's whereabouts took on momentum when the antique clock on the wall struck midnight.

Melvia's grave concerns about Savanna's absence prompted her and Isaack to walk under the cover of darkness to Harry's house. The couple confirmed that Harry had also not returned home. Melvia forcibly entered the house through the front door. With Isaack's assistance, she ransacked Harry's belongings in search of clues. Their search, however, had not turned up any clues as to the whereabouts of Savanna. As Harry was also absent, the couple arrived at the foregone conclusion that Savanna was with him.

"Isaack," Melvia said, "it's now anyone's guess as to why Harry and Savanna would be out together in the dead of night." Melvia's mind became somewhat at ease, knowing that Savanna and Harry were away together.

Isaack once more attempted to quell the tide with his sound advice. "Leave them alone," Isaack said, "They will certainly return home—one way or the other."

As the couple conversed in the late night air, a slight contention ensued between them.

"Isaack," Melvia said, "how dare you think that way! The poor girl may be in trouble. We should not take her disappearance lightly." In Melvia's heart, that was certainly not the way to deal with the disappearance of her innocent daughter.

In the heat of their contention, the couple walked home under the cover of darkness. Melvia cried bitter tears that only a mother could cry for her missing child.

The midnight darkness enveloped Amerhurst, hampering further search efforts to find Savanna. Until Savanna's whereabouts could be determined, she'd remained a missing person. The Sevensen household therefore clung to a thin ray of hope that news of her whereabouts would be received as the night progressed or during the course of the next day. All ears therefore remained perked up amidst fear and suspense.

The long-awaited Monday morning finally arrived. When the first birds began to chirp their cheerful melodies, the Sevensen household was awakened to face their new day of mounting fears. The grieving family waited for any news of Savanna's whereabouts. Everyone waited to see her and Harry show up, in Isaack's words, "with some convoluted explanation for their absence."

Harry's absence from his rented house had raised further suspicions that he had a role to play in Savanna's disappearance. The golden glow of the sun gradually appeared in the eastern horizon when Harry arrived in his parents' carriage. No sooner had he alighted from the carriage than it promptly turned around, taking his parents back to their distant residence. Harry first noticed his opened door and was reluctant to enter his house. When Melvia and Isaack promptly appeared at the door and had refused to leave, Harry felt that something was brewing.

"Harry, where is Savanna?" Melvia asked.

Harry stood perplexed as he waited for the details of Savanna's absence. "Madam Sevensen," Harry said in astonishment, "I don't know where she could be. I last saw her past Friday when we kissed by the bus stop." Little did Harry know that he was the main person of interest in Savanna's mysterious disappearance.

Without further questioning of their suspect, Melvia and Isaack rushed home to alert their household of Harry's return without Savanna. At the departure of the Sevensens, Harry walked discreetly through the dew-drenched cornfield. He entered quietly into the nook to see if Savanna had been patiently waiting for him. Harry knew Savanna was a girl of sound wisdom. He therefore couldn't imagine her waiting beyond a certain hour if he did not show up the day prior. He checked out the nook nonetheless. It didn't take long for him to notice that the nook had been left in disarray. *What has happened here?* His heart pounded within his chest. *Where's my charming lady?* Harry immediately began to ponder the fate of Savanna.

Under the golden glow of the morning sunlight, Harry rushed through the cornfield and onto the quiet road leading to his house. At the spur of the moment, he diverted and cautiously walked toward the Sevensen house. His heart still pounding, Harry entered through the big gate, which had been left ajar. He walked hesitantly toward the main entrance of the house. Isaack and Melvia were seated on a bench beneath the redwood tree, sharing their grief at the disappearance of Savanna. With cautious expectation, Harry approached the couple.

"Good morning, Mr. Sevensen," Harry greeted his future father-in-law. "My heart grieves at the disappearance of Savanna. I know you and Madam Sevensen are in much grief."

Melvia was too emotional to speak. She sat with her face buried in Isaack's chest. She'd therefore left the talking to him but did not fail to take note of the conversation.

"Harry, we were quite certain Savanna had left Amerhurst to be with you the past evening," Isaack muttered, his tongue twisted as his voice trembled.

Harry stood motionless as his eyes wandered off in the distance.

"Harry, have you seen Savanna? Did she leave Amerhurst to meet up with you yesterday?" Isaack asked.

Melvia gave a guilty stare in Harry's eyes.

"No, sir," Harry said as he stood dumbfounded. "Last time I saw Savanna was past Friday evening when we said goodbye and I boarded the bus." It became crystal clear to Harry that he was a suspect in Savanna's disappearance. "I can assure you, Mr. Sevensen, that I do not know where Savanna might be," Harry added.

His voice trembled as tears trickled from his eyes. Harry was quickly reminded that school commenced at 9:00 a.m. Without further ado, he excused himself and walked along the road leading to his house. Harry was fully aware that he'd been walking under a thick cloud of suspicion.

Harry's failure to return to Amerhurst on Sunday, as he normally did, raised even greater suspicion in the Sevensen household. He'd walked in on the news of Savanna's disappearance and into the thick air of suspicion that surrounded him. What was his alibi? It was next to impossible to establish an alibi among the folk who felt he was guilty of the crime of kidnapping and possible murdering his future bride.

The Sevensen offspring had remained in the distance while they observed Harry's meeting with their parents. They'd remained hopeful that joy would come once more, not only to their hearts but to the grieving hearts of Melvia and Isaack and their grandparents, who'd been making every effort to suppress their emotions. At Harry's prompt departure, there were whispers. New tears began to flow.

Melvia looked at Isaack to sense his thoughts on Harry's actions as well as his demeanor. "Those were tears of guilt," Melvia whispered. Harry's prompt departure from their short meeting had left thoughts in Melvia's mind. "He knows the whereabouts of Savanna. Harry may be guilty of a crime." Melvia was overcome by cascading tears. Melvia also insinuated that Harry's tardy return to Amerhurst had left no doubt in her mind that he was responsible for Savanna's disappearance. "He couldn't have stood through the meeting bearing the guilt of knowing what he did with our daughter," Melvia concluded.

The offspring gathered around their parents to further discuss Savanna's disappearance. There was a strong belief that Harry remained a person of interest.

Isaack, being a man of straight thinking and plain talk, decided to put the matter to rest. "Harry is not guilty," Isaack said. "Savanna and Harry appeared quite amiable and affectionate. Harry had shown no indication of his intent on causing harm to her. He therefore should not be suspected in her disappearance."

Melvia and her offspring listened with mixed feelings. The offspring maintained their independent opinion about Savanna's disappearance. Despite Isaack's assurance of Harry's innocence, suspicion prevailed in the minds of Melvia and her offspring.

"A young man of such high leverage cannot be a suspect in any foul play," Isaack continued. After Isaack's meeting with Harry, he remained adamant that he was innocent of any wrongdoing.

News of Savanna's disappearance began to spread among the folk of Amerhurst and places around the mountain. The folk became panic-stricken at the disappearance of the beautiful Sevensen girl. All the teachers and students of Amerhurst Villa School were saddened by the news of the disappearance of their fine teacher and mentor. The staff pledged to assist in whichever way they could to find Savanna. As he was also a teacher of the school, all eyes remained focused on Harry.

Concerned folk from distant places joined forces under the midmorning sunlight as a search went into full force. Melvia and her older offspring had a break from their house chores as they joined the search for Savanna. A thorough search was conducted around the farm and along the road passing through Amerhurst. Rex and Spicer, the keen sniffing dogs, were made to take the scent from Savanna's shoes and let loose across the fields to carry out their search. The dogs' frantic sniffing and shuffling of the leaves turned up nothing.

Folk around the mountain joined the search of the spring; peradventure the missing young lady had slipped and fallen between rocks or into a deep section of the spring. The searchers' thorough search, however, failed to turn up a body or provide a clue as to Savanna's whereabouts. The search was further hampered by Savanna's failure to inform her household of her planned meeting with Harry in the secret nook. Concerned searchers therefore had no idea as to where to focus their search.

Had Savanna been a victim of kidnapping by the Red Vipers? This was a thought that went through the minds of the folk who'd joined the massive search. No one in Amerhurst and beyond, recalled hearing or seeing a vehicle in the vicinity during the prior Sunday afternoon. No one had ever had an encounter with the legendary Red Vipers; nor had anyone ever reported a missing person in Amerhurst or anywhere else. Nonetheless, everyone believed in a "first time," and this could be such a time for Amerhurst when a victim had been kidnapped by the Red Vipers. In the minds of the concerned folk, this could also be the first time one of their beautiful ladies had been murdered by a jealous lover.

Words of Savanna's disappearance quickly reached Addriana and Henry, Harry's parents—and so did the rumors. When they'd further learned that Harry was a suspect in Savanna's disappearance, the couple immediately traveled back to Amerhurst with one intent: to clear their son's name from the allegation that he'd likely kidnapped and murdered Savanna.

Under the heat of the Monday midday sun, the folk were alerted to fast galloping horses and a carriage traveling at high speed heading toward Amerhurst. The horses came to a halt in front of the Sevensen gate. Addriana and Henry quickly alighted from their carriage and headed to the main entrance of the Sevensen home. Melvia's and Isaack's eyes and ears were perked up for the ensuing altercation with their future in-laws. The couple had scarcely taken a seat beneath the redwood tree before words began to fly in every direction.

"Harry is not a murderer," Addriana and Henry blurted out in unison. "We shall fight to clear his name."

Isaack obtained Melvia's permission to address the overly irate couple. "Mr. and Mrs. Lovethon, Harry came to our door early this morning and made his point clear about Savanna," Isaack said. "We accepted his reasoning and his explanation that he had nothing to do with the disappearance of our daughter Savanna." Isaack went through great lengths to make his point clear.

Meanwhile, Melvia listened in silence, hoping she could nudge Isaack's shoulder or land a kick on his feet. In her heart, Melvia felt that Harry was fully aware of the whereabouts of Savanna. Harry had remained committed to his teaching position. He was therefore in school when his parents had arrived at the Sevensen home. During the Lovethons' altercation with the Sevensens, concerned searchers waited with perked-up ears. In the distance, there were shouts of "Murderer! Shame, shame, shame!" as the folk shouted in unison.

"*Where did he hide her body?*" a voice yelled from the rear of the crowd.

The constant cries of "Shame!" from the crowd caused the Lovethons to be more defiant. They'd come to Amerhurst to clear their son's name from the allegation that he'd murdered his bride-to-be. Despite Isaack's effort to assure the Lovethons of Harry's perceived innocence, the remaining Sevensens and the concerned searchers continued to point fingers at Harry. In the opinion of the folk, Savanna was murdered by her husband-to-be, although there had been no evidence to confirm their allegation. The folk arrived at the conclusion that Harry had murdered Savanna as he'd found another young lady elsewhere. The concerned searchers remained in front of the Sevensen gate, hoping to gather more facts about Savanna's likely whereabouts.

Amidst a moment of silence, Henry stood to further address the eager crowd. "Addriana and I strongly believe that the truth will come to light someday," Henry said. "Harry would not have harmed the young lady with whom he'd been in ardent love."

Henry gave his firm assurance while Addriana uttered a resounding "Amen." Addriana was sure to have the final say when she once more stepped forward to speak. "Harry made a bad decision to have come to Amerhurst. We'll do whatever is within our powers to clear his name and get him away from this place," Addriana said.

With those words uttered, Addriana and Henry walked toward their carriage, feeling defeated in their effort to clear Harry of the false accusations made against him. The couple remained defiant as they pledged to continue their fight to clear their son's name. In the midst of the chanting crowd, the frustrated couple quickly climbed onto the carriage and took their seats. The horses trotted off slowly toward their home.

The volunteer searchers had exhausted all search options in their effort to find Savanna. A last-ditch effort had drawn their attention to the towering heights of Deadman's Mountain, but would they dare to conduct a search up the treacherous mountainside? Deadman's Mountain, with its rugged terrain and unexplored summit, extended toward the heavens and cast its shadow over the villages below. For many years, the majestic mountain had inspired a perplex fascination among the folk of the villages located around its base. From the vantage point of the folk below, its peak appeared to nudge the sky and was often obscured by the clouds that continuously formed at its crest. Under the night sky, the mountain extended into the heavens like a monolithic monument.

There'd always been a fear of the unknown, hence careful thoughts about the imminent dangers on the mountain. Though it appeared stunningly beautiful, no one dared to venture up the sides of a mountain so high or around its sides of impassable and rugged terrain. The older folk around the base of the mountain had told tales of haunting sounds around its sides. The unidentified sounds solidified the folk's belief of its hauntings while they remained constantly reminded of the many caveats.

In the minds of the folk searching for Savanna, there'd been a strong belief that humans existed on the mountain peak. However, no one dared to venture up its treacherous paths to bring truth to its legendary tales. With their limited knowledge of the mountain, the searchers feared venturing up its paths in search of Savanna. During their frantic search, the folk scoured the villages in the most likely places but failed to find her. When all their efforts had failed, further searches became those for a washed-up body along the banks of the spring or a body disposed of among thick shrubs or in a shallow grave.

Savanna's whereabouts remained a mystery to Melvia and Isaack as well as their offspring, whose hearts yearned to see her return home. The Sevensen household as well as concerned folk who'd joined the search, called off their search. Nonetheless, they'd pledged to remain vigilant in their daily walks. Meanwhile, young Perry was put on the town train to convey the news to Cecelia. Victoria rushed into Bragerston to send a telegram off to Kladius in the UK. This was certainly not the news Cecelia and Kladius had hoped to receive from home.

CHAPTER 12

Attempted Escape

Back on the mountain, Savanna lapsed in and out of her shallow sleep while she pondered her fate in the hands of her kidnapper. She awoke to the sounds of chirping birds and noises she did not readily identify. After her long night of troubling thoughts, Savanna felt as one waking up in the land of nowhere. Surprisingly, she'd remained unscathed during the night. Golden sunlight beaming through a fissure of her small window was further attestation that she'd survived her first night in captivity. Not knowing what to do or where to turn, Savanna remained in bed as one in a dream, although she was wide awake.

As she became conscious of her surroundings, great fear gripped her heart. There hadn't been an antidote that could have eased the pain of separation from her family. Her heart yearned for Isaack and Melvia, her parents, who'd been so dear to her. At the tender age of nineteen, Savanna still maintained a close attachment to her parents and her grandparents, who'd continually pampered her with love and words of sound wisdom. Savanna still felt the need to cuddle close to her siblings to maintain the warmth of the bloodstream of their tightly knit family. Most of all, her heart yearned to return to Harry; the love of her life. Her wedding day was fast approaching while she was held captive in a secluded log house miles up the treacherous mountainside. Savanna had been looking forward to commencing the first day of her new life with the love of her life, Harry.

The brilliant glow of the rising sun began to cast its rays around the mountainside. Savanna regarded the sharp bright rays shining through the crevices of her room. Her mind became inundated with a myriad of questions. Would it be her first and last day in captivity? Was Tom waiting on the outside with his accomplices to wage an attack? Savanna felt that only time held the answers to her many questions. She perceived each moment as her last—unless she could find a way to make an escape.

She mustered up the courage and got out of bed. After changing into her dress, Savanna thoroughly scrutinized the room in which she'd slept. Her curiosity was further sparked when she peeped through a crevice of the rugged door of her room and noticed that the door to Tom's room had been left ajar. There hadn't been a stir in his room or anywhere else in the house. Had Tom ventured down the mountain to kidnap another victim? This was another of Savanna's greatest fears when she looked into his empty room.

She continued to scrutinize her room while her ears kept vigil for sounds of movements in the house. There wasn't much that met her eyes. There was the small bed on which she'd slept and a wooden chair covered with the skin of an animal. By the side of the bed, there was a round log table on which personal items were placed. A long rope lying on the floor in one corner of the room sparked her curiosity and sent chills flowing down her spine.

Savanna had hoped to scrutinize the house in its entirety, but fear had put a damper on her endeavors. She'd also become leery of encountering dark dungeons and what they could reveal. With no obvious signs of movement in the house, Savanna stepped cautiously from her room. In response to the call of nature, she made her way to the outhouse compartment. She quietly snuck back to her room without incidence.

The silence was quickly broken when Savanna heard a sound at the rear entrance of the house. She snuck cautiously outside her door and peered into the area lined with black soot. To her astonishment, she saw Tom rallying by the fireplace. He was preparing a large bird he'd apparently hunted at the crack of dawn. Savanna quickly snuck back into her room. Shortly thereafter, the aroma of roasted meat ignited her sense of smell and set her taste buds on high alert. She'd remained quietly in her room when Tom's voice echoed from the kitchen.

"Madam, your meat is ready."

Savanna walked cautiously into the second hall, where she saw Tom already seated at the table. As a gesture of good hospitality to his new guest, Tom placed on the table, two metal plates containing slices of the roasted bird, surrounded by slices of tomatoes. He gestured to her to take her place around the table. Savanna's fears were gradually subsiding as she sat at the opposite side of the table.

"Eat your meat, madam," Tom said. He'd been ravenously devouring his serving of the meal.

"Thank you, Tom," Savanna said.

Amidst her dilemma, her stomach had been running on empty. She therefore gladly partook of the savory breakfast. Tom also ate his meal in silence while his eyes kept vigil around the hall. His occasional eye-piercing stares placed Savanna in a precarious position. She became uncomfortable while seated in his immediate view.

The breakfast session quickly ended. Tom rose to his feet as if he had an important errand. He promptly exited the house through the rear door. Savanna remained at the table to ponder his prompt departure. Was he alone on the mountain? Did he have accomplices lurking in the vicinity? She had many other unanswered questions.

In the absence of Tom, Savanna scrutinized the house for whatever her eyes could detect. Her constant fear of the unseen, coupled with suspicion that Tom could be lurking around in conspicuous corners, put a damper on her thorough scrutiny. She therefore reverted to observing the outdoors from the small window of her room.

Thick fog shrouding the mountain had dampened the atmosphere. The mist gradually evaporated as the morning sunlight spread around the vicinity. The misty morning air was permeated with fragrances of the myriad of trees, shrubs, and flowers around the house. The compelling morning fragrances had been prompting Savanna to step out and entertain her addiction to the outdoors. She, however, was mindful of the endless possibilities of endangerment from creatures of the wild and therefore chose to remain in the safety of the house. From her small window, Savanna viewed distant places, as far as her eyes could see and her mind could perceive. She looked down at Amerhurst in the distance and perceived the closeness of her home to the log house, yet she felt so far away from home. Time had elapsed since Tom made his exit through the rear door. The sun was on its downward journey toward the horizon when he returned home. Savanna cautiously joined him in the soot-lined kitchen as he was occupied with preparing the evening meal. It was a meal of smoked rabbit and tasty dried corn on the cob he'd taken from a pot beside the fireplace.

In the second hall next to the kitchen, Savanna joined Tom at the table to savor the meal he'd prepared. It was an unusual but appetizing meal. She quickly replenished her stomach, which had been, once more, running on empty. The dinner session had ended when Tom retreated to the first hall. Savanna promptly made her way to the safety of her room.

Soon after they'd parted, a voice resonated throughout the house: "Madam, please come this way."

Savanna anticipated another night of suspense as she continued to ponder Tom's motive for snatching her from her nook. She promptly entered the hall at his command and took her seat on the bench she'd occupied the night prior. The atmosphere remained charged with fear and suspense. Tom sat in silence while his eyes surveyed the ceiling of the hall. As the evening shadows fell, the atmosphere under the early dusk had become calm and quiet, except for the creatures scurrying to find a safe resting place for the night.

Savanna had grave concerns about Tom and his solitary life on the mountain—whether he'd been living alone or there were other humans at the crest of the mountain. Whatever lay at the summit or below the log house was left to her imagination. She'd maintained her fears of being surrounded by mountain warriors or by the legendary Red Vipers—assuming Tom was one of them. Savanna further feared that, if other humans lived on the mountain peak or elsewhere, unbeknownst to Tom, his life could also be in jeopardy.

Savanna's curiosity took on momentum when she began to ask questions of her seemingly quiet kidnapper. She had her suspicions that he held a pent-up rage which she feared could explode at a moment's notice. With much precaution, Savanna bolstered up the courage to face him with the questions on her mind.

"Tom, do you live alone in this house?" Savanna asked, fearing greatly his response.

She noticed his arched eyebrows shifting in every direction. Not certain as to whether he would respond to her question or in what manner he would respond, Savanna decided to put her inquisitive mind to rest. The silence, however, was promptly broken when Tom finally responded.

"I no longer live alone, madam," he blurted.

From Tom's unexpected response, Savanna felt she didn't have a chance of being released from his strong hold. Tom quickly resumed his silence as if he were awaiting further questions from his cunning interrogator. Savanna pondered his silence as she contemplated her next action. As the night advanced, Tom remained sprawled on his bench as one overcome by fatigue. He unexpectedly rose to his feet and commenced making quick strides across the hall.

"Good night, madam," his gruff voice resounded in the quiet atmosphere of the hall.

"Good night, Tom," Savanna said.

She watched as he entered the second hall leading toward his room. Savanna was greatly relieved at Tom's departure. She had a sense of assurance that her life would be spared yet another night. At Tom's departure, Savanna was left alone in the hall. It was much too early for sleep, but she retreated to her room nonetheless. Tom's presence in the house had inhibited her further scrutiny of the strange surroundings.

By the light of the faint glow from a candle still burning in the second hall, Savanna walked quietly toward the room that was slightly larger than the rest. She quickly reached for the candle and held its glow at the entrance of the room. With ardent curiosity, she peeped into the pitch-black room. Nothing stirred. There wasn't a puff of air to rustle the soot-covered curtain hanging listlessly at the window above the bed. While she stood to peer into the room, goose bumps popped up all over her entire body. The fear of being caught peering into the mysterious room sent her rushing into her room.

The quietness of her room aroused her senses to the myriad of sounds in the night air. Beneath the night sky, Savanna had become intrigued by the sounds of creatures she could not readily identify. She lay awake, unable to fall asleep while the creepy night noises continued to stir up further fear and panic.

The quiet night advanced. Savanna lay restlessly awake. She wondered what lurked in the shadows within and without the house. She continually pondered whether Tom would take a turn for the worse, thus revealing the monster within. Was he a villain? Would he be as a lion waking from its sound sleep to pounce on her while she slept?

In her state of restlessness, there was that constant yearning in her heart to go back home. She perceived the impossibilities of attempting an escape but was determined to free herself from Tom's strong hold. Despite the preconceived impossibilities following Tom's trails, crisscrossing down the mountain, Savanna hadn't been daunted in any way. She'd remained preoccupied with charting out her plan of escape when sleep gradually took hold of her.

At the emergence of the dawn of another new day, Savanna was once more relieved of her fears that terror could have struck during the night. Her eyes were opened to face the new day and to begin another day of hope in the hands of her unpredictable captor. While she remained trapped in the secluded mountain log house, hope was the guiding light for her life of uncertainties and ensuing imminent danger.

At the crack of dawn, Savanna had heard Tom's footsteps as he exited the house through the rear door. The silence left by his departure had given her the opportunity to conduct further scrutiny of the house. Her effort, however, was abruptly impeded when Tom promptly returned. Upon entering the kitchen, Savanna was joyously overwhelmed by his brisk movements as he prepared breakfast.

Tom reached for the suspended leg of smoked meat in the ceiling lined with black soot and spiderweb. He commenced carving thin slices of the meat and heating them over a coal fire he'd kindled in the fireplace. Warm slices of the meat were served with sliced tomatoes.

Upon savoring the meat, Savanna tasted burnt spiderweb and black soot. The meat Tom had generously prepared was unlike the spicy and delicious barbecued steaks or the sizzling chicken legs Savanna prepared at home. Nonetheless, it was good enough to appease her hunger. She'd been reluctant to eat, but her growling stomach had left her no other choice. Savanna was also reminded of her anticipated escape down the mountain and felt that she needed the added energy.

At the end of their smoky breakfast, Tom commenced pacing the halls as one overcome by anxiety. He promptly exited the house through the rear door as he made his way into the outdoors. At Tom's departure, Savanna entered her room. She stood by the window to observe the mountain through the panoramic view the small space allotted her. As she weighed her chances of escaping, many unanswered questions flooded her mind. Where was Tom? What were her chances of making it down the mountain without being attacked by creatures of the wild?

From the small window of her room, Savanna watched an eagle spread its wings and commence soaring high around the mountainside. She wished she had wings like the eagle's. She would soar above the barriers, above any dangers that lurked below, and make an escape down the mountain. By chance or sheer luck, Savanna thought she could slip, slide, and tumble until she made it down the mountainside to her home. The sound of the flowing streams in the spring at the foot of the mountain would serve as a compass as she would make her way down.

Despite the perceived consequences of attempting an escape, the constant yearning in Savanna's heart to go home prompted her to make a run for her life. With Tom away from the house, she felt there was a good chance of making her escape before he returned from wherever he'd wandered.

With very little time to spare, Savanna quickly discarded her night accessories and changed into her own garments. She securely tightened her shoelaces and swiftly escaped through the main door through which she'd entered at the time she'd arrived at the house. With much urgency, she escaped among the tall rocks, between the trunks of huge trees, and among thick shrubs. Amidst fear and anxiety, Savanna began to lose her sense of direction—if ever there were directions. Before gaining distance, she became disoriented, not having the perception of up or down. Not knowing where to go, she crouched behind a thicket a short distance from the house.

Savanna became panic-stricken as she remained in hiding. She'd least suspected that Tom had held her under his close surveillance when a large strong hand placed a firm grip on her arm. Savanna lay sprawled on the ground, trembling from fear. In a fit of anger, Tom forcefully pulled her back up the mountainside. With great force, he quickly shoved her through the entrance door of the house. She stumbled before landing on the floor with a loud thud. Savanna lay on the floor in great fear and tremor as she awaited her fate. For the first time since her capture, she'd seen Tom in a rage and noticed his display of vented anger.

"Where did you think you were going?" Tom said in utter disgust.

Savanna noticed his glaring eyes as they were focused directly on her face. Tears immediately flowed from her eyes as she remained on the floor in fear and agony. Tom stood speechless as if he'd been contemplating what punitive action to take against his stubborn captive. Savanna waited in anticipation of Tom's harsh reprisal for her attempted escape.

In a last-ditch effort to gain her release, Savanna pleaded in sincerity, "Please, Tom. I have to go back home to my parents. My wedding day will be soon. I must marry the love of my life."

His eyes glaring, Tom stared down at his trembling victim. He continually took deep breaths and sighed heavily, a gesture of relief that Savanna had not escaped. Savanna remained in a fetal position on the hard log floor, reeling from the traumatic effects of being recaptured and returned to the log house. While she gasped desperately for air, Savanna realized that the light she'd seen at the end of her tunnel was no shining star of hope. Her attempted escape had failed miserably.

A moment of sustained fury elapsed before Tom once more began to speak. "Madam, you will stay in this house. I can't let you go. It could be a matter of life and death if you try to escape."

Added fear sprang up in Savanna's heart. She lay on the hardwood floor, begging for mercy from her dominant captor. Savanna reverted to silence while she waited for Tom's further reprisal for her attempted escape. She'd been expecting the worse when his big feet made giant strides across the hall. He headed toward the rear exit and wandered off into the outdoors.

With cautious expectation, Savanna rose to her feet. She sat on her bench in the hall. She tried to remain calm as her fate was now being weighed in the balance. In light of her attempted escape, there was no doubt that she would be kept under Tom's closer scrutiny. Whatever punishment he had in store for her would be even more severe, should she attempt another escape.

At the spur of the moment and being prompted by a constant yearning to go home, Savanna became defiant. Despite her first failed attempt, she became determined to attempt another escape. She, however, remained fearful that raising a revolution would result in Tom's most severe retaliation. While she pledged to attempt another escape, Savanna was constantly reminded of the severe consequences. She therefore felt she had no other choice but to walk the thin line. Savanna waited in unwavering hope that someday she would be free from the strong hold of her adamant kidnapper.

CHAPTER 13

Scrutiny and Exploration

There wasn't much to see living in a mountain log house surrounded by tall rocks and trees with wide-spreading branches. From the confines of her room, Savanna therefore listened to the harmonious sounds of the mountain forest—the wind rustling the leaves of the surrounding trees and the creatures of the mountain making their strange bleating and chirping sounds.

With nothing to keep her occupied in the house, Savanna developed an appetite for scrutiny and exploration. She'd perceived that Tom's fascination with the mountain jungle had kept him wandering around the mountainside. His absence had therefore given her the opportunity to closely scrutinize the strange house and its contents.

After scrutinizing certain items in the house, Savanna was faced with the difficult task of unraveling a tangled and complex web of clues. She further felt compelled to unravel the mysteries surrounding Tom's solitary existence in a mountain jungle. Her constant memory of the dark room into which she'd peered the night prior, had immediately triggered her curiosity. Savanna had an anxious desire to further scrutinize the room.

Her sharp and curious eyes scrutinized the shoes neatly placed by the entrance of the first hall. The male shoes were obviously worn by

Tom, except for the style of others that suggested they'd been worn by an older male. Savanna was curious about the beautiful pairs of female shoes that were a perfect fit for her average-sized feet. It was obvious that the smallest pairs of shoes were those of a young girl in her mid-teen years.

In the quiet atmosphere, Savanna explored the strange spooky interior of the log house. With Tom in the outdoors, she quickly conducted a thorough scrutiny of his room. If there were secret weapons stashed away in his room, she would be sure to find them, and who knows what else she would uncover in his mysterious sleeping quarters?

Closer scrutiny of Tom's bed revealed the thick logs stacked in layers on the floor. For added comfort, wood bark and dry leaves were placed on the layers of logs. The bed was then covered with the skin of animals. Further scrutiny of the room revealed clothes hung on long cords along the wall opposite Tom's bed. Other items in the room were strewn around in every corner and crevice. At the completion of her scrutiny, Savanna hastily exited Tom's room.

She carefully checked the entrances of the house to ensure that he hadn't been secretly watching her movements. Savanna had the assurance that the way was clear when she cautiously entered the spooky room into which she'd peered the night prior. She commenced her full scrutiny of the double-sized bed, also made of layers of logs. A gray woolen blanket seemingly appropriate for the mountain climate was spread at the foot of the bed.

According to Savanna's standard of neatness, the bed was unmade. The blanket had been pushed aside and left in disarray. The mattress on the bed was made of layers of thick linen folded to further enhance its thickness. Her closer scrutiny of the mattress revealed small pieces cut from the linen, as if someone had tried to cut away soiled patches. Parts of the blanket were carefully pulled over the unmade bed. It appeared that someone had tried to conceal the patches that had been cut from the linen. A tattered dark-brown spread, sewn with golden thread, was also left in disarray halfway across the bed. Savanna once more noticed the soot-stained curtain suspended at the only window in the room.

There were many troubling thoughts and questions in Savanna's mind as she scrutinized the room and its contents.

There were male and female garments hung on a cord along an entire wall of the room. The sight of the garments left her to assume that the room had once been occupied by Tom's parents. Savanna scrutinized two elegant dresses on the cord. She immediately flaunted her flair for fashion as she held each dress against her body. While she scrutinized the dresses, her thoughts immediately went back home. Tears flooded her eyes as she thought about the elegant wedding gown she wouldn't be wearing. Her wedding day was fast approaching. Two pairs of elegantly designed shoes on the floor immediately caught Savanna's eyes. She felt they were the type of designer shoes to die for. Never had she seen shoes of such style and elegance. There were no other items that sparked Savanna's curiosity. She therefore cautiously exited the strange room.

By comparison, Savanna's room was the smallest in the house. It was a room equipped with a narrow bed, also made of logs. The round log resting on the floor beside her bed, had a surface with a diameter wide enough to accommodate a small stone candle and a few personal accessories. The wall on the opposite side of her bed was lined with dresses that appeared to be those of a young adolescent. As Savanna further scrutinized her room, she continued to be intrigued by the long rope that lay partly coiled up by the side of the bed.

At the completion of her close scrutiny of the room, Savanna returned to the first hall. She scrutinized the old brass clock suspended from the wall opposite the bench on which Tom habitually sits. He routinely wound the clock to ensure that its hands traveled from one to twenty-four each and every day. There were no pictures on the walls to depict any human presence in the house. The items on the walls were trophies of the dried heads of animals—a goat, a wolf, and birds of beautiful plumage.

On the wall, just below the clock, hung a tattered calendar displaying the months of the year. The calendar was equipped with a pointer, suggesting that it was designed to give the day, month, and year for many past and subsequent consecutive years. On one side of the calendar were pictures of male soldiers, a bright golden sun, and a rugged mountain Savanna did not identify. An old tattered magazine and a bundle of newspapers were stacked on a dusty wooden shelf on the eastern section of the hall. Savanna perused the magazine, but only pictures of fine ladies and their elaborate lifestyles appealed to her.

For a short period, her eyes remained riveted to the newspapers. Their pages were partially stained by watermarks and black soot. Savanna strongly believed that the newspapers held the missing pieces of the puzzle of Tom's strange and solitary life on the mountain. She curiously read the headlines and topics in search of clues, but nothing aroused her suspicion. She therefore vowed to continue her quest to uncover more clues and artifacts that could explain Tom's solitary existence on the mountain.

Savanna had completed her scrutiny of the items in the first hall. She promptly returned to the second hall, where she'd sat to eat her first and subsequent meals. The small wooden table surrounded by four log chairs, she assumed, was the meeting and eating place of Tom's household—whoever they might have been.

Savanna once more entered the small kitchen space adjacent to the second hall. Black soot lined the walls and the ceiling of the entire area. The fireplace was a carved-out rock close to the rear exit door. Careful scrutiny of a wooden box on the floor uncovered matches, spices, medicinal items, and preserved foods for Tom's daily consumption.

Upon close scrutiny of another area of the kitchen, Savanna stumbled upon a large metal barrel containing kerosene oil. It was quite similar to the barrels the folk in Amerhurst used to store their supply of fuel. Fear struck Savanna's heart as she thought of the consequences of the fuel igniting. But it appeared that, Tom had learned safety from his parents or from whoever had provided guidance during his childhood years.

Immediately outside the kitchen space was an area with stone flooring. The solid-rock flooring was carved out of a rock at the time the log house was built. A wooden tub resting in one corner of the space suggested that it was utilized when the season became too cold for outdoor baths in the flowing mountain streams.

Savanna almost stumbled over miscellaneous items strewn on the floor in another corner of the space. She noticed a metal bucket, which she assumed Tom had been using to fetch water from one of the mountain streams nearby. There were hunting and fishing apparatuses: hunting spears, slingshots, two army knives, and coils of long ropes left in disarray on the floor. Among the items were tools that were obviously used during the building of the log house.

Immediately outside the exit door, on the right side of the house, Savanna needed no further reminder when a familiar stench seeped into her nose. With added precaution, she exited the house through the narrow rear door and entered the back area. Savanna was careful not to be noticed by Tom, should he be lurking in the woods to keep her under his watchful eye. There was the possibility that he'd been vigilant around the house, should she attempt another escape. Wherever he'd been, his absence allowed her the opportunity to scrutinize the interior of the house.

From her new vantage point at the rear of the house, the sound of the spring at the foot of the mountain was faintly audible. Savanna admired the frisky waterfalls careening down the mountain. She reflected on the estuaries along the bank of the spring. They continuously received fresh and new water from the mountain streams.

Amidst fear and misgivings, Savanna took in the sights and sounds while she breathed in the fresh mountain air. She'd been quite certain that the continuous squeaky sounds she had heard were made by bats. The little creatures often found a sanctuary in places that were warm, dry, and abandoned. It wasn't long before she found herself looking up at the faces of dozens of little bats hanging beneath the exterior edges of the house. She immediately learned to love and admire the little creatures hanging in an upside-down position. They curiously scrutinized her while she stood to admire them.

In the center of the backyard, two wooden benches rested beneath the branches of the overhanging trees. One of the benches was made just for two individuals. The other seated three or more. The benches were conspicuously situated to facilitate a family discussion beneath the cool shade of the trees.

Steps from the location of the benches, in a small cleared area, Savanna stumbled upon an abandoned fireplace. She could not have ignored a strange sight that caught her eyes. A closer scrutiny of the fireplace revealed the charred remnants of bedclothes, as if someone had tried to burn stains from the clothing. There were layers of charred bed linen, a pair of charred pajamas, and a charred nightgown strewn over a rock by the side of the fireplace.

Savanna was unable to differentiate bloodstains from burns on the items as, over time, they'd become decomposed by the elements of sunlight and rain. The charred items left no doubt in her mind that some strange mishap had occurred on the mountain and in that quiet log house. She stood in fear and trembling, pondering her own fate—whether she would become a victim of whatever the circumstances had been.

With cautious expectation, Savanna continued to survey the rear of the house. When she stumbled upon discarded bones strewn around the vicinity, the feeling that gripped her heart was much more than she could have borne. At first, she perceived that they were human bones; however, her careful scrutiny of their origins confirmed that they were the bones of animals. They were most likely the bones of animals Tom had slaughtered for his survival. On the north side of the house, she noticed a vegetable garden Tom maintained for his mountain survival. The foods and vegetables grown in the garden were similar to those grown in the gardens of Amerhurst. Tom had already fully reaped the produce in his garden for the autumn season.

Further scrutiny of the exterior of the log house revealed that it had been structured from thick logs. The house stood wedged between incredibly huge rocks and was further secured by the trunks of tall forest trees. It was also shielded by the branches of overhanging trees. As added protection from outside elements, its roof had been carefully covered with thick canvas.

The house stood carefully camouflaged from the aerial view of anyone who might be searching the mountain for structures or manmade hiding places. It lay nestled in a conspicuous location from which point, Tom could observe occurrences in a panoramic view of the mountain. The house further permitted a view of Bragerston Town in the distance below.

Savanna hadn't been able to fully survey the outdoor vicinity for the trees, thick shrubs, and rocks. There was also the possibility that Tom had been hiding in the woods close by, watching for any sign of her attempting another escape. She therefore returned indoors to resume her scrutiny of the unusually strange house.

Further scrutiny of the interior of the house ended abruptly when Tom entered through the rear door. His presence quickly put a damper on Savanna's curiosity; however, she vowed to continue her search for clues once Tom left on his next undisclosed errand.

Savanna was quickly reminded that she hadn't eaten since Tom served her the meal of smoked meat and sliced tomatoes. As a way of appeasing him at the end of his day of frustration, Savanna entered the kitchen, where she rallied to prepare a satisfying dinner meal. She'd been searching around the soot-lined kitchen when Tom stepped forward to assist.

"Madam, you must be hungry," he said, insinuating that he too had been feeling the pains of hunger.

"I am hungry," Savanna said. "You must be hungry too, Tom. May I prepare the meal?"

"Sure, you may, madam," Tom said, still showing a willingness to assist.

Tom poured a few drops of fuel over the dry logs stacked in the fireplace and immediately struck a match. While the logs burned, he subsequently lit a stained oil lantern suspended from the ceiling by a rope lined with thick soot. Black soot lining the surface of the semi-dark kitchen was quickly illuminated by the glow from the flame beneath the shade of the lantern.

Under the flickering glow of the flame, Savanna became perturbed by a network of spiderweb. The swift-moving spiders scurried across the ceiling on webs lined with black soot, fragments of dust, and remnants of the skeletons of flies and bugs. The roasted leg of goat suspended from the ceiling of the kitchen, was barely noticeable in the soot-lined ceiling and among the network of spiderweb crowded with fragments of insects. Tom reached for the leg of goat and carefully placed it on the stone counter beside the fireplace.

Savanna commenced cutting slices of the smoked meat and warming them in a shallow pot Tom had placed over the fire. He'd brought a potato, which Savanna also cooked in the pot. In a jiffy, a meal of smoked meat, cooked potato, and sliced tomatoes was placed on the table in the second hall. At the sight of the soot-covered ceiling, the network of spiderweb, and fragments of the skeletons of insects, Savanna could not build up an appetite. However, she hesitantly partook of her serving to avoid shunning Tom's kind hospitality.

Dusk was slowly engulfing the mountain as the dinner session progressed. With his big appetite, Tom devoured his meal in silence. As a way of showing his appreciation for the appetizing meal, he gave a pleasant smile as he left the table. No sooner had he excused himself from the table than Tom retreated to the first hall—but not before barring the doors and windows of the house. Savanna remained alone at the table to finish her unsavory meal. She reflected on her earlier attempt at escaping and perceived how short a memory Tom might have had as he'd shown no sign of leftover anger.

Cautiousness was the order of the evening as Savanna left the table and entered the first hall. She found Tom seated in silence in the comfort of his bench. Savanna took her usual seat on the bench opposite Tom's and waited for any gesture of his intention to communicate, particularly to exercise his reprisal for her attempted escape. Whether Tom had been passing the time or contemplating his next plan of action, it was anyone's guess. With his eyes twitching and head turning in either direction, he continually stared at the ceiling of the hall with that "What now?" look in his eyes. Savanna cunningly commenced asking the questions she felt would unravel some of the mysteries surrounding Tom's mountain existence, and bit by bit, he began to disclose sketchy bits of information.

"Tom," Savanna said.

His eyes twitched as they surveyed the ceiling of the hall before they were focused on his interrogator.

"Do you have relatives in Amerhurst?"

While his surveying eyes once more circumvented the hall, Tom responded with a look of annoyance. "No! Never," he said. His glossy eyes gave piercing looks from beneath long strands of hair suspended from his head and flowing over his protruded forehead.

Savanna's heart pounded within her chest. She was fully reminded of the earlier event, her attempted escape, for which she was yet to be punished. When she'd least expected, Tom surprisingly began to speak after he'd vented his anger.

"Don't you dare ask me this question again, madam," Tom blurted.

He promptly left his bench and commenced pacing the hall as one in an uncontrollable rage—growling, snapping, and uttering sounds like a snarling animal waiting to wage an attack. Savanna observed in silence while she permitted him to release his pent-up anger. Tom returned to his bench no sooner than he'd vented his anger or portrayed the signs of a mere coward. In her heart, Savanna felt her persistence would eventually pay off. She therefore continued to ask the questions she knew would provide the answers she sought.

"I'm sorry to have hurt your feelings, Tom, but I need to know who you are and from whence you've come to this mountain."

Tom once more reverted to his usual silence. As they remained beneath the pale glow of the lantern suspended from the ceiling, Tom shook his knees as one under a spell of convulsion. He'd made every effort to avoid eye contact with Savanna. At the spur of the moment, Savanna began to perceive Tom as one having evil intentions. She therefore had great concerns for her safety. What if he decided to wage an attack as a reprisal for her attempted escape? Bold as she was, Savanna wouldn't dare to get into a scuffle with a monstrous giant of a man. Despite the likelihood of Tom's reprisal, Savanna remained adamant. She would not be deterred by her stubborn intimidator and therefore continued to press for more details about him.

"If you weren't born in Amerhurst, from where did your parents come?" Savanna asked.

She waited to obtain the answers she hoped would provide more clues about Tom. He'd been quite candid about his origin and his reason for being on the mountain, but Savanna remained hopeful that time would reveal his mysterious existence. She further remained hopeful that she would gain her release unharmed. Moments passed. Tom had still not responded to Savanna's question but appeared to have a barrage of questions for her. He showed a keen interest in her background, particularly about her family. The table was quickly turned when Tom began to throw questions at his brave interrogator.

"Were you born in your home, madam?" he asked.

To appease her intimidator, Savanna promptly responded. "Yes, I was born in my home in Amerhurst. Did you know the name of my village?" Savanna asked, hoping that Tom was a total stranger to the places below the mountain.

"You've just responded to your question, madam," Tom said with added assurance that Savanna had been providing the information he sought about her.

"My parents as well as my grandparents have been longtime residents of Amerhurst," Savanna said.

Her prompt response further sparked Tom's curiosity. "Do you have brothers and sisters?" he asked. Tom's eagle-like eyes peeped from beneath bushy eyebrows and thick matted hair as he waited for her response.

Savanna shivered as she recalled Tom's first eye-piercing look while she had sat in the nook. "I have many siblings," she said.

Tom's eyes twitched repeatedly while he continued to press for more details. "And do they all live in your house?" His curiosity was further sparked as he candidly pried into Savanna's background.

"Three have left home," Savanna said. "I'm soon to be married and will also be leaving home." She spoke with a tremor in her voice.

With a sneaky smile on his face, Tom began to throw more questions at his unsuspecting victim. "Are Victoria and her husband happily married?" he further asked.

"Yes," Savanna said, "they're happily married."

She immediately lapsed into a state of shock. Her thoughts were on Victoria and Aldbright, who'd walked frequently by the edge of the woods. The young lovers had habitually sat on the tranquility bench by the side of the pond while they enjoyed the ambience of the crisp afternoon sun. Savanna became dumbfounded when she realized that Tom had been lurking along the edge of the woods. He'd eluded the folk's detection for, who knows how long. Savanna soon realized that she'd given too much information about her household. She'd left her siblings vulnerable to kidnapping by the prowler who'd snatched her from her secret nook.

Tom's curiosity was further sparked as he weighed in on Savanna's response. "When will you get married?" he asked.

Savanna lapsed into abrupt silence as tears flooded her eyes. It was an awkward question to ask and an awkward response to expect as she realized that she'd been held captive, far away from her home and from her future husband. Upon realizing that, Savanna immediately refrained from providing further information. Tom quickly reverted to his mode of silence, thus bringing the dialogue session to an abrupt end. He'd cunningly evaded Savanna's questions about his origin as well as his solitary existence in the mountain log house. She therefore looked forward to their subsequent evening dialogues, with hopes of obtaining the information she sought. As Savanna had perceived, darkness enveloped the entire mountain and the plains below. Tom had quickly developed an intolerance of the dialogue session and therefore retreated to his room. Savanna followed suit, retreating to her room. Fatigue had begun to take hold of her after a full day of activities.

It became difficult adjusting to her new environment in the wild. The buzzing mosquitos continually interrupted her sleep throughout the night. Tom had made every effort to expel the annoying insects by adding leaves and trash to the dying embers in the fireplace. The burning leaves on the embers generated tons of smoke that engulfed the house during the early hours of the night. As expected, the stubborn creatures had not been deterred. They returned with greater force after the smoke dissipated. Savanna carefully shielded her face to escape the feeding frenzy of the determined parasites. She had no other choice than to adjust to her wild environment while she remained in captivity. Amidst the buzzing sounds of the annoying insects and her attempts at fending off their vicious attacks, sleep quickly took hold of her.

CHAPTER 14

Reflections on Home

Savanna woke up to face another new day and her continuing dilemma. She'd been involuntarily adjusting to her new environment as each new day arrived. Amidst a state of restlessness, she occupied her time trying to make good of a bad situation. She'd still not unraveled the mystery of Tom's solitary existence on the mountain and therefore continued to live amidst doubts and mistrust. Savanna faced each new day and night hoping for her release from the mountain environment, most of all, from her mysterious kidnapper.

The days turned into a week since Savanna was forcefully carried up the mountain. She spent her first Saturday performing house chores while remaining under Tom's close scrutiny. Tom had spent that particular Saturday making short trips in the outdoors, but he'd remained in the house for the greater part of the day, seated on his bench in a quiet atmosphere.

With Tom's assistance, Savanna prepared the day's meals. At the end of that quiet Saturday, after Tom had eaten the savory meals she'd prepared, he retreated to the first hall. As customary, Savanna followed suit. Unlike the dialogues of the nights prior, the Saturday night's dialogue in the first hall was short and brief. Tom had rarely spoken before making an early retreat to his room. With nothing in the hall to occupy her time, Savanna retreated to her room.

The quiet night advanced while Savanna remained confined to her room. She'd been having her ample dose of solitude, being confined to the mountain sanctuary and away from her home. Savanna lay in her bed to reminisce on the joyous life she'd had back home. Most of all, she thought about her wedding day, which was fast approaching.

The Saturday night had been the quietest Savanna could recall. Saturday evenings at home were usually full of cheers and laughter, particularly during the barn dances. Whenever there were no Saturday night events, she and her siblings remained in the safety of the house to read new books they'd purchased in Bragerston. In light of her disappearance, Savanna felt Saturday nights back home would never be the same.

Her siblings had often been engaged in frequent exchanges of gossip about their potential soul mates. They revealed their secret rendezvous with the sons or daughters of the wealthiest farm lords. Savanna and her hopeful siblings were quite aware that they would be kissing frogs in their effort to find a soul mate. Victoria had kissed only one frog. Aldbright was her childhood sweetheart. Savanna thought about her short love affair with Bentley. When she had met Harry, she was quite certain she didn't have to kiss another frog. Her thought of Harry suddenly brought tears cascading down her cheeks. She was quite certain he would be the last frog she kissed. She'd found her soul mate.

Each passing day, the search for a soul mate continued among Savanna's remaining hopeful siblings. They'd all been waiting on time and providence to see what would unfold for them. Her siblings continually found solace in their belief that patience is a virtue. As she lay sleepless, Savanna reflected on the prior Saturday before she was taken from the nook. She, along with her siblings, had displayed their elegantly designed garments, fancy shoes, and complementary jewelry. They'd been preparing for the most lavish wedding ever to take place in Amerhurst—Savanna's wedding.

In the still dark room, Savanna reminisced on the joyous time she had had with Harry. It was a prelude to their future lives as a happy couple. Whenever Harry didn't visit his parents for the weekend, he'd always taken her to Bragerston to the movie shows. She'd often taken proud steps by his side as they walked along the busy streets. In the quiet atmosphere, Savanna wept bitter tears for Harry, and her big wedding day, which she knew she would be missing. In the midst of her restlessness and the yearning to return home, sleep had taken hold of her being.

Savanna was awakened by sounds from the flurry of activities that greeted the dawn of a new day and another Sunday in captivity. The Sunday morning atmosphere buzzed with the activities of the seemingly cheerful creatures of the forest. Beams of sunlight streaked through the cracks and crevices of the tiny window in her room. She unwillingly greeted the dawn of another day of suspense, not knowing her fate in the hands of Tom and in the strange mountain environment.

Savanna had been busy preparing the Sunday breakfast when she was alerted to the faint peal of the church bell at the foot of the mountain. The church in Amerhurst was a short distance from her home. The peal of the bell was a reminder to everyone except her, that it was the day to gather in the place of worship. The periodic peal of the bell also kept the folk aware of the time, particularly folk who habitually showed up late.

The peal of the church bell continued while Savanna reflected on the Sunday church service. She thought about the memorial services held for those who'd passed on. There was no doubt in her mind that the bell tolled numerous times for her, the missing girl who'd been presumed dead, hence a memorial service in her honor. Savanna sincerely wished that the peal of the bell had been for her joyous wedding, but it was to the contrary.

She perceived the tears, coupled with the grieving hearts, of those who'd been mourning her passing—particularly her grandparents, whose hearts might be failing from grief and sadness. She imagined a beautiful bouquet of flowers placed in the sanctuary in her memory. Melvia, Isaack, and her siblings would be sure to place a beautiful bouquet on the pew where she normally sat. Savanna became even more nostalgic as her heart yearned to be with her family in the beautiful church sanctuary.

She was quite certain Cecelia had taken the long train ride home to attend the memorial service for her presumed deceased sibling. Her thoughts were on Kladius's telegram of condolence, unless he'd purchased a plane ticket to fly back home for the memorial service. Fresh tears flowed as Savanna reminisced on her household and her grandparents, who would be shedding volumes of tears at the presumption of her disappearance and death.

Savanna reflected on her parents and their favorite seat in the pew. She recalled where Cecelia sat prior to her departure; in her favorite seat by the northern window. Victoria and her husband would be seated in the center row of the left pew. Savanna knew where the other siblings took their favorite seat in the sanctuary. Her seat had always been on the second row beside Melvia and Isaack. She wondered who would take her favorite seat in the pew once the memorial service ended. Should no one take her seat, it would become a vacant seat in the pew. Savanna felt strongly that, amidst the superstition of her seat being haunted by her ghost, no one would dare to take it. With the wide skirt of her dress, Savanna wiped the tears flowing down her cheeks.

Tom watched with compassion and with a feeling of guilt. He knew quite well that his act of kidnapping had resulted in Savanna's predicament. "Why are you crying, madam?" Tom asked. Tears began to flow down his cheeks as he pondered the welfare of his crying companion.

"The peal of the bell has brought back memories of home," Savanna said. "Tom, I must go back home." New tears cascaded down her cheeks.

Tom immediately ceased from prying further into the cause of her melancholy mood. The faint peal of the bell continued in the distance below the mountain as Savanna wept profusely. It hadn't been for her absence from home or her presumed death that she cried. She perceived the tears flooding the eyes of her parents and her siblings. She shed tears for her grieving grandparents. Most of all, she perceived the tears flooding Harry's eyes. His wedding day was fast approaching, and she would not be walking down the aisle.

Instead of a celebration of her most joyous occasion, she perceived her parents gathering to have a memorial service for their presumed deceased offspring. Among the village folk, Savanna perceived that she would be remembered as one of the charming young ladies growing up in the Sevensen household. She thought about the kind words of the neighboring folk and her past school peers. She would be remembered as a fine student, particularly in their home economics class. Savanna perceived the consoling words and honor bestowed upon her by the staff of her school, where she'd taught for a bit shy of two years.

Meanwhile, as Savanna reflected on Sunday in Amerhurst, as she'd imagined, a memorial service was held in her honor. Reverend Moutray, pastor of the church, had met with Isaack and Melvia to schedule a memorial service for Savanna. There was no doubt that he'd numbered her among those who'd passed on. The folk of Amerhurst gathered in the church sanctuary to pay their due respects to the missing girl who'd been presumed dead.

Harry had not dared to join the folk, who strongly suspected that he was responsible for Savanna's disappearance. He'd chosen to spend the Sunday at his parents' home. Addriana and Henry therefore attended the memorial service on behalf of their grieving son. During the Sunday memorial service, devoted teachers, scholars, and members of many communities, gave their honorary reflections on Savanna's life and her devotion to teaching. Gorwald Thomary, principal of the school, stood to address the grieving congregation.

"You folk will agree that Savanna was a perfectionist. She was a mentor, not only to her scholars, but also to the entire school community," the principal said.

The audience shouted their acclaim with a resounding "Amen!"

Reverend Moutray stepped up to the pulpit to honor another departed member of his congregation. There wasn't a dry eye in the sanctuary while he delivered his sermon on the life of Savanna.

"Savanna Sevensen was one of the adorable young ladies of the Sevensen household. She will be certainly remembered as the beautiful bride-to-be whose wedding has been put on hold," the reverend said.

"On the day of reckoning, the one who's responsible for her passing will be severely judged."

Members of the audience once more shouted their acclaim with a resounding "Amen!"

While the reverend spoke, necks craned, and eyes rolled as the folk made gestures of suspicion among themselves. Addriana and Henry moved to the edge of their seats. Addriana remained poised to speak in defense of her son but was prevented by Henry's constant nudging.

Mrs. Gravenhurst, a prominent member of the Amerhurst community, gave her summary on the life of Savanna. "Savanna was regarded as one of the beautiful and charming ladies of the Sevensen family. Her short life had touched the heart of all the folk who knew her. Her gifts of arts and many other talents had drawn many closer to her. Savanna had won the hearts of all who knew her. She'll be greatly missed."

The audience applauded with another resounding "Amen!"

Melvia stood to address the audience on behalf of her household—Isaack, her many offspring, and the grandparents. Melvia was immediately overcome by a constant outburst of emotions, which impeded her usual wordy speech. Amidst tearful sobs, a few words finally escaped from her lips. "Savanna has left her siblings a legacy of humor to brighten their day and the spirit of caring and endeavoring to rise to their dreams. Isaack and I, Savanna's grieving siblings, and her grandparents strongly believe she'll return home someday." Melvia was overcome by a spell of convulsive weeping, which prompted Isaack to escort her from the sanctuary.

The service ended—but not before Reverend Moutray pledged to continue his ardent prayer for the soul of the deceased. Despite Savanna's death presumption and the memorial service held for her, Melvia and Isaack as well as their entire household, continued to wait for any news of her whereabouts. As they waited, the light over the Sevensen farm slowly went dim. The entire household continued to endure their grief and anxieties. To their great astonishment, Savanna had vanished without a trace. The household arrived at the general consensus that life wouldn't be the same without Savanna, who'd been the bright shining star of the family. Despite their dwindling hope, everyone maintained a strong belief that someday, she would return home.

The Sunday atmosphere in the log house was pleasantly calm. The breakfast session had ended when Tom retreated to his bench in the first hall. It was Savanna's perception that he habitually spent his Sundays within the confines of the house, except for the prior Sunday, when he ventured down the mountain and snatched her from the nook. Throughout the day, Savanna carried out her chores while her heart continually yearned to return home to the joyous life she'd once lived—most of all, to marry the man of her dreams.

The golden glow of the Sunday evening sun lit up the horizon. Savanna prepared the appetizing dinner of smoked meat and tomatoes. At the end of the evening meal, Tom retreated to his usual place of comfort, on the bench in the first hall. The evening dialogue was limited to discussions on the church bell and Savanna's desire to return home. Tom persistently shied away from the subject of permitting her to go back home. He therefore maintained his silence for much of the evening.

Meanwhile, Savanna had thoughts percolating in her mind but had not the opportunity to spark up a conversation. Darkness had settled on the mountain when Tom excused himself from the hall and retreated to his room. Savanna was left alone in the quiet hall. With no other activities to occupy her time, she retreated to her room.

Another night of turmoil began as Savanna lay in bed to reminisce on her life back home and ponder her new life in captivity. She'd become nostalgic and traumatized at the realization that she had no chance at escaping or gaining her release. The Sunday morning peal of the church bell had further stirred up grief and a yearning to go back home.

The hours of darkness slowly drifted as Savanna lay in bed in a serene atmosphere. The silence was continuously interrupted as sounds of footsteps were heard in Tom's room as well as across the halls. The intriguing sounds triggered fear and caution. Savanna also became perturbed by the rear door, which opened and then shut repeatedly in the dead of night. She continued to entertain her fears that Tom was meeting with a gang of Red Vipers under the cover of darkness. Savanna wondered whether it was the moment she'd feared the most—a sudden attack by Tom and his accomplices while she slept.

Savanna perceived infinite possibilities that Tom had accomplices in the mountain peak. Was he a member of the Red Vipers? She continued to entertain fears that Tom's accomplices could show up under the cover of darkness, thus bringing an end to her hope of being released. Amidst fear and uncertainty, she placed her head on the rough pillow of trash and waited for some well-deserved sleep.

Before the much-coveted sleep took hold of her, Savanna once more reflected on her home and the turmoil and unrest in her household. What would they be thinking and doing? She imagined the frequent moans and groans of Isaack and Melvia as their hearts yearned to see her return home. She imagined Isaack going about his daily farm chores, shedding teardrops whenever his thoughts were on her. Savanna had no doubt that her siblings as well as her grandparents had been spending sleepless nights fearing for her safety and pondering her whereabouts.

Savanna was overcome by added grief at the sad separation from her siblings. She perceived the bitter tears shed by Harry at her disappearance. She missed the secret hideout where she'd hung out with him. Most of all, her dreams of a happy life with Harry had begun to fade with each passing moment. There wasn't a doubt that her siblings had been yearning to see her home, alive and unscathed. Savanna imagined the joyous reunion at her sudden reappearance through the big gate of her home, but she wouldn't allow her thoughts to wander astray. What if she never made it back home? There would remain only disappointed hopes and faded memories.

As she reminisced on home and her separation from her household, Savanna wished she had the opportunity to thank Melvia and Isaack, her grandparents, and her beautiful siblings for the good times she'd had with them. In the silence of her room, she wept and sighed as she reminisced on the good life she'd had back home. In her moment of grief, Savanna continued to reflect on her household's unrelenting search to find her. She recalled that Kladius had, on occasion, tried to scale the mountainside to compensate his appetite for adventure. He'd often climbed short distances up its treacherous side, searching for clues to the existence of humans and strange creatures.

Had Kladius been home, Savanna felt strongly that he would have turned every stone and searched every path for clues leading to her whereabouts. In his quest to locate her, Kladius would have certainly ventured up the side of the mountain, accompanied by Rex and Spicer. Rex and Spicer possessed the uncanny ability to search for and retrieve stranded animals around the foot of the mountain. The dogs, however, had not been trained in applying similar traits to find humans. If they were sent alone up the mountainside, they wouldn't likely return displaying sprawling and barking signs that suggested that they'd picked up on her scent. Besides, no one had reasons to suspect that she would have crossed the spring and ventured up the mountain alone—or with anyone having good intentions.

Savanna reflected on Bentley and the possibility of his parents being suspects in her disappearance. She recalled the day Bentley had formally informed her that his life in Amerhurst had come to an end. His parents were sending him to study in America. Savanna had had no animosity toward Bentley as he prepared to leave Amerhurst for his new life in a foreign land. Her chances of joining him were rather slim—so too were Bentley's chances of returning to Amerhurst. The news of Bentley's plans to leave Amerhurst had been a foregone conclusion that he'd severed ties with her. In Savanna's mind, not many ex-lovers have the opportunity to reunite. This, therefore, had been the case with her and Bentley. Amidst mounting grief, sleep gradually crept in, bringing much relief from her constant reminiscing on life back home.

CHAPTER 15

A Mother Figure

After a long night of shallow sleep, Savanna awoke at the commencement of the dawn with a readiness to take on the day. She realized she'd been wasting valuable time on the mountain and had therefore gladly taken on the day's activities—preparing meals and maintaining the log house. Amidst fear and suspicion, she'd been slowly adjusting to her new and structured lifestyle, surviving on roasted and smoked meats with a meager serving of vegetables.

Savanna realized she'd been in an unfortunate dilemma and therefore pledged to turn her misfortune into opportunities. Back home in her household, she was a girl of great courage and commitment, one who had the audacity to succeed in all of her undertakings. She'd striven to foster good discipline among her younger siblings, to ensure that they were equipped to manage their own future. It therefore wasn't long before she'd voluntarily assumed a similar role in Tom's household.

Savanna's confinement in the log house with Tom had further inspired her loyalty to attend to the needs of his household, now made up of himself and her, his captured victim. She'd been inducted into a world governed by chores and routines and had therefore pledged to perform her household duties expeditiously. Being equipped with her housekeeping skills, Savanna commenced serving her seemingly delinquent kidnapper in a motherhood capacity.

Tom habitually commenced each day by wandering off into the outdoors. Savanna remained alone in the house to carry out the daily duties she'd assumed—preparing the meals and maintaining the log house. Each day she routinely observed the outdoors through the small window of her room. She looked forward to the evening dialogues with Tom before he retired to his room. This had become the order of each day in the log house sanctuary.

Tom habitually exited the house during the early dawn, but he always returned for his morning meal. At the commencement of each day, Savanna routinely prepared and served his breakfast. Thereafter, she watched him make his usual prompt departure through the rear door. Toward the evening, she prepared his dinner with whatever meats she had found in the ceiling of the soot-lined kitchen. At the end of his long day, Tom routinely arrived home with the expectation to be served his evening meal. Savanna prepared savory meals that tantalized his palate and ignited his taste buds. Each day, Tom therefore commenced waiting at the table to indulge in the appetizing meals Savanna had prepared.

At the end of each day, after dinner, Tom habitually took his place in the first hall. Savanna routinely joined him, taking her place on the bench directly opposite where he sat. She waited in anticipation of their fact-finding dialogues. She always sought the opportunity to obtain whatever facts she could during their dialogue sessions. In Tom's absence from the house, Savanna occupied her time scrutinizing the contents of each area in the house. By a stroke of luck, she felt she might stumble upon hidden clues.

The task of laundering Tom's stained and tattered clothes was one Savanna particularly enjoyed. She took advantage of the opportunity to venture outdoors each time she had to launder his clothes in the streams flowing among the nearby rocks. Prior to washing Tom's clothes, Savanna was careful to scrutinize his pockets. By chance, she might detect hidden tools or other items that could pose a threat to her safety.

In the pockets of his pants, loaded with dry leaves and broken sticks, Savanna began to notice pieces of leaves having notes scribbled on them. She soon realized that the leaf fragments contained parts of notes written by Bentley and Harry. She stumbled upon her own handwritten notes that she'd left on the leaves of tree branches overhanging the nook. It all began to come together as Savanna stumbled upon more torn leaves in Tom's pockets.

On each bit of leaf, there were key parts of the notes missing: "To Harry, my lo . . . You bring me sunshine to brighten . . . Love, Sav." On another torn leaf, a partial note read, "Sav, we're madly in . . . Ben—" Savanna clearly recalled the last note Harry had left on the leaf of an overhanging tree branch beside the nook: "Sav, my angel, my bride-to-be, please wait here for me tomorrow, Sund . . . Love, Har—" There was no further element of surprise when Savanna read the remaining partial notes on the leaf fragments.

Close scrutiny of the pockets of Tom's other garments revealed more torn leaves with similar partially written notes on them. Savanna clearly recalled the times when the leaves on which she and Bentley had left notes to each other had been partially torn. She was quite certain that the leaves were torn by creatures of the wild, but Bentley had thought otherwise. He'd suspected that the leaves had been torn by an intelligent being and had therefore pledged to find the culprit.

As Savanna recalled, Harry had only theorized that the leaves on which he'd written notes to her, had been partially eaten by creatures of the wild. Savanna perceived that Harry's thoughts had been focused on his ardent love for her. He therefore hadn't given much credence to the fact that, an intelligent being could have been deliberately destroying the notes he'd left for his soul mate. Savanna had no perception of the fact that someone had been deliberately tearing away at the leaves on which she'd left notes for Bentley and Harry, as well as notes they'd left for her. She was appalled at the realization that the leaves were being torn by Tom. Most of all, she'd been kept under surveillance by a culprit who'd subsequently kidnapped her.

Upon her discovery of the torn leaves in Tom's pockets, Savanna recalled the strange behavior of Spicer and Rex each time they visited her in the nook. While she sat with Bentley and, subsequently, Harry, the dogs had raised suspicions that went unheeded. Spicer and Rex had often growled and sniffed frantically around the nook whenever they dropped by to pay her a friendly visit. Savanna had often felt that Spicer had been on to something each time he growled and kept his eyes focused on some sighting in the vicinity of the nook, particularly on the opposite side of the spring. She surmised that the dogs had been seeing animals of the mountain venturing to the edge of the woods to have a drink from the spring. Savanna had least suspected that the dogs were alerting her to the presence of someone in the vicinity. Whether it was a threatening wild animal or a human being, nothing had passed in Savanna's view while she sat in the nook with Bentley and, subsequently, with Harry.

From the torn leaves found in Tom's pockets, Savanna concluded that he'd been roaming rapaciously around the mountainside and in the vicinities below the mountain. He'd been no doubt prowling about the communities, searching for whatever he could scavenge from the unsuspecting folk. The grim discovery of the notes in Tom's pockets further shed light on her kidnapping and subsequent confinement in the mountain wilderness. Amidst her grief and anger, Savanna pledged to keep the discovery of the notes on the leaf fragments a secret. By so doing, she hoped to unravel more of the facts surrounding Tom's mysterious existence on the mountain.

In her mountain environment, time was passing slowly. For one held in confinement, time appeared to move at a much slower pace. The days seemed longer, while the nights lengthened. This allowed Savanna particularly long nights to reminisce on her life back home and ponder her fate in her mountain confines. Savanna spent the long days performing her assumed duties in the log house. She felt as though her life had come to a standstill, but her life had been revolving around Tom and his constant need for care and nurturing. Each day, there was a renewed passion to take on more responsibilities in the house. Savanna had therefore willingly assumed her role as the devoted mother of the household. She prepared Tom's meals, made his bed, and continually arranged his room in an orderly fashion. She often stepped aside to regard his neatly arranged room, which was a far cry from its usual sloppy appearance.

As each day arrived, Tom exerted tons of energy hiking around the mountainside in his quest for survival. Wherever he roamed in the night hours, particularly during the prior night, was anyone's guess. That prior dark and warm Thursday night was like every other night on the mountain. After their short dialogue, Tom retreated to bed. Not long thereafter, his footsteps were heard in the halls. As the night advanced, around the midnight hour, footsteps were heard once more. As usual, Savanna heard the rear door open and quickly close. The atmosphere had returned to silence, allowing her to assume that Tom had left on another of his undisclosed night errands.

The silence did not last for very long. Soon thereafter, she heard the rear door open. Savanna was alerted to a loud thud. Someone had entered the house through the rear door. With cautious expectations, she left the safe confines of her room to investigate. Upon entering the kitchen, to her astonishment, Tom was seated on the floor. Savanna could have heard every beat as his heart consistently pounded against his chest. She couldn't ignore the distraught look on his face. Before conducting an investigation, she quickly shut and barred the door.

Upon close scrutiny, Savanna noticed that Tom's old tattered and bloody pants had been ripped in several areas below the knees. The rips and tears in his shirt left her to think that he might have been attacked by beasts of the wild. Savanna could only conclude that things hadn't gone well on that attempted trip down the mountain or wherever was his intended destination.

Tom's demeanor and his bloody clothes raised many questions. Where did he go? Had he encountered wild creatures of the night? He couldn't have reached the foot of the mountain during his short absence from the house. Savanna therefore could not conclude that he was attacked by dogs in the villages below the mountain. Had he been viciously attacked by his secret accomplices on the mountain? Her guesses were just as good as anyone else's.

Savanna had always maintained caution each night she listened to wild pigs and wolves lurking in the vicinity. They were no doubt, scavenging for household refuse that Tom habitually left in the rear of the house. No sooner had Savanna attended to his wounds—his legs and arms, which had sustained cuts and bruises—than Tom promptly made his way to his room.

Savanna returned to her room but kept an ear perked up for any signs that Tom might need her assistance. Meanwhile, as she pondered Tom's dilemma, her ears constantly kept vigil for any signs of one attempting to enter the house. As she lay on her bed, Savanna perceived that life on the mountain was not for the fainthearted. Amidst great courage and bravery, she realized that there were no other options but to adapt to her new life in the mountain environment.

The next morning, at the breakfast table, Tom was duly reminded of the incident the night prior. Sadly, he didn't appear to have any recollection of what had transpired.

"Tom," Savanna said, "what happened to you last night?"

Tom wasn't stirred by her thought-provoking question. His eyes remained focused toward the ceiling of the hall. "Nothing, madam," he said.

Savanna wondered whether he'd woken up from his night's sleep. "Shortly after you left the house, you returned with ripped clothes and cuts to your hands and feet," Savanna said. "Can't you see the bandages on your legs? Tell me what happened last night. Why did you venture out into the outdoors in the dark night?"

Tom sat and gazed at the soot-lined ceiling. He either was incognizant of the incident or chose to remain tight-lipped. For the greater part of that day, Tom remained in the house, reeling from the excruciating pains he'd sustained from his mysterious nighttime injuries. Savanna carefully attended to his wounds while she carried out her house chores.

It was the end of another day of routines in the house. The sun had slowly sunk over the horizon after its brilliant rays beamed onto the forest floor. Thick dark clouds overshadowed the mountain, forcing Tom to return from wherever he'd wandered off in his semi-incapacitated state. Tom struck a match that he'd taken from the log table in the kitchen. He promptly lit the lantern suspended over the log table in the second hall. A tiny flame flickered beneath the shade of the lantern, casting its glow within a fair circumference of the hall.

Savanna served up roasted bird, potatoes, and tomatoes—Tom's favorite meal. At the end of the dinner session, he retreated to the first hall, the place for relaxation and anticipated dialogues. Savanna had become inducted into her routine of appearing in the first hall for her usual evening dialogue with Tom. She therefore promptly joined him as he waited in anticipation of whatever would transpire.

CHAPTER 16

The Refugee Ship

Under the early dusk, swift flashes of lightning lit up the log house. Loud claps of thunder roared in the heavens. The late evening rain began to pound the mountain with a fury. There were thundering sounds such that Savanna had never before heard. Her senses were aroused by the orchestrated rhythm of raindrops hammering on the leaves of the surrounding trees. The constant hammering of raindrops on the mountain forest quelled the tide of the sounds of all living creatures. Under such unfavorable weather conditions on the mountain, Tom always sought refuge in the safety of the log house while he waited out nature's fury.

The glow from the small candle was inadequate to provide sufficient light in the hall. Tom therefore struck a match and lit the oil lamp resting on the log table. The lamp and the suspended lantern were his last resort as oil had become one of his scarce commodities. To prepare Tom for the night's anticipated question session, Savanna served sizzling hot tea made from fresh herbs she'd gathered in the garden.

Savanna was always on a quest for more answers to her many questions about Tom and his solitary existence. She was fully aware that he'd never shown his willingness to respond to her frequent questions.

She therefore chose the right time to conduct her question sessions, the time Tom lapsed into his comfort zone.

Tom had been amusingly sipping his tea, but it seemed he wasn't in the mode for a dialogue. Silence therefore dictated the order of the evening until Savanna ceased the opportunity to commence her question session. She'd developed the insatiable appetite for wanting to know more. Tom, however, was willing to disclose only limited information from the barrage of questions she'd thrown at him.

There'd been incidents in Tom's place of origin that remained indelibly on his mind, such as the day his school was raided by soldiers. He'd once spoken of the incident but had not disclosed the details. At Savanna's prompting, Tom began to share his recollection of what had transpired during that horrifying moment.

"The soldiers were on the search for the enemies who, it was alleged, had been hiding in the school among the students. I watched innocent folk being captured and taken away. Whether or not they were enemy soldiers, they were arrested and dragged away by the authorities," Tom said.

Savanna listened with keen intent as she asked her next question and waited to obtain more details. "How and why did your parents get away?" she asked.

Tom's demeanor quickly changed. Savanna observed tears flowing down his cheeks. For what he was willing to disclose, Tom began to relate tales of his escape from his country of origin.

"I remember the day Father rushed home and ordered my mother to gather my sister and me and whatever items she could take. Minutes later, we were running in the direction of the seashore, where a big ship had docked."

Tears continued to flow profusely down his cheeks. Savanna felt she'd been getting some of the facts she sought. Tears began to flood her own eyes as she listened to Tom's elaborate details.

"There was a great struggle as the terrified crowd scurried to get on board the ship. Father lifted me and my sister, Caroleena, into the ship. He then pulled my mother on board."

At this point, Tom lapsed into abrupt silence. It appeared he'd become overwhelmed by the grim memory of leaving his homeland and whatever else was on his mind. Tom paused for a breath as Savanna waited impatiently to obtain further details about his escape.

"Many frightened civilians clung desperately to a meager supply of items they were able to grab before making their escape," Tom said. "There were mothers who desperately clutched their crying children as they struggled to climb aboard the ship."

Savanna's ears were perked up like those of a hunting fox as she waited to hear more of Tom's heartbreaking details. Her patience was wearing thin as she waited for the details of Tom's arrival on Deadman's Mountain.

There was a brief head-scratching and knee-shaking session before Tom once more began to speak. "Everyone scrambled to climb on board, but many hadn't been lucky. Once we got on board, Father clung to his family while he scrambled to get below the deck of the ship. We remained cuddled together in a dark corner below deck until the vessel pulled away from the shore. Its interior was packed with civilians stricken by fear and confusion."

In Savanna's mind, she knew she was getting closer to solving the mystery of Tom's presence on the mountain and in a secluded log house. "On what shore did the ship dock?" Savanna asked as Tom's tales further sparked her curiosity.

Tom hung his head forward as if he'd suffered a sudden loss of memory. "The ship came ashore in our town of Grecko Bay. That's the town where I lived with my parents and my sister, Caroleena," Tom said. His eyes were focused on the ceiling of the hall. He held his face as if he were trying to control the tears flowing down his cheeks.

Savanna began to develop her own fears about the overcrowded ship. There was the possibility that it could have sunk into the deep ocean. "Overcrowded ships often sink or capsize," she said. "Tell me about the voyage."

Tom gazed once more at the ceiling as he reminisced on the turbulence and the voyage that appeared to have taken forever. "The ship was tossed in every direction by great gushing waves," Tom said.

"All on board clung to whatever object was within reach. Those who were not able to find a safe place to hold were thrown to the floor, where most remained throughout the voyage. To ensure that my mother, Caroleena, and I survive the voyage, Father taught us how to sit in a swaying ship on a tempestuous ocean."

As Tom spoke, Savanna nodded repeatedly to assure him that she'd been following his every detail. "Did you know where the ship was heading when it left Grecko Bay?" Savanna asked.

"Not until it docked on the shore and Bragerston Town was seen on a post planted on the beach," Tom said. He let out a sigh of relief as he reminisced on the day the ship's voyage finally ended.

Tom's tale of the refugee ship docking in her town of Bragerston further sparked Savanna's curiosity. She sat at the edge of her bench while Tom took a series of deep breaths. "Who were your parents?" Savanna cunningly asked.

Tom scratched his head as if he'd been sharply bitten by a louse or a crawling insect. He hesitantly began to give the names of his parents. "My father was . . . Hornett Brentkham." Tom further hesitated before disclosing the name of his mother. "And my mother was . . . Kalister Brentkham. And, madam, I earlier mentioned my sibling, Caroleena Brentkham."

Tom stopped abruptly. He took a series of deep breaths as if he'd been traumatized by the memories of his past ordeals. Savanna knew Tom had a lot more details about his past, particularly about his sibling, whose name he'd frequently mentioned. As she waited, Tom continued his sketchy recollection of the refugee ship.

"The ship came ashore, across the bay over yonder." Tom pointed in the direction of the town of Bragerston in the distance below the mountain. "There were curious eyes scrutinizing everyone who'd stepped down from the ship onto the shore. The large number of passengers was taken to an enclosure where the head of each family had to produce documents to confirm their identity. Father held the documentation for his family while he waited to be processed as a refugee." Tom sighed amidst deep breaths before he continued to disclose more details of his escape. "While the officers were kept busy counting and recording the refugees, Father gathered his family and his belongings. He discreetly slipped away from the crowded harbor. We immediately boarded a bus heading toward this mountain."

As Tom spoke, a look of great sorrow shrouded his demeanor. Savanna felt she'd struck gold and therefore waited for the much-sought-after information.

"My father, being a soldier and a great mountaineer, got off the bus with my mother, Caroleena, and me," Tom continued. "He quickly took cover among tall shrubs and small trees before heading up this mountain he'd charted out on a map." Tom continually wiped his flowing tears as he spoke. "As a brave soldier, my father was equipped with the skills of survival on sea and on land, particularly in rugged terrain. He therefore immediately applied his survival strategies as well as his expertise to build this log house; with whatever help I could give."

Savanna listened with keen interest. Anxiety had taken her to the edge of her bench. A brief silence ensued. Amidst tears of apparent grief, Tom continued to provide further details.

"Father made several trips to the town to fetch essentials for our survival on the mountain. Most times, he traveled alone. Whenever she was up for the journey, Mother accompanied him to shop for the household essentials." Tom once more took a deep breath before he continued to speak. "Whenever Caroleena and I needed special things, we followed Father to town and climbed up the mountain to get back to the log house."

The heavy rain gradually let up. Fatigue was slowly taking hold of Tom. It appeared he'd been running out of steam and out of breath as information became fewer and far between. From Tom's brief account of his arrival on the mountain, Savanna quickly concluded that, Hornett had escaped with his family before the authorities in Bragerston could capture and record their identity. After they'd settled on the mountain, Hornett and his family had taken the local bus passing below the mountain, to the town of Bragerston. Since no one knew his identity, he'd ventured into the town at will without being noticed. Savanna had also obtained her answer for the tools, materials, long ropes, and other household items that were present in the log house.

As if his thoughts had bounced back into focus, Tom continued to provide details of his family's survival on the mountain. "My father and I perfected our hunting skills using long ropes and the tools in the back room," Tom said. He was under the assumption that Savanna had closely scrutinized the items in the room next to the kitchen. Savanna had also noticed the wall in the first hall, lined with trophies of the heads and skeletons of creatures on the mountain.

Tom extinguished the flame from the lamp and promptly lit a small candle resting on the table. The night was still new when the information session abruptly ended. He had been displaying signs of fatigue and a grievous demeanor. Amidst frequent yawns and falling eyelids, the brass clock on the wall showed nine o'clock, a reminder that he'd passed his bedtime. Tom had had a long day roaming around the mountainside in his incapacitated state. His painful wounds, coupled with a long evening relating the incidence of his escape from his war-torn homeland, had left him no other option but to retreat to his room.

The rain had quickly induced sleep, giving Tom another reason for retreating to his room. Savanna remained hopeful that the rain would put a damper on Tom's ventures in the outdoors in the dead of night. As she remained alone in the hall, Savanna followed suit and entered her room—not necessarily to enjoy a good night's sleep. She faced a night of restlessness, pondering the horrendous tales Tom had told.

It was quite a wet and saggy night in the mountain forest. Savanna lay in bed to reflect on Tom's tales of the refugee ship and his family's escape to the mountain. The mystery of his solitary existence on the mountain, she strongly felt, was soon to unravel. As Savanna remained sleepless, it wasn't long before sounds of footsteps were heard in the hall. She subsequently heard the rear door open and then promptly close. There wasn't a bit of doubt in her mind that Tom had ventured out into the dark rain-drenched forest.

From Tom's sketchy details of his escape from his country of origin, Savanna concluded that, Hornett Brentkham had escaped on the ship that had left the shore of Grecko Bay, Korenith. The ship was laden with refugees who'd escaped atrocities in their war-torn country. After weeks on its turbulent voyage, the ship, with its cargo of refugees, arrived in her homeland of Heiden, docking in the port of Bragerston Town. Its hundreds of refugees had sought asylum in Heiden. However, with his sharp wits and cunningness, before Hornett's belongings could be searched and his authenticity recorded, he evaded the border authorities and quickly disappeared in the crowded harbor with his family. Hornett's destination was Deadman's Mountain, where he built his hideout—a log house halfway up the mountainside.

Hornett built his log house, wedged between incredibly huge and tall rocks and among tall forest trees. Savanna perceived that the rocks and surrounding trees provided an ideal location for Hornett's log house. The house, surrounded by large rocks, served as a perfect hideout from the view of the folk in the villages below as well as the folk in the distant town of Bragerston.

There were many questions about the family's rationale for seeking refuge in an isolated mountain log house. As Tom had revealed, his father, Hornett Brentkham, was an army sergeant who'd allegedly escaped the war and imminent atrocities. As a former army sergeant, Hornett learned to survive in remote and treacherous places. He'd therefore sought refuge on the mountain and adopted a primitive lifestyle as a means of survival. He, along with his family, had become part of the wildlife in the mountain jungle.

Tom had conceded to being on the mountain with his parents, also his sibling. However, he'd stopped short of revealing their whereabouts, particularly the whereabouts of Caroleena, whose name had become his household word. Savanna's curiosity sparked even brighter as she felt there'd been many gaps in Tom's tales of his arrival on the mountain. As the perky interrogator, she vowed to pry further into his past with hopes of bridging the remaining gaps.

C H A P T E R   1 7

The Search Intensified

As the night progressed, Savanna lay awake, unable to fall asleep, particularly after Tom's sketchy tales of the refugee ship and his family's escape to the mountain. Savanna continued to entertain added fears for her safety after hearing Tom leaving the house in the late-night hours. She was reminded of the night prior when he had returned from the outdoors with sustained cuts and bruises. Tom's frequent groans and moans in the night had become unbearable, but she gradually developed a tolerance of them. She'd remained leery of Tom's nightly activities and therefore kept a constant watchful eye. Whenever the audible groaning ceased, either Tom had fallen asleep or his footsteps were heard as he exited the house through the rear door. His errands in the outdoors during the night remained shrouded in secrecy.

Savanna continued to entertain her thoughts that Tom had been making trips down the mountain with the intent to capture another victim. Whether he ventured down to the villages in the pitch-black night or he remained on the mountain, Savanna feared for his safety. She also feared for her safety, particularly while she remained in the house, with its rear door left unlocked in the dead of night. Amidst her fears and restlessness, Savanna quickly lapsed into a melancholy mood. Her thoughts went back home, on her siblings, on Melvia and Isaack, and on her grandparents. Most of all, tears flowed down her face as she imagined the joyous life she could be living with Harry. She'd missed her wedding day.

The lingering night allowed Savanna ample time to reminisce on the joyous pleasures she'd had back home. Fond memories of the barn dances lingered in the recesses of her mind. Each barn dance had offered the young folk the opportunity to meet their future partners. Savanna thought about her siblings, whether they'd been living their lives in pursuit of happiness, also whether another of her siblings had found a soul mate and another wedding plan was in progress.

It was a surety that Victoria and Aldbright were enjoying their married life and should be looking forward to seeing their first child. Cecelia, she imagined, was stuck in a faraway town, not knowing the fate of her sibling who'd failed to return home. *What would Cecelia be thinking?* Savanna perceived that Cecelia as well as Kladius would have been in on whatever her household speculated about her disappearance. Savanna had become lost in her thoughts of the happenings back home when sleep took hold of her.

Meanwhile, back in Amerhurst, the grief and sorrow that followed Savanna's disappearance had weighed down heavily on the Sevensen household. As each day came and left, Melvia's heart yearned to see Savanna back home. Without word of her whereabouts, Melvia presumed her dead but continued to cling to a thin ray of hope that one day, providence would come knocking on her door. The faithful volunteers carried out yet another search that came up empty, but they'd pledged to continue their search for the missing Sevensen girl.

In the meantime, there were mounting speculations and theories as to the whereabouts of Savanna. The concerned searchers began to direct their speculation at Harry's parents. The fact that the Lovethons had not been directly involved in the search for Savanna, was a sure sign that the couple had hidden secrets. Harry had failed to inform the Sevensens of his planned meeting with Savanna in the secret nook and on the day she disappeared. Had he done so, the news of her disappearance would have sparked further speculation and solidified the folk's belief that he'd kidnapped and murdered his future wife.

As the days came and went, Harry's heart grieved at the disappearance of his soul mate and beautiful bride-to-be. Many thoughts and questions began to flood his mind: *Why? When? Where? How? I'm innocent!* In his heart, he questioned whether he was at fault for Savanna's disappearance. The entire village thought so, except Isaack, who refused to resonate his thoughts of guilt. Isaack had found Harry clean of any wrongdoing, but Melvia and the remaining offspring, as well as the concerned volunteer searchers, felt otherwise. Savanna's grandparents, of sound wisdom, felt that the facts of her disappearance would come to light someday. They therefore held back their outright accusation of Harry being responsible for Savanna's disappearance. As the search continued, her grandparents maintained high hopes that someday, she would be found alive.

There had been mounting accusations of Harry being a suspect in Savanna's disappearance. The charming ladies, who had once been contenders for his love, expressed thankfulness that he had not chosen them as his future bride. The parents of the contending ladies expressed thanks to God above that they weren't the ones searching for their daughter. In the minds of the parents of the fine contending ladies, the innocent girl chosen by the handsome bachelor, a seductive murderer, had become his victim of foul play.

"If Savanna hadn't said yes to Harry, she wouldn't have vanished," one folk said.

"Did he suspect that she was still in love with Bentley, her ex-lover, and had found justifiable cause for murdering her?" another folk said.

The accusations took on momentum as each day passed and Savanna remained missing. There was a stagnant air of suspicion among the folk of Amerhurst that Bentley's parents held information vital to the whereabouts of Savanna. It was common knowledge that Savanna had parted with Bentley. Everyone knew Bentley had migrated to a foreign country. Nonetheless, the folk felt that Savanna may have eloped to join him as she didn't love Harry as she thought she did. Despite mounting speculations, the whereabouts of Savanna remained shrouded in mystery.

It hadn't been the norm for the folk of Amerhurst and beyond to contact the law authorities in their town of Bragerston. The folk around the mountain were quite settled in their daily lives. Likewise, their offspring had a well-structured existence. In a small community setting, the folk adhered to the laws of the land. They maintained strict adherence to the rules laid down: "Be good and kind to one another. Love thy neighbor as thyself." With the folk adhering to the strict rules, there was no justification for summoning the town authorities to the villages. As a result, in the matter of their missing daughter, Melvia and Isaack felt it was much too soon to engage the town authorities in the search. The couple strongly believed that Savanna would return home.

Weeks passed. Isaack had still refused to implicate Harry as the one who'd done harm to his daughter. He'd made every effort to protect his future son-in-law from the scrutiny of the town authorities. Finally, at Melvia's prompting and after thorough searches had proven futile, Isaack made his way to the town authorities to officially report the disappearance of Savanna.

Upon receiving news of a missing person, two officers arrived in Amerhurst to commence an official investigation. During the course of interviews and careful scrutiny, Melvia and Isaack were thoroughly interrogated. As the facts were gathered, Bentley Skaffer had become a person of interest. Had he shown any signs of resentment or jealousy toward Savanna at the time of their separation? Were there envious signs to indicate that Bentley had not willingly parted with Savanna? Had Bentley shown signs of jealousy toward Harry?

"Mr. Sevensen, had Mr. Skaffer resented the fact that Savanna left him for someone else?" one officer asked.

Isaack remained silent, leaving the dialogue to Melvia. In Melvia and Isaack's opinion and in their discussions with the officers, at the time of their love affair, Bentley was just a young boy. So was Savanna.

"The lad was much too young to be engaged in the things that the birds and the bees do," Melvia said. "They were much too young to be engaged in a serious love affair and to understand what a breakup entailed."

Despite Melvia's reasoning, the authorities further looked into the possibility that Bentley could have returned from America and eloped with Savanna. Melvia was quick to assure the authorities that Bentley had had no contacts with Savanna since leaving for America. In the outset, Bentley had become a suspect in Savanna's disappearance. However, the officers reluctantly cleared him of any wrongdoing after they'd thoroughly interviewed his parents.

It didn't take long for the officers to stumble upon a key piece of the missing puzzle as well as evidence leading to a crime. Beneath a rock by the side of the Sevensen gate, the officers found a note written by Savanna and carefully placed for Harry, obviously on the day she disappeared: "Harry, my love, I'm on my way to the nook. Don't forget our plan to meet in the nook as soon as you get home today. I'll be waiting there for you. Love, Sav. Diary note of Sunday, October 4." This was additional information that shook Amerhurst and further justified the folk's belief that Harry was responsible for Savanna's disappearance.

The officers immediately drove to Harry's house. A barrage of questions was directed at him. The officers questioned Harry to determine whether he'd actually met up with Savanna on that bleak Sunday evening. Harry had also been asked to lead the officers to the nook mentioned in the note Savanna had left for him. The officers, upon their arrival at the nook, found it in disarray. There'd been no doubt that whoever had met Savanna in the nook that day, a great struggle had taken place. The officers therefore concluded that Savanna had been taken away, amidst fierce struggles and altercations with her captor.

Harry immediately looked at Isaack and Melvia to attest to the fact that he'd left Amerhurst on the Friday evening prior to October 4 and had not returned until the subsequent Monday morning. The couple had no knowledge of Harry leaving Amerhurst that Friday evening prior. They therefore could not attest to his whereabouts before the subsequent Monday morning, when he returned to Amerhurst. The officers therefore could not accept Harry's alibi.

Knowledge of Harry's planned meeting in the secret nook with Savanna on the Sunday evening of her disappearance, prompted the officers to interview his parents. Under the midday sun, they arrived at the home of Henry and Addriana Lovethon. The officers were on a mission to investigate Savanna's disappearance, most importantly, to establish a time frame and confirm Harry's alibi. Where had he been on the evening of Savanna's disappearance? If he did not return to Amerhurst that Sunday evening, as he habitually did, why hadn't he returned? Where had he been on the Sunday afternoon and on the Sunday night of Savanna's disappearance?

The contents of the note left by Savanna were clear confirmation that Harry had been in Amerhurst on that day and had met up with her, whether or not he'd retrieved the note. Amidst accusations and implications of Harry's guilt, he'd been stricken by a double whammy. He'd not only been devastated by the disappearance of his bride-to-be. He now faced the accusations of kidnapping and possibly murdering her.

The officers completed their investigation but still had not found evidence that linked Harry to a crime. They hadn't been satisfied that he had a sound and credible alibi. The lack of credible evidence that could have linked Harry to the disappearance of Savanna resulted in the officers returning to Bragerston. They treated the disappearance as a cold case. In the minds of the folk of Amerhurst and beyond, as long as Savanna remained a missing person, Harry remained the key suspect in her disappearance.

Isaack and Melvia as well as their grieving offspring remained hopeful that someday Savanna would return home. As time passed slowly, it seemed their hope was slowly fading. Devoted searchers worked alongside the Sevensens to erect a structure in Savanna's memory. A large rock was placed inside the nook. The folk generously planted flowers around the rock, the most brilliant flowers Savanna had always adored. The "Flower Garden of Hope" was only fitting as the nook was alleged to be the place where Savanna had been at the time of her disappearance.

Harry had established a good rapport with the folk of Amerhurst. Some folk therefore had no reason to believe that he would have kidnapped and murdered his future bride. Despite the honor previously attributed to Harry, whether he walked the paths of Amerhurst or sat in seclusion in his rented house, words of insult and accusations were continually directed at him.

"Kidnapper!" one passerby shouted in disgust.

"*Where is Savanna?*" another shouted in the most disrespectful manner.

The accusations delved Harry excruciating pain and agony. He kept his silence nonetheless and maintained the noble status he'd portrayed when he had first arrived in Amerhurst. Amidst mounting accusations, Harry began to have second thoughts about his future in Amerhurst. He contemplated resigning his teaching job and promptly leaving Amerhurst but vowed to remain defiant. Harry vowed to pursue his profession as a devoted teacher and not walk away like a coward.

CHAPTER 18

Wolves of The Night

Back in her mountain log house, Savanna awoke from her short sleep to face another day. She carried out her usual activities as the day progressed. Tom had been out roaming around the mountainside but had returned before the sun slid down the western horizon.

Savanna had prepared the usual appetizing evening meal. Immediately after the dinner session, Tom took his usual seat on the bench in the first hall. Savanna remained in the kitchen to prepare tea. Tom had become accustomed to being served his delightful cup of tea at the end of each day. The evening's anticipated dialogue was complemented by sizzling tea served in metal mugs. Savanna entered the first hall bearing the mugs of aromatic tea.

"Have your tea, Tom," she said.

Tom promptly took his cup and commenced sipping the savory hot tea while his eyes scoured the ceiling of the hall. Savanna promptly took her seat on the opposite bench as she sipped tea with her companion. After a long period of proper grooming, Savanna began to notice Tom's receding hairline that made his protruded forehead more pronounced. His facial features had also become more revealed.

As the evening progressed, Tom lapsed into his usual silent mode. He continually made eye-piercing stares around the hall and occasionally toward Savanna. His actions had left her with a feeling of insecurity. Savanna was uncertain as to whether Tom had been waiting for the opportunity to pounce on her or if he'd been going through the motions.

While sipping the aromatic tea, the warmth in his stomach had no doubt, placed him in a more relaxed mood as he sat in anticipation of a dialogue. The usual evening dialogue began after Savanna poured an additional serving of warm tea. The calm atmosphere was conducive for a session of dialogue. Savanna therefore cunningly commenced asking questions she felt, would unravel more of the mysteries surrounding her companion, and bit by bit, he began to provide more sketchy details.

The dialogue session commenced with inquiries about Caroleena, the sibling Tom continually mentioned even while he slept. Savanna knew that Tom's release of information about Caroleena was contingent upon stating the whereabouts of his parents. She therefore played the cards quite well. Tom knew she'd been on to something when she had posed her first question.

"Tom," Savanna said, "in our prior conversations, you'd spoken so much about Caroleena." Savanna set her gaze toward the small window above his head. "Where is she?"

Tom's eyes remained focused on the ceiling of the hall. He commenced making a series of quick blinks before responding to her thought-provoking question. "Madam, I told you my family arrived in this country on a refugee ship." Tom spoke in a rather contentious manner. He kept his focus toward the second hall, as though he intended to make an escape.

Savanna kept her ears perked up for whatever was forthcoming.

"We all lived in this house until something happened," Tom said unexpectedly. Tears began to flow profusely from his eyes. He continually repositioned himself on the wooden bench as one overcome by a fit of restless anxiety. As if a compelling force had gripped his thoughts, he continued to speak. "On the night my parents passed, I was asleep and wasn't aware of what had transpired." Fresh tears began to flow down his cheeks and over thick facial hair.

Savanna maintained her silence as she too had been overcome by anxiety of a different kind.

"Madam, I had a terrifying dream that I went out hunting for a large bird to prepare dinner for the family. I followed the bird to a tall rock and suddenly realized that I was being chased by a pack of ferocious wolves." Tom paused briefly as he took a series of deep breaths.

It was a conversation Savanna dare not interrupt. She therefore listened intently while attending to every detail.

"In a fit of fright and with stern determination, I began to wrestle with the charging wolves. They'd quickly turned around to make their escape, but I cornered and fenced them in." Tom became overwhelmed by the incident as if it had occurred the night prior. "I took one of the long thick ropes Father and I used to tie the wild animals we caught in the woods. I recalled tying the first creature around its neck and wrestling it to the ground. By my quick thinking, I took the second creature and tied it up with the other end of the rope." Tom made a quick pause, as if he deserved an applause for the great feat he'd accomplished.

Savanna cringed at his narrative, which began to shed light on what had transpired in the night. She continued to maintain her silence, not affording even a blink.

"I had quickly tied two of the wolves with my rope, but one escaped." Tom once more paused for a fresh breath. He continually wiped new tears flooding his eyes. "I followed in hot pursuit to capture the third wolf, but it escaped. The next thing I knew, the two wolves I had tied up lay on a rock, gasping for breath. Madam, I still hold great fears that the wolf that escaped will return to attack me." Tom paused for a series of deep breaths while he stared at the opposite wooden wall.

Savanna sat dumbfounded as she listened to the gruesome tales of Tom's horrifying nightmare. While she listened, her heartbeat became more pronounced in her chest. She'd perceived something much more sinister than tying up two wolves and chasing a third. "Had the third wolf been injured during the scuffle?" Savanna asked.

Tom sighed as he once more took deep breaths. He spoke effortlessly as his memory of the dream unfolded. "No, madam. It quickly escaped before I could unravel my next rope. In the midst of the commotion and in my effort to capture the third wolf, I woke from my sleep. I felt disappointed that one of the wolves had escaped among the rocks." Tom felt that he'd accomplished a great feat that night, although it was just a dream.

Tom had provided sketchy details of his encounter with wolves while he slept. However, he'd not responded to the question of Caroleena's whereabouts. Savanna therefore revisited the question with hopes of obtaining more details.

"Where's Caroleena?" Savanna asked once more.

Tom struggled to maintain a measure of composure before he continued to speak. "The next morning, I woke up to find the town authorities in the log house, Caroleena standing by their side," Tom said. "The authorities later discovered Mom and Dad in their bed, strangled by one of the hunting ropes in the back room." Tom quickly wiped his tearing eyes with the palm of his hands. "Based on the evidence, one of Dad's hunting ropes used during the strangulation, I was accused as the perpetrator who'd strangled my parents while they slept. I did not strangle my parents." Tom repeatedly stomped the wooden floor with his heavy feet. He sat remorseless because of his apparent lack of admission of guilt.

With great intensity, Savanna listened to Tom's tales of his encounter with the wolves while he slept. He repeatedly denied the allegation that he'd strangled the two victims.

"I didn't strangle my mom and dad! I swear, madam!" Tom yelled. He continued his odd behavior, stomping his feet like a child throwing temper tantrums. "I wrestled and tied up the wolves when they came to attack me while I slept. I didn't attempt to strangle Caroleena. She's my only sibling." Tom blurted out pleas of his innocence while he wept buckets. "The next thing I knew, I was taken into custody by some officers and carried down the mountain to a waiting vehicle," Tom said.

Savanna's curiosity sparked brighter as the moments ensued. She therefore continued to ask the questions she knew would provide details of his parents' whereabouts. "Why did the authorities take you into custody?" Savanna asked.

"The officers felt that I had strangled my parents while they slept, but I swear I didn't do it," Tom said. "I was quickly driven away to town and locked up in an institution." It appeared that Tom had placed his breath on hold, but he once more began to speak. "I was in the institution for a short time before I was set free," he said.

The information Tom provided lacked details and credibility, but it had given Savanna a glimpse into that night of his horrifying encounter with the wolves. Savanna perceived that there was much more to Tom's story than his encounter with wolves while he slept. As for Tom's reason for returning to the mountain, Savanna still sought an answer. She therefore continued to prolong her interrogation session in her quest for more details.

"It has been a lonely existence on this mountain, Tom," Savanna said. "Why would you have even thought of returning after being set free from the correctional institution?" Savanna watched in grief as Tom's eyelids buzzed like the tiny wings of a hummingbird.

He persistently wiped his flowing tears with the palm of his hands. "I knew no one, madam, and no one knew me," Tom said. "When I was taken into court by the authorities, it was my last time seeing Caroleena." He continued to shed tears of grief.

Savanna became empathetic for the fact that Tom had arrived in a strange country, not knowing anyone except his parents and his sibling. He'd subsequently lost his parents. Not knowing the whereabouts of his only sibling, he was left alone to fend for himself in his mountain sanctuary—the only place he knew, away from his country of Korenith.

Tom's tales of his strangulation of the wolves had brought Savanna to tears. She consistently wiped her eyes with a white handkerchief that she'd retrieved from her bosom. Tom watched with added grief as he too sobbed uncontrollably. Like a sobbing child, he promptly excused himself from the hall and retreated to his room. Savanna reluctantly left the hall and retreated to her room. After listening to Tom's tales of strangling the wolves while he slept, Savanna became leery and afraid of falling asleep in her room. She'd become possessed by a sudden feeling of added insecurity behind the locked doors of the house.

In the midnight hour, when sleep had failed to take hold of her, Savanna remained preoccupied with thoughts about Tom. He'd been no doubt, traumatized by the passing of his parents and separation from his sibling. Savanna thought about Tom's parents, whose bodies were no doubt, buried on the town's public property it kept for the "Have-nots." Without fanfare or any condolence expressed, his parents had been buried in silence. She perceived Tom grieving in silence at the passing of his parents and the disappearance of his only sibling.

The frightening tales had given Savanna a glimpse into Tom's shady past. Savanna began to perceive that his demeanor portrayed a constant telltale of some traumatic occurrence. She further perceived that, whatever had transpired in the mountain fortress, had its genesis in Korenith, the land of his origin. In her time of sleeplessness, Savanna pondered the details of Tom's twisted dream. She tried to piece together some of the convoluted facts. Tom had related a recollection of his encounter with the wolves, but he was unaware of Caroleena's escape from the log house during the night of the incident. He'd had no knowledge of her escaping down the mountain to report the commotion in the house in the dead of night.

At the crack of dawn, Caroleena had made it to the town to report the commotion she'd heard in her parents' room during the night. She'd also reported Tom's attempted strangulation when he entered her room with his hunting rope. Under the early morning sunlight, at Caroleena's guidance, the town officers commenced their climb up the mountainside. They were carefully led to the log house, wedged between the rocks. At the time of her escape, Caroleena had left the rear door open, thus facilitating the officers' entry into the house.

Upon entering the house, the officers found the evidence clearly laid out. There were stunning scenes in every room. The officers first established that there hadn't been evidence of a break-in or forced entry into the log house prior to Caroleena making her escape. In the smallest room of the house, close to the bed, a long rope lay coiled up on the floor, evidence of an earlier commotion. The bedclothes were strewn around the room, further evidence of a struggle in Caroleena's room prior to her escape.

The officers entered a slightly larger room that had been ransacked, the bedding strewn around the floor. Dresses, a pair of slippers, and toiletry items were also strewn across the floor. The items left in disarray were evidence of a struggle in the room. On a log bed in the room, the officers found the lifeless bodies of a couple. A long rope had been wound around the two victims' bodies as they lay on the bed.

Caroleena was taken into the room to identify her parents. She immediately collapsed and was taken outdoors, where two waiting officers administered first aid. In an adjoining room, the bedclothes and a small log chair had been left strewn across the room, as if the occupant had left in a hurry. Upon entering the room, it didn't take long for the officers to notice an occupant asleep beneath layers of bedclothes on a ransacked bed. The sleeping male occupant was awakened after the officers had made their discovery.

"Hello, sir," one officer said.

The sleeping male turned slightly before rolling over in the bed.

"Sir, get up," the officer said.

The male struggled until he finally sat upright on the bed.

"Sir, what's your name?" another officer said.

"Tom Brentkham, sir," the man said in a rather groggy voice. It was obvious from his demeanor that he'd had a long night of activities that contributed to his fatigue and sleeplessness.

Tom sat on the bed with his shoulders held upright, giving due respects to the uniformed officers. Without further interrogation, the officers placed him on his feet. They immediately took him into custody. Tom was promptly taken outdoors and handed to the remaining officers. He was further identified by his sibling, Caroleena.

A quick scrutiny of Tom's room revealed compelling evidence that prompted the officers to conclude that he'd committed the crime. Tom was further identified by Caroleena as the one who'd entered her room with his rope prior to her escape. The presence of the rope in Caroleena's room confirmed her allegation of his criminal intention. Upon the conclusion of the officers' investigation, Tom was immediately bound by his hands and feet. He was led down the mountain, Caroleena leading the way. The bodies of the victims had also been carefully transported down the mountain.

The folk of Amerhurst had faint knowledge of a strange occurrence up the mountain. A curious gentleman walking along the road below the mountain, had suspicions that a mishap had occurred when, he noticed early morning activities. He'd given a sketchy account of a young man who was tied by his hands and feet as he was carried down the mountain by four officers from Bragerston.

Before the eyewitness had an opportunity to observe further events, the man was shoved inside a waiting vehicle. A young girl who'd been weeping profusely, had also been placed inside. The witness reported seeing the four officers place two large objects into the trunk of the vehicle. Before he could get further details, the vehicle had quickly driven off. Whether the incident had taken place on the mountain or by the side of the quiet road, the eyewitness did not obtain the facts. As no one dared to venture up the mountain, this was all the eyewitness had seen of the incident that had taken place that day.

In the small court of Bragerston, Tom was tried for the strangulation of his parents and the attempted strangulation of his sibling. Based on the evidence presented by the officers and Caroleena, Tom was found guilty of the heinous crimes. For his crimes, he'd received a prison sentence of five years, subject to early parole. Savanna perceived Tom's actions as a brazen, yet innocent act of violence. Had Tom been having nightmares? Was he having weird dreams that had caused him to act and be on the defensive? Savanna pondered these and many other questions for which there weren't immediate answers.

Knowledge of Tom's acts of violence had left Savanna to feel that she was slowly unraveling the mysteries surrounding her strange captor and his solitary life on the mountain. Savanna had once had a sense of safety behind the thick heavy wooden doors of the log house. However, in light of Tom's tales of strangling wolves while he slept, she'd become leery of the continuous sounds of footsteps in the house during the still night hours. The disturbing sounds had often dissipated once she heard the exit door open, then close some time thereafter. Savanna had refused to take the sounds for granted and had therefore pledged to remain on high alert under the cover of darkness.

As she obtained knowledge of the strangulations, Savanna didn't ever perceive the log house as a haunted environment. There were times when she was quite certain she'd heard someone speak when no one else was present in the house, but she quickly ignored the voice. There'd been nights when she thought she'd seen shadows in the crevices of her eyes. She, however, quickly reaffirmed her senses and her thoughts that it was just a figment of her imagination. In light of her knowledge of what had transpired seasons prior, Savanna felt she must reaffirm her thoughts that she hadn't been living in a haunted environment.

With the passing of his parents and the disappearance of Caroleena, Savanna perceived Tom as a prisoner confined to the mountain. He was a young man with no place of belonging. Tom had become a derelict in his mountain forest hideaway. Savanna was reminiscing on his tales of encountering wolves and the unfortunate outcome, when sleep slowly took hold of her.

C H A P T E R   1 9

The Revelation

It was the morning after Tom's gruesome tales of strangling the wolves while he slept. Savanna rose out of bed without incidence. Throughout the night, she had been kept awake by the sound of Tom's footsteps in the halls. She'd heard him leave the house through the rear door and reenter shortly before the dawn. It was anyone's guess where he'd ventured under the cover of darkness.

Savanna had been fully inducted into her world of routines. She performed her daily routines while trying to fathom the pains, heartaches, and miseries of one who'd sought refuge on a rugged mountain. It had become a part of her daily routine to prepare the usual breakfast. Tom always had his fill before wandering off into the outdoors. Savanna perceived that his life revolved around the great outdoors. His absence had therefore given her the golden opportunity to further scrutinize the contents of the house.

It was her strong belief that, under the light of the sun, Tom wandered expeditiously around the mountainside. She abhorred his lifestyle of wandering around the mountain like the wind blowing wherever it lists. He'd adopted the lifestyle of the animals in their mountain habitat, wandering around aimlessly and gathering whatever he could scavenge. Savanna often wondered whether Tom's fascination for the outdoors kept him wandering around the mountain.

She further perceived his intent to avoid her presence by being in the outdoors. He hadn't been hunting and bringing his daily catch to the house. At the end of each day, he often returned empty-handed. Savanna therefore concluded that Tom's absence hadn't been only for the sheer pleasure of hunting for survival. Her mind was bent on unraveling more of the mysteries surrounding Tom's place of confinement. Savanna felt there were artifacts she could unearth that would shed new light on the man and his mysterious secluded log house. She therefore rekindled her curiosity and, room by room, commenced her closer scrutiny of the contents of the house.

There was nothing exquisite about the small log house, but Savanna had been slowly uncovering a treasure trove of artifacts. A ray of sunlight suddenly beamed through a fissure of her solitary surrounding when she unearthed letters and artifacts in secluded locations in the house. One particular wall of the second hall was lined with shelves made from rough logs and thin slabs of wood. During her prior scrutiny of the items on the shelves, Savanna had noticed a small stack of folded newspapers and an old tattered book about wars and brave soldiers. She cautiously revisited the folded newspapers and commenced scrutinizing and perusing their contents. She soon realized that the newspapers were written in the foreign language of their origin. This discovery quickly put a damper on her curiosity.

Two other editions of the newspapers, Savanna noticed, were written in English. They were local newspapers purchased in Bragerston more than two years prior. She curiously perused a few pages of the newspaper. On the front page of one of the newspapers, she read sketchy details of a fugitive who'd been on the run from authorities in Korenith. Upon her close scrutiny of a newspaper clipping attached, a paragraph caught her attention:

SGT. DEFENBUM KENKORRY, THE SUBJECT OF A WORLDWIDE MANHUNT

> Sgt. Defenbum Kenkorry, a once honorable army chief, has become the world's most wanted. His outstanding performance had gained him promotions up through the ranks to become an honorable army sergeant. Sergeant Kenkorry was a high-ranking soldier with power and authority. He possessed authoritative powers to give orders that had to be executed.
>
> Throughout his career, Sergeant Kenkorry was engaged in unscrupulous practices. He'd earned a tolerable fortune through bribes and kickbacks. By the nature of his character and the powers vested in him by the authorities, Sgt. Defenbum Kenkorry ruled by the gun, punishing his subordinates who'd refuted his commands. He'd hunted and obliterated families of soldiers who'd questioned his hangings and decapitation of his subordinates. Sergeant Kenkorry's corruptive actions had turned him into a tyrant. The fugitive is being sought for his atrocities committed against humankind and for his defection from the army.

Savanna read without showing much interest, but she endeavored to continue reading the article in its entirety. The article further read,

> Sgt. Defenbum Kenkorry escaped with his wife, Dafariena Kenkorry, their son, Christopher Kenkorry, and their daughter, Graciena Kenkorry. Should anyone see him, Sgt. Defenbum Kenkorry, do not approach. He's considered armed and dangerous.

Savanna did not give much thought to the article; nor had she taken note of the photograph of Sgt. Defenbum Kenkorry. In her view, by taking a note of the photograph, she had no basis for comparison. She did not find any other photograph that identified the current and previous occupants of the log house.

The brass clock in the first hall indicated ten o'clock. Savanna's heart thumped heavily against her chest when she was alerted to the time. Tom had eaten an adequate breakfast prior to leaving the house. He therefore had no reason to return during the morning hours. Besides, his days were usually spent mostly in the outdoors. With that thought in mind, she resumed her close scrutiny of the house and its contents. Savanna's curiosity prompted her to further scrutinize the items she'd seen while carrying out her daily chores. She'd found herself out of her comfort zone when she scrutinized the artifacts and relics in the large room she assumed, had been once occupied by Tom's parents.

On the log table in the room, there was a trendy collection of perfumes. Her close scrutiny of the vials revealed their origins as the UK and Paris, France. Savanna opened one of the vials and fanned the fragrance toward her nose. She could readily smell rancid perfume, a fragrance that was unpleasant to her smell. There were other vials she opened to smell their intriguing fragrances. She once more scrutinized the elegant garments hanging on a cord, and the fanciful pairs of shoes on the floor in one corner of the room. The contents of the room portrayed the characteristics of a sophisticated couple who'd had a flair for fashion and a taste for luxury, one who'd once pursued a glamorous lifestyle.

Savanna cautiously remained in the room while she commenced her close scrutiny of the old green canvas bag she'd seen hidden behind the bed. Her closer scrutiny of the bag revealed a cache of items worth investigating. Carefully stashed away in the bag were maps displaying the mountains of many countries. There were maps also displaying mountain passes and hiking trails. Savanna had never heard of the countries she noticed on the maps. She therefore quickly and carefully folded and replaced them in the bag.

Bright stars sparkled in her eyes when she opened a tiny black box and noticed an elegant gold ring. The ring had lost its golden glow from lack of use, but it had maintained its sentiments as well as portrayed the outlandish lifestyle of the one who'd once worn it. Savanna carefully removed the ring from the box and held it under her close scrutiny. Her sharp eye detected the engravings on the inside of the ring: "DK to DK, with love." She immediately perceived the genuine love of two folks locked up in a circle of pure gold. Savanna carefully returned the priceless ring to its box and continued her search of the canvas bag.

A closer scrutiny of the items in the bag raised suspicions and kindled added fears and caveats. Nonetheless, Savanna felt she'd stumbled upon facts and artifacts that would likely unravel Tom's mysterious existence on the mountain. She'd been closely scrutinizing each item in the bag and promptly returning them. Should Tom walk in unexpectedly, she could leave the room quickly without raising any suspicion. Carefully folded in the false bottom of the bag were birth certificates of four individuals. The documents were moth-eaten and tarnished by brown stains and dead termites. The lack of a photograph on each of the documents rendered them useless in identifying the past and present occupants of the house.

Savanna began to carefully unfold each birth certificate; peradventure she could find one belonging to Tom Brentkham. The first certificate contained the name Defenbum Kenkorry. The birth date suggested that the document was that of an older adult male. The second certificate had the name Dafariena Montrieve, with a date of birth that suggested the owner was an adult female. The third and fourth birth certificates having the names, Christopher Kenkorry and Graciena Kenkorry, were those of children born to Defenbum and Dafariena Kenkorry. Closer scrutiny of Christopher's birth certificate indicated an age of twenty-two. Likewise, the date on Graciena's birth certificate indicated an age of eighteen. The certificates stated the place of birth as the town of Grecko Bay, in the country of Korenith. The absence of Tom's and Caroleena's names on any document in the house made it difficult to connect them to the birth certificates in the bag.

Savanna curiously scrutinized the birth certificates and immediately recalled the newspaper article about the fugitive Sgt. Defenbum Kenkorry. She felt she'd struck gold when she connected the birth certificate of Defenbum Kenkorry with the name in the newspaper. Nonetheless, she could only assume that Defenbum Kenkorry, along with his family, were left behind in Hornett Brentkham's country of origin. Savanna became puzzled that Hornett had maintained ties with Defenbum Kenkorry, a fugitive he'd left behind in his country of Korenith. Further scrutiny of the canvas bag also revealed a small stack of dollar bills neatly folded beneath the birth certificates. Savanna had never seen such currencies. The dollar bills were written in another language; each having the word Korenith clearly printed across its face.

Carefully hidden in the false bottom of the bag were items of gold. There were gold watches, gold badges with names engraved on them, the engraved names having "Sgt." in front of them. Savanna perceived that the items were Hornett's memorabilia of the treasures he may have stashed prior to making his escape on the refugee ship. She'd pondered the fact that Hornett Brentkham had so many sergeant badges in his possession.

Savanna felt she'd struck gold as she continued her close scrutiny of the canvas bag. Newspaper clippings further detailing the crimes of Sgt. Defenbum Kenkorry were carefully stacked in the false bottom of the bag. One such article written in English sparked further curiosity as Savanna began to read its contents:

> Villain Defenbum Kenkorry, an army sergeant, executed innocent civilians to exert his authoritative powers. During the war, Defenbum Kenkorry took pleasure in decapitating his fellow sergeants and their family. He'd carefully disposed of his victims after concealing their identity. He'd also executed civilians for financial gains.

Another newspaper article read,

> Defenbum Kenkorry discarded the bodies of many of his victims in the ocean. He'd lain most of his victims in deep trenches. A worldwide hunt is on for Sgt. Defenbum Kenkorry, who may have fled Korenith with his wife, Dafariena Kenkorry, his son, Christopher, and his daughter, Graciena. Defenbum Kenkorry is wanted for his heinous crimes against humanity.
>
> While he was out on bond, Sergeant Kenkorry had failed to appear for his court trial. He was therefore tried in absentia for the deliberate slaughter of his fellow officers and more than a thousand innocent civilians during the war. There's a reward of a million dollars, payable to anyone who turns in fugitive Defenbum Kenkorry, dead or alive. Should anyone

see the former Sergeant Kenkorry, do not approach. Contact your local authorities. He poses danger to himself and others.

Savanna continued to question Hornett's reason for gathering information about a wanted fugitive. Further search of the canvas bag uncovered other items that continued to spark her curiosity. Neatly tucked away in the bag was a book that appeared to have been a treasured possession of Sgt. Defenbum Kenkorry. The title of the book, *The Years of War*, was inscribed in gold. Behind its cover was written, "Presented to Sgt. Defenbum Kenkorry." The signature had been decipherable and was therefore not of interest to Savanna. Closer scrutiny of the contents of the book revealed that it was written in the language of the recipient's country of origin. Should Savanna conclude that Sgt. Defenbum Kenkorry was left behind in Korenith? Had this been the case, Hornett Brentkham had a connection and a likely vested interest in the fugitive, Sgt. Defenbum Kenkorry. Savanna continued to hope that, time and Tom would unravel the mystery surrounding the two persons of interest.

A magazine Savanna had found in the canvas bag, contained photographs and articles about the lavish lifestyles of movie stars and opera singers. Although the language of the magazine was foreign to her, each of its pictures painted many more than a thousand words. The magazine depicted picturesque scenes and great people of show business flaunting their elegant attire. The foreign language on the pages deterred Savanna from reading the articles. She'd no doubt overlooked the name and photographs of the glamorous lady Dafariena Kenkorry.

When Savanna stumbled upon a stack of letters in the canvas bag, she felt she'd uncovered hidden treasures. She curiously leafed through the stack of letters and noticed that most had been written in English. As Savanna stood poised to read the letters, she felt strongly that she would be engaging in facts and gossip that would shed new light on Tom's past.

Her heart was suddenly gripped by the severe pain of separation as she opened the first letter. If only she could have received letters from her family down below the mountain. Sadly, no one knew her whereabouts.

Savanna thought about letters Cecelia might have sent to her, which she could not receive while on the mountain. She reminisced on the pains her disappearance dealt to Isaack and Melvia and how much her siblings had endured. Savanna cried bitter tears as her thoughts were on Harry and the wedding she'd missed. If only she could receive news from him or be able to send a letter home. Most of all, she wished she could go back home.

The first letter she read was sent to Hornett by his brother, Ummerald. It read thusly,

> My brother, Hornett: Our new chief, Sgt. Gerrard, has pledged to continue the worldwide search for the fugitive. There's still a bounty on his head. The highest reward awaits the one who will turn him in to the authorities. Take extra care, my brother. And don't forget that we all miss you dearly. P.S. If at all possible, I would love to hear from you. There're always wishes to be made—if they would all come true. Signed: Ummerald.

Savanna's inquisitive mind prompted her to open and read the contents of each letter as long as the language permitted. A second letter—dated June 10, two years prior, written by Meiszer—had its origin in Sudsfort, Korenith. The letter read,

> Hornett, my dear son: I must first of all become comfortable with your name. I'm so sad that we parted in that manner. Your father must be rolling in his grave at the thought that you're caught up in these circumstances, causing you to leave home so unexpectedly. I'm quite certain that you're following the news. Stay safe, son. I hope that someday soon, the way will be cleared and I'll see you back home. Signed: Meiszer.

The page of Meiszer's letter was smudged and stained from large apparent teardrops. Whether they were the teardrops of Hornett or those of Meiszer, only they could tell. At the sight of the teardrops,

Savanna's eyes were flooded with tears as she thought about her own parents, her siblings, and her grandparents, whom she'd left behind. Most of all, she'd missed her wedding day with the love of her life, Harry. Like one in a feeding frenzy, Savanna curiously unfolded another letter that read,

> My dear grandson, I miss you very much. Your grandfather passed away last month. He didn't quite make his ninety-eighth birthday. I'm so sorry you didn't have the opportunity to see him before he passed. This could be my last letter to you. I'm very ill. It's not known how much longer I'll live. I may never see you again, but remember that I love you dearly. If I didn't see you again, don't worry about me. I'll be gone to my rest and will join your grandfather in the afterlife. Love you. Kiss your wife and the children for me. If at all possible, please write to me so I'll know you received this letter. Love, Grandma Georginette.

The scraggly lines of Georginette's signature were telltales of her shivering hands and the existence of a deteriorating age-related condition. She'd no doubt dictated the contents of her letter to someone else. Lastly, Savanna opened another letter, written by Iriena Kennester. The letter read,

> Dear Hornett: August 5 was the court date. The trial by Justice Armistice was in absentia. Many witnesses had come forward to testify of the torture and termination of their husbands, wives, children, their dear fathers, also their uncles. Dr. Doughally and many others submitted evidence of the torture and massacre of their relatives and friends. The folk of Korenith gathered in the courthouse to seek justice for their loved ones who'd been murdered. On August 5, there was a guilty verdict brought down by Justice Armistice. A sentence of one hundred years for the massacre of innocent civilians, plus five years for defecting from the army, was also brought down by the justice. There's a reward payable

to anyone who successfully brings the fugitive into custody.
Be safe. Signed: Iriena Kennester.

Savanna read the letters stashed away in the canvas bag, but she was
left with more unanswered questions on the twisted saga of Hornett
Brentkham and Sgt. Defenbum Kenkorry. She'd established that the
letters were sent to Hornett Brentkham. However, she continued to
ponder his connection to the fugitive, Defenbum Kenkorry. Savanna
was particularly pondering the fact that Hornett had had such interest
in securing details on the affairs of Defenbum Kenkorry. She continued
to question Hornett's motive for maintaining documents, including the
birth certificates of the Kenkorry family.

Savanna further perceived that Hornett had been a confidant of
Sergeant Kenkorry. She could only maintain her suspicion that Hornett
had hoped to cash in on the reward offered for the capture of the fugitive,
Kenkorry. No other clues or suspicion crossed her mind. The contents
of Meiszer's letter had left Savanna wondering whether Hornett was
also in trouble. Being unable to connect the two subjects, her shallow
focus quickly deflected back to the fugitive, Sergeant Kenkorry. There
hadn't been any new correspondence, English or any other language,
found in the bag since Hornett's receipt of Iriena Kennester's letter,
dated two years prior.

Savanna perceived the log house setting as a place where time had
stood still. Moth-eaten documents and newspapers, stained by soot
and water drops from the humidified ceiling of the house, were a
reflection of abandonment and decay. Relics found in the house had
once supported the lifestyle of its inhabitants, who'd once basked in the
sunshine of luxury. Abandoned garments, fine jewelry, and elegantly
designed shoes mildewed by constant humidity—all were reflections
of the end of a dynasty. The backyard had been littered by the dry
bones and carcasses of animals that had once supported the lives of the
mountain inhabitants. The sole survivor in the log house remained as
the derelict who'd fallen between the cracks of a lost dynasty.

Before returning the canvas bag, Savanna reopened the small
jewelry box. Her eyes once more sparkled at the sight of the beautiful

gold ring. The ring brought bittersweet memories of her wedding, which had been put on hold since her kidnapping. She carefully returned the ring and neatly arranged the documents in the bag. With the bag and its contents safely returned to their hiding place, Savanna quietly exited the room. Caroleena's room had not sparked much of her curiosity. This had been the room Savanna occupied since arriving in the house. In her view, Caroleena was just an emerging sixteen-year-old adolescent and therefore had nothing of much significance to attract a curious eye.

The sun had commenced its descent over the western horizon when Savanna exited the large room. There hadn't been much time remaining to further scrutinize the artifacts in the house, but Savanna felt that she had to have a closer scrutiny of the items in Tom's room. She felt there might have been items that evaded her view each time she tidied his room. While keeping her eyes and ears on high alert, she cautiously entered Tom's room.

A sound at the rear of the house had suddenly put a damper on her attempted scrutiny. Tom's giant steps could be heard as he entered the kitchen. Savanna quickly exited his room and made her way toward the kitchen. Upon Tom's arrival, she promptly commenced preparing the evening meal. Tom took his usual place at the log table in the second hall. It had become his delight to be served dinner at the end of his days roaming around the mountainside. Savanna promptly served his dinner of roasted meat with potato. At the end of their appetizing dinner session, Savanna prepared herbal tea, which she poured into the mugs. She carefully served Tom his sizzling cup of tea. She'd been preparing for another evening session of dialogue and fact finding.

CHAPTER 20

Love Sparked

The Friday evening sun once more displayed its orange glow as it slowly slid behind silver-lined dark clouds in the western horizon. Darkness was slowly bearing down on the mountain. A warm gentle breeze rustled the leaves of the surrounding trees. Meanwhile, creatures of the wild hustled to find a place of rest before the darkness fell. Savanna felt secure after Tom had carefully barred the doors and the small windows of the house.

Tom sat comfortably on his bench, where he'd retreated immediately after the dinner session. He was sipping tea from his metal mug while entertaining his usual habit of staring at the opposite window in the hall. Tom was taking every step to avoid eye contact with Savanna as she sat on the opposite bench. Savanna had subtly created the atmosphere for another night of dialogue. Her thoughts were preoccupied with the contents of the letters she'd earlier discovered. However, she was constantly reminded of Tom's likely reprisals should he become aware of her scrutiny of his secret possessions.

They'd been sipping tea in the semi-dark hall when she noticed his trembling knees, as if he'd been shaking to music his mind had been creating within. While Tom amused himself, he periodically made eye contact with Savanna. The continuous shaking and trembling of his feet left her in a precarious position. She felt that his rapacious wanderings around the mountainside had no doubt, left him with fidgety feet and quite often, uncontrollable tremors. Lately, Savanna had begun to notice Tom getting into his jovial moods while he relaxed on his bench.

In her quest for answers to her numerous questions, Savanna sat ready for another night of dialogue. She felt there was much more that Tom had to disclose and was therefore determined to delve deeper for whatever facts she could obtain. Amidst Tom's continued rhythmical motion, Savanna ignited his thoughts by commencing their usual evening dialogue.

Caroleena was not the best subject matter to discuss while Tom remained in his pleasant mood. Nonetheless, Savanna felt it was a good place to start. He'd mentioned seeing Caroleena for the last time during his court hearing in Bragerston. Savanna had her doubts as to whether Tom had been telling the truth about anything. The subject of Caroleena's absence was therefore placed, once more, on the table.

"Tom," Savanna said, "have you any idea where Caroleena might be?"

Tom quickly lapsed into a state of discontent as he pondered the question. He slowly regained some measure of composure before he began to speak. "As much as I could remember and as I have told you, Caroleena was taken away by the officers while we were at the courthouse."

Savanna heard the slur in his voice as he attempted to recall the incidence of Caroleena's departure.

"That was my last time seeing her, madam." He couldn't hold back the flowing tears. Like a child throwing tantrums, Tom's feet pounded the thick wooden floor. No sooner had he released a sufficient measure of tantrum than Tom quickly retreated to his room.

Savanna perceived Tom's unwillingness to disclose much about Caroleena, also about himself. His refusal to speak about his sibling was a sure sign of a cover-up. It therefore became clear that he and his sibling had made a pledge to secrecy. There was no other ploy Savanna could have applied to obtain the crucial information she sought. She therefore strongly believed that time would uncover the mystery of Tom's solitary existence. The facts surrounding the mysterious documents hidden in the canvas bag also remained shrouded in mystery. Savanna remained hopeful that someday she would unravel the mysteries surrounding the mountain dweller and the relics of the shabby log house. On that thought, she retreated to her room.

The creatures of the wild had long settled into their secured resting place for the night. Soon, they would succumb to a night of restful sleep, except for the nocturnal creatures that roamed around the mountainside, seeking their night's meal among their unsuspecting sleeping prey. Whether Tom had plans to roam around the mountainside in the night hours remained to be heard.

Savanna had spent her long day scrutinizing and sifting through the documents she'd uncovered in the canvas bag and elsewhere. She was quickly overcome by fatigue and the perplexities of not being able to uncover Tom's secrets. While she lay in bed, her mind resumed its difficult task of analyzing the items found in the house, particularly in the canvas bag.

There was nothing exquisite about the log house, but within its walls lay a treasure trove of artifacts and a tangled web of mysteries. There were relics that remained frozen in time, scenes from a past livelihood of those who'd made the log house their sanctuary. There were clues revealing something much more sinister than a young man living a solitary life on the mountain—if only Savanna could join the pieces of the puzzle.

The dark night lingered. Savanna reflected on the contents of the newspaper clippings Hornett had allegedly collected and stored. Her thoughts were on Sgt. Defenbum Kenkorry, the fugitive who'd once taken pleasure in the massacre of innocent victims. The newspaper articles painted Defenbum Kenkorry as a ferocious leader who had enforced submission to his authority by applying his iron fist. Torture and ultimate death had been the punishment meted out to his victims for noncompliance with his orders.

There was a myriad of other thoughts that bombarded Savanna's mind as she lay awake. She'd remained deep in thought when the tiny glow from the candle finally flickered and died. Darkness immediately enveloped her room, creating innumerable pictures that evaded her inner vision. Savanna had been waiting for much-needed sleep when her thoughts were on the motherhood role she'd been playing in the log house, also the mother figure Tom perceived in her. It was her heart's greatest desire to be regarded as the fine young lady in need of love and affection, not just to be perceived as a mother figure.

Savanna was devoting her young life to a labor of love and care for a seemingly, young adult child whose parents' lives had been cut short before he was groomed into manhood. Tom readily embraced her warm affection, the affection only a mother could offer to her child. Whether he had subtle intentions, he always eluded the subject of romantic love. Tom lived a young adult life of self-pity, with a feeling of neglect and a constant need of attention. However, deep within, Savanna perceived love and passion percolating. Manhood was gently knocking at his heart's door.

In the quiet and secluded log house, Savanna remained preoccupied with her life of portraying motherhood, but her heart yearned to be perceived as Tom's romantic lover. Tom's quest for mothering had no doubt, obscured his perception of the fine lady who was fit for a prince—if only he could perceive himself as the young prince of the lost Brentkham dynasty.

At the crack of dawn, Savanna habitually woke up and adorned herself in the elegant garments Tom had brought her from the large room. She often waited in the second hall, adorned in one of the elegant dresses. Whenever Tom entered the hall, she stood poised for her session of admiration. In his admiration of the young mother, as he'd perceived her, Tom often stopped in the hall to shower her with his kind words.

"You look lovely today, madam," he often said.

Savanna was playing her motherhood role quite well, but she wished Tom would perceive her as a young lady whose heart yearned for his love. She'd been living in a somewhat glorious delirium, maintaining her hopes that Tom would look beyond a motherhood image to find her charming and attractive.

There were times when Tom seemed to be in need of a shoulder to cry on, an outlet for his apparent ravaged emotions. Over time, Savanna realized that he'd clung to her emotionally like a stamp to a letter. From her point of view, Tom's actions were quite understandable. His parents had passed. His only sibling's whereabouts were unknown. As Tom had conceded, he'd been left alone to fend for himself in a small log house on a rugged mountainside.

Having Savanna on the mountain had therefore become his only hope of survival. She'd been living her structured life, performing motherhood duties—the greatest needs of her kidnapper. At the end of his day roaming the mountain, Tom routinely changed from his rugged mountain clothes and into clean garments from his meager wardrobe. He sometimes salvaged whatever he could find in the large room. Savanna had coached him on routinely shaving his face, using an antiquated razor that, surprisingly, had still maintained its thin edge. The once long matted hair on his head was kept to a reasonable length.

She habitually massaged Tom's hands and his feet, which were often calloused from his constant wandering around the mountainside. As she carried out her motherhood duties, she often gave him a manicure and a pedicure, using the army knife she'd found in the back room. Tom often radiated his most pleasant smile as he admired his freshly cut nails. After each grooming session, Tom admired his appearance in the mirror on the wall in the second hall. He always expressed his appreciation in the most profound way.

"Ma'am, this is heavenly to the touch," he often said.

In Savanna's mind, every picture paints a thousand words. She therefore perceived Tom's heartfelt gratitude for her difficult tasks of caring and nurturing him. She'd given him her tender loving care in a way only a mother could to nurture her child. Her motherly care and nurturing groomed and molded Tom and set him on the path to become the fine gentleman he ought to be.

Savanna often admired his radiant charm beaming forth, particularly after each grooming session. She'd begun to admire his display of gentlemanly mannerisms, a reflection of his noble heritage. It seemed Tom had been slowly acknowledging his heritage. He was once the well-disciplined young son of a high-ranking army sergeant, Hornett Brentkham, whose mountain confinement had brought an end to his family's dynasty.

As each day came and left, Savanna pondered Tom's lack of romantic love. She always noticed his habitual avoidance of eye contact. She felt that he'd always been in secret admiration of her poise and stature and other traits that had captivated his imagination. His gazes, stares, and quick glances had no doubt gone unnoticed, while she remained preoccupied and fully absorbed in her daily house chores.

Whenever Savanna spoke, she'd always made eye contact with Tom, but her stares had no doubt, left him in an awkward position. Lately, she'd been noticing changes in his demeanor. Tom's infectious stares had left her in an uncomfortable position and with more unanswered questions. How should Savanna react to Tom's frequent stares each time she walks by him? She'd once had bright hopes of a happy life of marriage with Harry, the love of her life. They'd each had hopes of a good life together as man and wife. Their marriage plans, however, ended abruptly when she was snatched away by her mean and rugged kidnapper.

To become the focus of eye-piercing stares of love by the man who'd so viciously taken her away from her nook, was beyond her wildest dreams. Throughout her many months in captivity, Savanna strongly believed Tom perceived her as a mother figure. He'd continually sought from her, the care and nurturing that only a mother could offer to her child. Tom's continuous stares, however, portrayed a deeper meaning than his quest for motherly care and nurturing. Savanna perceived a new day dawning in her life.

Lately, Tom had been getting into his frisky moods. Upon returning from his mountain chores and while he sat in the first hall, he'd been singing cheerful songs, often in his mother tongue. His songs stirred up Savanna's emotions and often brought tears to her eyes. Savanna did not quite understand the language in which Tom sang; nonetheless, the songs exposed his innate feelings. Tom's actions while he sang, spoke volumes. His songs stirred up Savanna's emotions and brought tears to her eyes as he sang with such a deep expression of exhilaration.

Tom acknowledged the childish nature in which he sang. He'd often made silly grins after each song. At her age of early adulthood, Savanna was in pursuit of pleasures beyond childish behaviors. In the still dark night, Savanna lay sleepless as she reminisced on her life in captivity. Time passed since she had arrived on the mountain. According to the secret marks she'd been making on the calendar, autumn, winter, spring, and summer came and left. It was the beginning of another autumn season, a grim reminder of the season in which she had been taken away from the nook. The new season sadly brought memories of the joyous autumn wedding she'd missed. As far as she could see, the leaves had begun to show signs of brown, yellow, red, dark green, and whatever other colors signaled the season of change.

The long days passed slowly while each night brought new thoughts about love and belonging. Each day, Savanna's heart yearned to be close to Tom in a passionate way. Persistent rainfall often brought cold and damp weather conditions on the mountain. On a chilly night, Savanna wished she could cuddle up beside Tom, who did not appear to be affected by changes in the mountain atmosphere. During dark and blustery days, when Tom was forced to remain indoors for the day, Savanna wished he would caress her against his broad hairy chest while he sat on his comfortable bench in the hall. As each new day arrived, she developed a yearning to be touched by Tom's strong hairy hands and to be held in his warm embrace.

Despite her eleven months in captivity, away from a civilized society, Savanna maintained her elegant looks and graceful charm. It had become her deepest wish that Tom would adore her charming looks and, by so doing, express his love for her, the only lady in his presence. As she'd perceived, Tom was not the Prince Charming that every girl would die for, but he appealed to her in many ways. He radiated the charm of a handsome prince. She'd become mesmerized by his charming and overpowering looks. Amidst the yearning in her heart to be in Tom's embrace, Savanna endeavored to continue playing the cards well, with hopes that someday, love would spark. While her heart yearned for Tom's love, the dark and quiet night finally brought sleep to her eyes.

The Saturday morning sun crept up quietly from the horizon, waking all creatures that had fallen asleep at its departure the evening prior. Its long rays beamed among the branches of the mountain trees and shone through the crevices of the house. Savanna felt that she'd slept but not the desired deep sleep she'd expected. She rose out of bed and promptly commenced her morning chores nonetheless.

The mountain atmosphere was calm and quiet, except for the creatures of the wild that continually made their presence known by their constant amusing sounds. It was one of Tom's typical days when he lapsed into his usual mood swings—on-again, off-again silence. Savanna perceived his inner state of emotional turmoil that would have given him reasons to be discontented. She therefore exerted every effort to appease him in his time of woes.

Tom quietly made his exit through the rear door but returned promptly from his Saturday morning stroll. It was his Saturday custom to take brief walks around the mountainside, but he always returned to the house, where Savanna catered to his eating needs. The Saturday breakfast of roasted bird and corn was served. Tom ate his serving with a big appetite. At the end of the short breakfast session, he made a non-routine exit through the rear door. It appeared that he'd left on another of his brief Saturday morning outdoor errands.

At his departure, there wasn't much to do indoors. The morning sun was crisp and inviting for a short stroll in the outdoors. Savanna felt that she should bask in the warm sunlight within the vicinity of the house and therefore followed suit. Upon venturing into the outdoors, she found Tom seated on the bench made for two, beneath the branches of the overhanging trees. He sat basking in the warm glow the sun cast around the vicinity. It was rather out of character for Tom to be seated in the outdoors instead of his habitual roaming around the mountainside. Savanna walked toward him as he stared steadfastly into her eyes. For the first time, his eyes met hers with eager curiosity. At her gentle approach, Tom's heart became overwhelmed. A drastic change appeared in his demeanor as he welcomed her presence.

"Don't be shy," he said. "Sit beside me."

Savanna's sparkling eyes glowed as tears of joy began to flow. In her heart, she felt that hers had been the first dreams to ever come true—Tom was in love with her. Savanna promptly took her place by Tom's side. She knew it was the moment for which she'd waited when he slowly shuffled his body close to hers. Tom's mind couldn't have contained the comforting words that began to escape from his lips and no doubt, from his trembling heart.

"Sav, you've brought a ray of sunlight to my solitary life," he said. "I had once basked in life's sunshine my parents brought to me, but I've been alone, having no hope of leaving this mountain. I've been living the dark days of my life and felt that I would never see another sunlit day, but you came along and have given me hope." Tears suddenly flooded his eyes.

Tears filled Savanna's eyes as she too became overwhelmed by emotions. "I didn't come here willingly," Savanna said as she wiped her flowing tears. "I was kidnapped and brought here. You took me away from my home, my parents, and my beautiful siblings. You took me away from Harry, my soul mate and husband-to-be." Savanna hung her head between her knees as bittersweet tears cascaded from her eyes.

Tom watched helplessly as the tears flooded her eyes. Whether Savanna had hoped to receive Tom's expressed remorse for his act of kidnapping and forcible confinement, he'd shown no remorse. "Savanna, I took you away because I love you," Tom said. "Now that you're with me, I want you to stay."

At Tom's uttered words of consolation, the tears dissipated from Savanna's eyes. She quickly lapsed into her usual charming demeanor and ceased from expressing sadness or regrets for Tom's act of kidnapping and subsequent confinement. The morning breeze softly rustled the leaves of the trees around the bench. There was an atmosphere of serenity as the two overwhelmed young adults sat on the bench built for two.

Tom reached out his strong hairy hand and held her hand as if he would never let go. Savanna's heart pounded against her chest as she remained cuddled by his side. She felt love and passion as Tom softly smoothed her hands while he showered her with words of love.

"Sav, your smile has always cast rays of sunlight around me," Tom said softly. "You're the sunshine that wakes me up in the morning and sends me to bed at night. You're the one who gives me pleasant sleep in the night hours."

Savanna had her qualms about Tom's claims to having pleasant sleep during the night. She was fully aware that he'd spent his nights pacing the floor and wandering off in the outdoors. Nonetheless, she cherished his tender touch and was elated by his assuring words of love. As Savanna sat by Tom's side, she was intrigued by his tantalizing charm and comeliness. As she'd perceived, Tom had suddenly realized that a strange feeling had been welling up within his heart. His love had begun to emanate toward the charming young lady in his presence. For the first time, Savanna sensed Tom's love that had surpassed motherly love.

Savanna was suddenly overcome by a feeling of ardent love and desires that burned within her heart for Tom. An exchange of love and passion was the order of the blissful morning beneath the swaying tree branches. A new day had dawned in Savanna's world when Tom slowly released his ardent feelings of love for her. He began to admire her with sparkles in his eyes and a heart on fire. She perceived Tom as a bright light emanating from pitch darkness.

Savanna felt in her heart that her time on the mountain had been well spent. She reminisced on her months of hard labor and devotion to Tom's well-being. The moment for which she'd long waited had finally arrived—love sparked between them.

"I've always been here for you, Tom," Savanna said. "I've earnestly played the role of a mother and a guardian to you. I'll always be here to love and care for you."

As she spoke, Tom further displayed his appreciation and passionate love by softly pampering her hands. A shade of a smile shone on his cleanly shaven face as he continued to shower his new love with assuring words. "I want to spend the rest of my life with you, Savanna," Tom said in sincerity.

While his love toward the beautiful lady seated by his side kindled, there was no doubt he'd abandoned his age of innocence. Savanna perceived the dawn of a new day in the log house. The soft touch of Tom's rough and calloused hands was heavenly as Savanna remained in his warm embrace. Her overwhelmed heart pounded within her chest when he gently shuffled his body closer to her side.

From the comfort of the bench, built for two, the new lovers cherished their time of togetherness. Tom, for the first time, reached for the bunch of brilliant flowers he'd gathered in the vicinity during his short morning stroll. When he presented the flowers to Savanna, it became quite clear that something within him had changed drastically. She gladly accepted Tom's heartwarming presentation.

"Thanks for the brilliant flowers, Tom," Savanna said gleefully. "They've brought cheerfulness and joy to my heart."

"You're welcome, my fair lady," Tom said bashfully. His smile extended from cheek to cheek while he watched Savanna admiring the brilliant flowers.

The new lovers exchanged love and a warm embrace while the morning sunlight cast its rays around the bench. Savanna continually wiped fresh tears that flooded her eyes. The tears flooding her eyes were no longer tears of wanting to go back home or for the wedding she'd missed. They were tears of love and ardent passion that had begun to burn within her heart for Tom. She had no doubt that passionate love had also taken hold of Tom's heart.

Amidst their exchange of a warm embrace, Savanna suddenly became aware that Tom's stomach was running on empty. She promptly excused herself from his presence and headed indoors. To maintain a close attachment to his new love, Tom followed close by her side. Savanna later took her place by Tom's side as they sat to dine on a savory midday lunch. At the end of their short lunch session, Savanna commenced her afternoon chore of preparing the evening meal. Tom, being a creature of habit, retreated to the first hall to take his customary Saturday afternoon rest.

The evening sunset quickly brought an end to Savanna's chores for the day. Another warm autumn day made its way into history. Just as the dusk began to cover the mountain, Savanna sat with Tom for their Saturday evening meal. She'd anticipated a dialogue spiced with the flavors of love and passion. In her attempt at creating an atmosphere conducive to the anticipated dialogue, Savanna prepared tea made from aromatic mint she'd cut from the garden.

Beneath the faint glow of the small lantern suspended from the ceiling, Savanna took her usual place in the first hall. She waited for any gesture to take a seat by Tom's side, but he'd chosen to sit on his bench alone. He'd not extended his invitation to her to join him on his bench. While they sipped tea in silence, a gusty autumn breeze rustled the leaves of the trees and whispered through the crevices of the log house. The stage was set for an evening of love and shared passion, but Tom lapsed into a mode of silence, as if he'd had a famine for words. As the night progressed, however, he continually played hide-and-seek with his radiant smiles and tantalizing glances of love.

Savanna did not take the initiative to spark up a conversation; instead, the ball was left in Tom's court. From her place on the bench, Savanna thought about Tom's sudden silence. She wondered whether the tide had turned on their love affair. Amidst his prompt silence, she'd become fearful that he would lapse into a state of regression. Savanna pondered Tom's earlier display of love and affection toward her. Did something go wrong? Why did Tom portray a sudden change in his behavior toward her? Savanna asked herself these questions for which there weren't immediate answers. She'd become broadsided by that which she'd been fearing the most—Tom withdrawing his love.

The atmosphere had gotten quiet and eerie when, without warning, Tom excused himself and retreated to his room. Savanna was left in dire straits. She quickly extinguished the flame from the lantern and promptly retreated to her room. As many young lovers do, Savanna wept in the quietness of her room. Her thoughts became inundated with many questions. If Tom no longer loved her as his soul mate, would he revert to regarding her only through the eyes of motherhood?

From her quiet room, Savanna pondered Tom's welfare and their future lives in the house. What if he still loved her romantically? Savanna began to perceive that Tom had just been going through the motions, having a dearth for words to further express his love for her. She therefore maintained high hopes that their love and courtship would be once more revived.

Many thoughts lingered in her mind as the night progressed. She remained overwhelmed by Tom's expressed love and affection for her.

What if he asked her to marry him? What if Tom offered to take her back down the mountain to her parents? Would he be regarded with disdain, or would he be welcomed and loved? Savanna became preoccupied with these questions, but she'd overlooked the issue of presenting a kidnapper to her parents. She'd further overlooked the fact that Harry had been waiting for her to take their marriage vows.

While her thoughts remained focused on love and marriage, Savanna's eyes were set on the elegant dresses and the adorable shoes she'd seen in the large room. She further reflected on the gold ring that was a perfect fit for her finger. Should Tom marry her, she felt there would be no need for a veil to cover her face. There would be no one else present to see her face, just her adorable bridegroom, Tom.

The still quietness of the Saturday night allowed Savanna a greater opportunity to focus on her dilemma. Should Tom really ask her to marry him, a reverend would be warranted to conduct the marriage ceremony. There ought to be a reverend present to implore upon them the blessings, joy, and happiness implored upon all newlyweds during their marriage ceremony. With the absence of a reverend, Savanna felt she and Tom could say their "I dos" to each other on the bench for two beneath the branches of the trees. Should she become Tom's wife, a son would be vital for the survival of his species. By giving birth to a son, she would be perpetuating the name of the Brentkham family, which had once lived as a dynasty.

The still dark night lingered. Savanna continued to dream dreams of her new life with Tom. She anticipated bearing her new name, Mrs. Savanna Brentkham. As part of a new married couple, she anticipated the love and affection in the embrace of her new soul mate. Savanna anxiously awaited the moment when two lovers are locked away in a secluded log house on a rugged mountainside, loving and caring for each other in their romantic environment. Her mind became overwhelmed with thoughts of love, kisses, and warm embraces when sleep quietly swept her away.

Beneath the warm, crisp sunlight, Tom had taken his habitual Sunday morning short stroll around the vicinity. Since he fell in love with Savanna, life had taken a dramatic turn on the mountain. For the first time, Savanna prepared and served breakfast on the bench for two beneath the overhanging branches of the trees. As Savanna waited for Tom, she was overcome by a feeling of uncertainty. Would he shun her generous hospitality by refusing to eat in the outdoor setting? Would he take his seat by her side as he did the morning prior? She was sadly reminded of Tom's actions during the night.

Tom returned from his short stroll to find his Sunday breakfast waiting on the bench in the outdoors. His new love had also been patiently awaiting his arrival. Tom's face was aglow with pleasant smiles as he presented a beautiful bouquet of brilliant flowers to Savanna. She gladly reached for the flowers but not before becoming the recipient of his longest kiss and a warm embrace. Savanna's heart was overwhelmed with joy and appreciation. Most of all, her ardent prayers had been answered—Tom had not withdrawn his love.

Without further hesitation, Tom tenderly held his adorable lady by her hand and gently placed her by his side on the bench. They savored the delectably delicious breakfast on the lover's bench beneath the swaying branches of the trees. The faint peal of the church bell could be heard in the distance below. The young lovers remained on the bench, where they exchanged dialogues, kisses, and warm embraces in the glow of the brilliant morning sunlight. Tom had become the only one for whom Savanna's heart yearned. It appeared that Tom's love had climaxed when he once more lapsed into silence, as if his actions had spoken much more than his words.

The sun had been quietly making its way toward the mid-sky when the lovers retreated indoors to resume their Sunday routine. There hadn't been a doubt in Savanna's mind that Tom was still in love with her, and while her heart yearned for his love and warm embrace, there hadn't been a doubt in her mind that love was kindling in Tom's heart.

Savanna remained occupied, preparing the Sunday evening dinner. Tom always enjoyed the fine delicacies she prepared. He often hunted for game, rabbits, and frogs, which he carefully prepared for his special meals. On his secret trips to the spring at the foot of the mountain, Tom habitually caught shrimps, which Savanna prepared for the evening meal. For his Sunday evening meal, Savanna had delightfully prepared frog's legs as a fine delicacy.

The savory Sunday evening meal was served on the bench beneath the glow of a brilliant afternoon sun. A soothing autumn breeze rustled the leaves of the overhanging trees, creating a serene atmosphere for the dinner session. To spice up the dinner session, Savanna promptly sparked up a conversation. The after-dinner dialogue continued as she served cold tea in the ambience of the outdoor atmosphere.

The golden sun slowly sank over the horizon. Dusk quickly enveloped the mountain. The fear of wild creatures and likely human predators rendered the outdoors unsafe and hence, non-conducive to their dialogue. Tom therefore promptly retreated indoors, his hand gently placed around the waist of his new love.

Tom entered the first hall, where he sat in a placid atmosphere. Savanna prepared fresh tea, which she brought into the hall. She promptly replenished Tom's mug with fresh tea and placed it in his hand. There was a sense of calm as Savanna sat on her bench in an atmosphere of uncertainty. Would Tom revert to silence, as he'd done the night prior?

Her thoughts were abruptly interrupted when he spoke softly—"Come over, my angel. Sit by my side."

Savanna's heart overflowed with delight. She promptly took her seat by Tom's side as they sipped tea in the still silence of the hall. The atmosphere was once more set for another evening of dialogue. Whatever turn the dialogue would take, Savanna waited with an open mind.

Tom was softly prodding her arms while his eyes surveyed the hall. It wasn't long before he began to speak. "Savanna, your eyes are bright and beautiful," he said in a soft voice. "Your hair is beautiful and soothing to the touch."

Savanna was fully aware that her hair hadn't been kept up to the grooming and styling standard she'd once maintained back home. While she remained in the mountain confines, she'd given it her best attention. Nonetheless, she gladly accepted Tom's compliments he'd bestowed on her.

"Thanks for the kind compliments," Savanna said.

"You're welcome, my angel," Tom said. He continually smoothed her hair with his long and calloused fingers.

The night was slowly progressing. Savanna remained cuddled by Tom's side. She'd never felt true love in that manner, not with Bentley, her first love, or with Harry, her former future husband. Tom had become mesmerized by the reality of having a companion and a beautiful young lady in his presence. The calm and quiet atmosphere had set the pace for love and a warm embrace; and dialogue that began to flood Tom's mind.

"Savanna, you're the sunlight that brightens my day," Tom said with a look of assurance and sincerity. He pressed her warm body closer to his side.

In Savanna's mind, it was a dream becoming reality. She happily cherished the warm and tender embrace she'd always hoped to receive from Tom. "Your loving embrace has kept me warm, Tom," Savanna said. "I'm delightfully intrigued by your warm affection."

She became overwhelmed by Tom's looks of love each time their eyes met. She no longer perceived him as the shy young adult in need of a mother's tender loving care. Tom was admiring her with love and passion in his heart.

At his tender age of twenty-two, Tom had finally emanated his love and passion toward the beautiful young lady he'd once perceived through the eyes of motherhood. Like a sly fox waiting to devour its prey, Tom took advantage of every opportunity to embrace his young love. Likewise, Savanna waited for every precious moment when Tom made a gesture of love and expressed his need of her warm embrace. As the night advanced, the lovers sat by each other's side, exchanging words of love and bashful glances.

CHAPTER 21

Adventurous Journey Down The Mountain

The faint sounds of the flowing streams in the spring were barely audible from the log house. The sound of the spring at the foot of the mountain was a constant reminder of the distance Savanna had been from her home. She estimated a distance of approximately two miles up the mountainside. Throughout her most frightful days and her darkest nights in captivity, the faint sound of the gently flowing spring in the valley had brought her serenity and calmed her fears.

Whenever the weather was conducive to taking a refreshing bath, the spring was the place where the village folk around the mountain spent their time of relaxation. The cool and soothing crystal waters of the spring were inviting to both human and mammals. Tom habitually spent time bathing in the crystal waters cascading from tall rocks on the mountainside. By his own admission, whenever he felt safe from the watchful eye of anyone who might venture downstream, he took a plunge into the soothing waters of the spring at the foot of the mountain. Tom had perfected the skill of venturing down the mountain and taking a quick bath without detection. He'd also fished for shrimps and small fish before safely making his way back up the mountain.

Darkness swiftly shrouded the mountain as Savanna remained cuddled by Tom's side. As ardent love burned in his heart, he'd no doubt been driven by strong desires to be closer to his new love. At the spur of the moment, Tom thought of the joyous pleasures he could have, frolicking in the spring with Savanna by his side. Without further hesitation, he'd succumbed to his wild imagination when he extended his cordial invitation to Savanna.

"Sav," Tom said in a rather seductive voice, "can you still hear the spring at the foot of the mountain?"

Savanna noticed his wild looks of suspicion. She did not question Tom's motive for directing her attention to the spring in the valley before promptly responding, "Yes, Tom. I'm joyously intrigued listening to the solacing sound of the spring in the valley. It reminds me of my days back home when I bathed in the crystal streams with my siblings."

Tom listened with keen interest. His first question had been weighing heavily on Savanna's mind when he posed his next intriguing question. "Will you come with me to the spring tomorrow? Please, Sav?" Tom said beseechingly.

Without giving further thought to Tom's offer, Savanna responded in the affirmative. "I'll be delighted to bathe in the spring with you, Tom."

Tom's eyes sparkled with delight. His joyous smile extended from cheek to cheek. At Tom's invitation to venture down the mountain to the spring, Savanna's heart danced with glee. Her eyes glowed beneath the flickering flame of the lantern suspended from the ceiling. She cherished the occasion when she and Tom would further ignite their passion toward each other while they frolicked in the crystal waters.

"When will you take me to the spring, Tom?" Savanna asked.

"Tomorrow, before the sun throws its hot rays over the mountain, we'll commence our journey," Tom said with added assurance of his intention to venture down the mountain with Savanna.

Their dialogue continued in the quiet Sunday night atmosphere. The clock on the wall had been swiftly ticking toward midnight when their conversation ended abruptly. Tom excused himself and retreated to his room—but not before planting a kiss on Savanna's cheek.

"Good night, my adorable lady," Tom said.

"Good night, my love," Savanna said. She admired Tom's large physique as he made swift strides toward his room.

There was no one else remaining in the hall but Savanna and her mind-boggling thoughts and imagination. She therefore promptly retreated to her room. In the quietness of her room, Savanna reminisced on her past days of love and affection in Tom's warm embrace. She envisioned her new world with two lovers in it—she and Tom.

The Sunday night atmosphere was serene and conducive to sound sleep, but sleep had failed to appear. Savanna's heart kindled with ardent love and affection toward Tom. Their love for each other was growing with great intensity as each moment passed. Tom continually approached her with that tantalizing look of love in his eyes. Savanna was mesmerized by his eyes, which sparkled with genuine love. After all, she'd spent the past eleven months nurturing Tom into adulthood. Each day, her heart yearned to be perceived as a young lady in need of his romantic love. His love had finally sparked beyond the motherly love he'd once perceived in her.

Amidst her moments of bliss, Savanna waited for the dawn of the day she would bathe in the spring with her new love. For the first time since she was kidnapped and taken away from her home, Savanna anticipated venturing down the mountainside. Her moments of anxiety and the myriad of overwhelming thoughts came to an abrupt end when sleep finally launched her into a state of semi-consciousness.

It was unlike any other Monday morning. Savanna was awakened to the enchanting and melodious chirps as the birds frolicked among the surrounding tree branches. In her mind, the birds were chirping their cheerful songs in an atmosphere that had been charged with love—the love that kindled in her heart for Tom.

Savanna carefully scrutinized a beautiful dress hanging on a cord in the large room. She felt confident that it would make a perfect substitute swimwear. She immediately changed into the dress. Savanna pulled on her shoes that she'd worn up the mountain on the day she was kidnapped. In anticipation of his adventurous journey down the mountain, Tom had promptly left his room at the crack of dawn. It was one of those rare nights when his footsteps were not heard in the house in the dead of night.

Savanna promptly prepared and served breakfast, which they ate in a rush. Beneath the warm glow of the Monday morning sunlight, Tom led the way as the adventurous journey began down the rough and rugged mountainside. Savanna anticipated impeding rocks and treacherous paths. However, with Tom by her side, she had no doubt that they would safely reach the spring at the foot of the mountain.

Savanna's spirit soared to new heights as the long and treacherous journey progressed. Meanwhile, Tom's strides were swift and sure as he held her firmly in his grasp. He'd been silently following a path among huge rocks, tangled withes, and thick bush until the journey ended on the bank of the spring.

Savanna was delighted to once more see its crystal waters and set her feet in the bubbling streams. The enchanting waters, coupled with the exuberant sounds in the atmosphere, were inviting to her as she took her first plunge. Tom could not resist the temptation to immerse himself in the bubbling waters with Savanna. He therefore followed suit and plunged in beside her. Like playing children, they frolicked in the flowing streams.

Their love and passion had climaxed when Tom reached out to her with his warm embrace. Savanna had forever waited for that moment when she would become lost in Tom's love and warm affection. It was a wish becoming reality when she felt Tom's smooth body snuggled against hers. She was mesmerized by the gentle touch of his rough and wet hands against her skin. Amidst soft giggles and serenades in the refreshing streams, the young lovers had no thought about their tomorrows.

Their most romantic moment, however, was suddenly interrupted when voices were heard downstream. Tom listened with great intensity. He'd begun to fear the worse as the voices became more audible. He quickly drew Savanna closer to his side.

"Tom, we must hide from whatever is heading upstream," Savanna said in a whisper.

In an instant, the sound became more overwhelming.

"Let's get out of here," Tom said.

Tom made a quick dash into the nearby woods, holding Savanna firmly in his grasp. How lucky they felt to have escaped whoever was heading toward them!

Tom commenced his treacherous climb up the mountain, desperately clinging to Savanna's hand. As the climb progressed, Savanna vividly recalled the traumatic moments of her kidnapping eleven months prior. It appeared that her memory had faded as she climbed up the mountain, clinging to Tom's body. The grueling journey of climbs, slips, and tumbles ended in the log house, where they both collapsed on the log floor.

Meanwhile, two hikers on their adventure trail along the banks of the spring, were quite certain they'd seen two mermaids. The men had become fearful after hearing a loud splash in the spring and seeing two images quickly vanish from their sight.

"Did you see that?" one hiker asked in astonishment.

"What was that?" the other asked.

"Quiet! Seems like two mermaids."

The hikers took off running in the direction from which they'd come. They were escaping from what they'd perceived as an ominous apparition. Legend had it that, whoever encountered a mermaid, would be plagued by an evil omen. The hikers wouldn't soon forget their encounter with the strange creatures in the spring and the imminent omens that awaited them.

Word of a sighting of mermaids in the spring began to spread among the folk around the mountain. The hikers had reported their sighting of two beautiful mermaids who'd quickly vanished in thin air. Whether they'd disappeared beneath the spring bed or into the deep woods, they'd simply vanished from sight. No one was prepared to have a sighting of a mermaid, fearing the consequences. The word mermaid, however, sparked curiosity among the folk. The hikers' report of their sighting of the mermaids in the spring had set the folk on high alert.

The older folk around the mountain listened to the mermaid tales with much skepticism. They'd read about mermaids in fiction novels, but the tales of a sighting of living mermaids in the spring didn't tickle their fancy. In the minds of the older folk, mermaids were legendary creatures. Tales of mermaids were designed to fascinate young minds. The older folk therefore saw the report as fictitious. They were therefore careful to maintain their separation of fact and fiction. The young folk nonetheless, believed that mermaids exist as living creatures that were half human and half fish. They'd therefore vowed to hide by the banks of the spring to catch a glimpse of a mermaid, should any emerge from below the spring bed.

Meanwhile, back on the mountain, Tom was revived after his strenuous climb up the mountainside with his companion. In the quiet splendor of that sunny afternoon, he sat on the bench beneath the trees. Savanna sat cuddled by his side in a most relaxed mood. She continually passed her fingers gently over Tom's large hairy hands. In his state of shock, Savanna's hands were heavenly to the touch. He therefore reciprocated as he pleasurably smoothed her hands. For the first time since attaining adulthood, Tom began to feel love emanating from a beautiful young lady. In his mind, he felt it was the best day of the rest of his life.

During their session of loving and exchanging passions, neither resonated their thoughts about the incident in the spring. That moment appeared to have been obliterated from their minds. However, Savanna's memory of her passionate moments with Tom in the spring remained indelibly in her mind. To entertain his addiction to his mountain adventures, Tom abruptly ended his caressing session. He promptly excused himself from Savanna's grasp and wandered off into the woods. At Tom's departure, Savanna promptly reentered the house. She commenced her usual chore of preparing the evening meal.

Just as the sun commenced its journey toward the horizon, Tom returned from his outdoor errand. It was quite out of character for him to return home before sunset. At his early return, Savanna promptly placed dinner on the table. The dinner session ended shortly after it had started. Tom's sudden change in demeanor raised many questions in Savanna's mind. Her answers came immediately when he exited through the rear door and beckoned for her to follow. Savanna promptly followed at his request.

They soon arrived at the rear of the house. Tom promptly took his place on the bench beneath the trees. He gestured for Savanna to take her place by his side. The crisp afternoon sun created an atmosphere that was conducive to their rest and relaxation. The moment of silence was finally broken when Tom sparked up his impromptu conversation.

"Savanna, I love you," Tom said with sincerity in his voice.

Tears flowed profusely from Savanna's eyes as he drew her closer to his side. "I love you too, Tom," Savanna said. There was a sudden famine for words to express her love.

As tears began to flow down her face, Tom rested her head on his broad chest. They sat beneath the shade, shedding tears of joy on each other's shoulders.

"Promise that you'll never leave me, Sav," Tom said. "I too promise that I'll never leave you. Never."

"I promise. Tom, I promise. I'll never leave you," Savanna said in earnestness as she wiped her flowing tears.

The evening breeze gently rustled the leaves of the overhanging tree branches while they exchanged kisses, amidst quick glances of love and warm embraces. Tom's kisses ignited flames of love in her heart. Savanna felt that her wildest dreams had become reality. Tom's genuine love for her had sprung forth. Their engagement in love and affection had made them oblivious of the dusk that had swiftly settled around the mountain.

Savanna had always been leery of being in the outdoors after sunset. She therefore aroused Tom's awareness of the surroundings, hoping he would retreat indoors. "Tom," she said, "it's getting dark. We must seek the safety of the house."

Tom held firmly to Savanna's hand as they promptly retreated indoors. He lit the lantern suspended from the ceiling of the first hall. Beneath the faint glow of the lantern, Tom placed a kiss on Savanna's cheek. He gently sat her down on his bench.

"Sit beside me, my damsel," Tom whispered.

Savanna gladly accepted his cordial invitation and sat comfortably by his side. In the ambience of the tranquil atmosphere, their dialogue continued amidst a warm embrace. The young lovers sat silently in the comfort of the hall as if they were anticipating their future lives together. Savanna had had frequent dreams of being in Tom's arms and being caressed by his long hairy hands. She'd always felt that each passing day and night had been taking her further away from realizing her dream. When she felt the warmth of Tom's embrace, she suddenly realized that her dreams did come true.

Savanna remained cuddled by Tom's side. She'd also developed an addiction to cuddling up with him in the outdoors, whether the venue was on the bench beneath the trees or in the spring at the foot of the mountain. She'd been reminiscing on their moment of bliss in the enticing waters of the spring and therefore waited in anticipation of their next visit, which had no doubt, promised more thrills. Would Tom say yes if she asked to be taken back to the spring? Savanna had her doubts but felt she had to give it a try.

"Tom," she said in her plainest language, "when will you take me back to the spring?"

Savanna realized that she'd interrupted Tom's deep and overpowering thoughts, when he quickly lapsed into his normal state of consciousness.

"What did you say, my love?" Tom asked. Savanna was quite eager to repeat her question, if it meant forcing him into compliance. "Will you take me back to the spring?" Savanna had become up close and direct the second time around.

"We'll return to the spring some other day when the weather is as perfect as it had been today," Tom said.

Savanna noticed the mesmerizing smile on his face. "Why can't it be tomorrow? Please, Tom?" Savanna had learned just how to have her way and get whatever she wished from her enthusiastic lover.

As she waited, Tom's face lit up with his broadest smile of approval. "We'll return to the spring tomorrow, my fine lady," he said.

With a cheerful heart overwhelmed with excitement, Savanna planted a kiss on Tom's clean-shaven cheek. "I love you, Tom. You're my greatest hero," Savanna said with that usual glow of love in her eyes.

"I love you too, Sav," Tom said.

In the quiet atmosphere of the hall, he shuffled his body closer to hers. Unbeknownst to Savanna, Tom had been slowly developing an addiction to frolicking in the enchanting waters with her in his warm embrace. There was no doubt that his memory of the earlier incident in the spring had been short-lived. Savanna had not taken the time to question Tom's quick escape at the sound of men's voices. Why did he not wish to be seen or greeted by the men who were approaching them while they bathed? Savanna pondered the fact that she too had no intention of meeting the men and had therefore sought cover by making her escape with Tom.

Love is blind. It also asks no questions. The love within Savanna's heart therefore left no room for questions as she anticipated her next visit to the spring. Likewise, Tom's ardent love for Savanna had obliterated his memory of the earlier incident at the foot of the mountain. The young lovers were therefore gleefully making preparations to return to the spring. The night was still new when Tom impulsively rose from his bench. He planted a kiss on Savanna's cheek before walking toward the second hall.

"I love you, Sav," Tom said as he retreated to his room.

"Good night, Tom. I love you too," Savanna said. She watched as Tom's feet pounded the hardwood floor.

Savanna had become overwhelmed by Tom's expression of love for her. As the moments passed, her heart yearned for more of his love and warm embrace. She perceived his abundance of kisses as an encore to solidify his genuine love for her. After Tom had unexpectedly exited the hall, Savanna had no reason to remain alone. She therefore retreated to her room. In the quiet atmosphere, she reminisced on her past days filled with pleasant surprises.

Throughout the night, her heart yearned for another moment of Tom's warm embrace in the refreshing waters of the spring. Most of all, she waited in great anticipation of another adventurous walk by his side down the mountain paths. During her most anxious moments, the long-awaited sleep had taken hold of her. Anxiety had afforded her only a series of shallow sleep while the night progressed. It appeared that the dawn had been taking forever to arrive, but Savanna kept her vigil.

At the chirping of the first bird, she rose out of bed and promptly commenced her morning chores. It was another morning when, to her great surprise, Tom had not exited the house in the still hours of the night. He also had not left at the crack of dawn on his daily outdoor errand. In an instant, Savanna prepared and placed breakfast on the table.

"Tom," she said, "your breakfast is ready."

She heard quick and bold footsteps as Tom made his way into the hall. To her great astonishment, he was dressed and ready for their spring adventure. Tom had been diligent in keeping his promise to take her for another adventurous trip down the mountain.

"Good morning, Sav." Tom gave his delightful greeting as he took his place at the breakfast table.

"Good morning, Tom." Savanna greeted him with her usual broad smile.

"Did you sleep well, Sav?" Tom asked with that brilliant glow on his face.

"I slept quite well, Tom. Thanks for asking," Savanna said. There hadn't been a doubt in her mind that Tom had slept well. He'd remained indoor throughout the night.

Without further ado, the breakfast session was in progress. Tom promptly ate his portion before leaving the table. Savanna followed suit. She stood in the first hall, ready for her next adventure down the mountain. The warm sunlight cast its glow around the mountain as the adventurers commenced their journey in great exhilaration and cheerfulness.

With Tom pioneering the journey, Savanna walked in confidence by his side. As she'd perceived, the journey down the mountain took less time and appeared less hazardous. It was a joyous and exhilarating moment when Savanna plunged into the bubbling and enticing waters of the spring. Amidst hugs and kisses, she frolicked with Tom in the soothing water. Savanna was once more reliving her dreams of being caressed and held in Tom's warm embrace.

While she remained snuggled by Tom's side, their hugs and kisses were sadly interrupted when men's voices were heard on the opposite side of the spring. The approaching voices quickly captured Tom's attention and sparked his curiosity. He looked across the opposite bank of the spring and noticed two men making their way among the thick bushes. Savanna remained hesitant, not wanting to interrupt her ecstatic moment in the spring. As the men drew closer to the opposite bank of the spring, Tom felt that their approach was too close for comfort. He took Savanna by her hand and immediately scrambled out of the spring.

"They're coming, Sav," Tom whispered.

When he made a mad dash into the nearby woods, Savanna had no choice but to follow his lead. Tom moved up the mountainside at lightning speed, holding Savanna's hand firmly in his grasp. They made their way up the rugged mountainside and soon reached the log house. Tom immediately collapsed on the floor, where he remained to recover from exhaustion and fright. Savanna remained by his side, gasping for breath.

Savanna had fled back into the mountain with Tom, but she questioned his actions. Why did he escape? Why could he not have greeted the men? These were questions for which she would soon find answers. Savanna had not perceived Tom's likely dilemma and had therefore failed to understand his reason for avoiding detection by the men walking in the woods. Tom had also avoided detection the day prior when he heard voices downstream. Savanna's memory was short-lived. She'd overlooked her own dilemma of being a kidnapped victim held by Tom in his mountain sanctuary. Meanwhile, she'd had more concerns about her thrills that ended much too soon. She had been less concerned with Tom evading detection by the men.

On that warm and sunny Tuesday, just before the noon hour, two woodcutters of Amerhurst were on their routine search for the perfect tree that would make furniture for the folk in Bragerston. Suddenly, an object caught the keen eye of one of the men.

"Oh, heavens," he whispered. "Look down there, Kearens."

There was a strange sighting that sparked their curiosity. The men were appalled when they saw a girl bathing in the spring while she cuddled by the side of a young man.

Kearens was particularly concerned about the young girl he'd seen. "Garreth," Kearens whispered, "it's the Sevensen girl who has been missing for several months."

The woodcutters cautiously drew closer in an attempt to make acquaintance with the fierce and frightened young folk. No sooner had the woodcutters gotten closer than the man quickly escaped into the woods, with the girl clinging to his hand. The woodcutters had no difficulty differentiating a human from a mermaid. Legendary mermaids were said to disappear beneath the surface of deep waters, but the girl and her companion whom they'd spotted, had taken off running into the mountain forest. Kearens therefore immediately identified the girl as Savanna, the girl for whom the villagers had searched over many months. The woodcutters were not in any way perturbed by the young folk's escape. Kearens was quite certain he'd seen someone the semblance of Savanna, the missing Sevensen girl.

"Garreth, there's no doubt the girl is Savanna," Kearens said. "Her hair is slightly longer. She seems a bit taller than when last I saw her; and just as beautiful. That's the Sevensen girl for sure."

Garreth was not too familiar with Savanna. He therefore couldn't attest to her sighting. "Have you seen that young man before? He appeared to be a stranger to the village," Garreth said.

Kearens also agreed that the man they'd seen with the girl was a stranger to Amerhurst. "I've spent my entire life in Amerhurst and have never set my eyes upon that big fellow."

The men were overcome by fright, but they endeavored to organize a search into the dense woods where the young folk had escaped. They immediately left their woodcutting task and headed toward the Sevensen home. The woodcutters arrived at the Sevensen home, breathless and somewhat disoriented. They immediately collapsed to the ground. Isaack and Melvia stood frozen, waiting for the bad news that had come knocking at their door, but it was to the contrary.

Kearens had been gasping for air, but he immediately broke the news of his sure sighting of Savanna. "Come!" Kearens said.

"We've spotted Savanna in the spring. We're quite certain it's your daughter Savanna," the men spoke in unison while they continuously gasped for breath.

The woodcutters' report rekindled new hope in the hearts of the Sevensens as well as the concerned folk around the mountain. They endeavored to do whatever they could to verify the woodcutters' report and bring Savanna home.

Meanwhile, on the mountain, Tom was revived from his traumatic encounter in the spring. He did not venture outdoors on his usual errand around the mountainside after the ordeal. He instead sat on the bench beneath the trees, cuddled by Savanna's side. In Savanna's thoughts, Tom was making the most of his new life with her as he basked in the comfort of the log bench beneath the tree.

At the end of their eventful day, Savanna served up the evening's meal of roast bird and vegetables. She served the meal on the bench beneath the trees. The dinner session was complemented by the warm and gentle breeze that constantly rustled the leaves of the surrounding tree branches. As the sun disappeared over the horizon, Tom retreated indoors with his charming lady by his side. In her quest for love and affection, Savanna sat snuggled up by his side on the bench in the first hall. It was dialogue as usual over their mugs of aromatic tea. They remained in perfect harmony, exchanging words of love for each other as the night progressed.

After their thrills in the spring had been unexpectedly interrupted, neither brought up further suggestions of making another adventurous journey down the mountain. Nor did they discuss the events that had taken place in the spring. Tom remained on his bench, deep in thought and with a demeanor that suggested he'd been shaken by the earlier incident in the spring.

Dusk had quickly engulfed the mountain. Savanna sat by Tom's side, in anticipation of the night's continued dialogue. She'd saved the questions she hoped would give her a closer look into Tom's secret world, but it appeared that he was overcome by fatigue and had lain sprawled on the hard bench. Savanna had sat poised to commence the evening dialogue when Tom promptly excused himself from the hall and retreated to his room.

With nothing else to occupy her time, Savanna retreated to her room for her night of rest. In the dead of night, she heard Tom's usual scurrying throughout the house. Whether he exited to the outdoors during the night, Savanna was unaware of such an occurrence. She'd succumbed to fatigue from her climb up the mountainside and therefore had a good night's sleep.

CHAPTER 22

Savanna Found

The Wednesday morning atmosphere around the mountain was charged with brilliant sunlight. A gentle breeze swayed the branches of the surrounding trees. Savanna anticipated having breakfast with Tom at their usual outdoor venue. She awoke to find Tom in his room, sprawled out on his bed. It was quite unusual for him not to be roaming around the mountainside, particularly at the crack of dawn. Savanna felt he'd taken the day off from his usual mountain chores.

With Tom remaining in the house, Savanna spent her time attending to his every need. She prepared breakfast, which they ate at their usual outdoor venue. At the end of the breakfast session, Tom promptly returned indoors. He sat on his bench in the first hall, while Savanna commenced her usual house chores. At the spur of the moment, she suddenly realized that she'd turned twenty-one. Eleven months had been added to her life while in the confines of the log house. Savanna carried out her chores while she perceived a happy future with Tom.

Meanwhile, in Amerhurst, news of a definite sighting of Savanna by the woodcutters began to spread like wildfire. A number of anxious volunteers joined the concerned woodcutters. They took to the mountain on foot, as far as they could have ventured up the mountainside. The woodcutters had vowed to do whatever they could to find the young folk who'd escaped into the mountain forest. Rugged terrain, coupled with the hot Tuesday afternoon sun, impeded their progress. The search party soon realized that walking up the mountainside was not child's play. They therefore abandoned their search effort—a great setback for the Sevensen household.

Word of a possible sighting of Savanna had reignited hope that she would be found alive. Hope, however, began to fade when the search up the mountainside was called off. The folk of Amerhurst began to have vivid recollections of the report given by the sole eyewitness. He'd reported the early morning incident of a young man who had been carried down the mountain by the town authorities. Piece by piece, the details of that incident more than two years prior, began to jog the memory of the concerned folk. The eyewitness's report reaffirmed the folk's belief that there was human existence on the mountain, hence the likelihood that Savanna was held in its peak.

Amidst panic and frenzy in the Sevensen household, Isaack rushed into Bragerston to alert the officials of a possible sighting of his daughter and the fact that she'd escaped up the mountain with a young man. The town officials quickly organized a search team, equipped with K-9s, to conduct a search of the mountain.

Under the warm Wednesday morning sun, a brigade of officers with their sharp-sniffing rescue dogs, converged on Amerhurst. The woodcutters led the officers up the mountain. They carefully pointed out the direction in which the girl and her companion had escaped. Being heavily equipped with their ammunition and four sharp-sniffing K-9s, the officers scaled the rugged mountain paths. Not knowing what they were approaching, they were poised for combat.

It wasn't long before the log house was spotted high on the mountainside. Documents held by the officers confirmed that it was the house from which they'd removed two strangled victims and their offspring less than three years prior. Documents also revealed that the convicted son of the strangled victims had been released from prison, his whereabouts unknown.

The search team immediately surrounded the log house, where they strongly believed the villain and his victim were hiding. The officers quickly pried open the front door. They first let the K-9s loose before cautiously entering the house. Two officers noticed a young woman making her escape through the rear door. She was immediately restrained and held in the custody of one of the officers. Kearens, one of the determined woodcutters, immediately identified the woman as Savanna, the missing Sevensen girl. The young woman wrestled to free herself from the officers' firm grip, but she fell to the ground as fear gripped her heart.

"Madam, what's your name?" one officer said.

When the woman remained reluctant to speak, the officers stepped up their interrogation.

"Tell us your name, madam! We won't hurt you," another officer said.

With a fierce look in her eyes, the young woman whispered, "My name is . . . Savanna." As the woman gave her name, tears cascaded down her face.

In his effort to positively identify her, the officer further asked, "What's your family name, madam?"

With much hesitation, the young woman responded, "Sevensen." Savanna wept profusely after reluctantly revealing her identity to the officer. She remained in custody while the search continued for other occupants of the house.

The jubilant woodcutters watched as Savanna was held in custody by the officers. They felt strongly that their mission had been accomplished. The girl they'd spotted in the spring was, in fact, Savanna. With weapons drawn, the other two officers, along with their sniffing K-9s, cautiously entered each room in the house. Their thorough search had not turned up another occupant. However, when the K-9s commenced their frantic climbs and continuous barks toward the ceiling of one of the rooms, there was no doubt that they were on to something. The officers remained on high alert as the dogs barked frantically, signaling that there was another occupant in the house.

Amidst the frantic climbing and barking of the K-9s, one officer shouted toward the ceiling, "*Is someone up there?*"

There was a slight shuffle, but no one responded. The K-9s continued their frantic barking and pouncing against the wall of that particular compartment in the house. The officers waited, but their patience was wearing thin.

"We know someone is up there. Come down now!" another officer said.

Another shuffle was heard until a large figure of a man made a loud thud onto the thick wooden floor. The vigilant dogs jumped gleefully as they set eyes on the man who'd been hiding in the ceiling of the room. Without incidence, the tall and sturdy young man was immediately taken into custody. He remained trembling on the floor, heavily guarded by the K-9s, while the officers commenced their thorough investigation. Their first task was to identify the young man. One officer therefore began his interrogation.

"Sir, what's your name?" the officer asked.

The man maintained his silence. He looked fiercely at the waiting officer. Being suspicious of the man attempting an escape, the K-9s stood guard around him.

"Tell us your name," another officer said.

Fearing a likely punishment, without further hesitation, a course voice spoke. "My name is Tomas Brentkham, sir," he responded bluntly.

The young man knew quite well that he was identified by the officers surrounding him. He also identified one of the officers from his first running with the law. The tensed and shivering young man remained in custody. He was subsequently removed from the room and placed in the rear of the house, close to his companion. The K-9s, along with two officers, kept their vigil around the detainees, observing their every move.

Meanwhile, two officers commenced their thorough search of the contents of the log house. Their search commenced above the ceiling, where the man had been hiding. It was determined to be a secret hideout built in the house. Savanna had no knowledge of its existence, although she'd thoroughly scrutinized the house. The officers' search of the hideout in the ceiling of the room came up empty. They did not uncover any items of interest or any other occupant. The house had been closely scrutinized when the officers stumbled upon documents in the old canvas bag. Piece by piece, they began to unravel the mystery of the log house and its past and present occupants.

Among the bundles of documents in the canvas bag were four birth certificates. The birth certificates as well as newspaper clippings found in the bag, revealed the true identity of the strangled couple the officers had previously removed from the log house. Hornett Brentkham was positively authenticated as Sgt. Defenbum Kenkorry, the fugitive who was the subject of a worldwide manhunt. His wife, Kalister Brentkham, was, in fact, Dafariena Kenkorry. Tomas Brentkham and his sibling, Caroleena Brentkham, were also authenticated as Christopher Kenkorry and Graciena Kenkorry, offspring of the deceased couple.

Among the artifacts discovered in the canvas bag were war badges and trophies that further confirmed the identity of the fugitive, Sgt. Defenbum Kenkorry. There were war badges containing the names of soldiers who'd been missing in battle. Further searches of the log house turned up more newspaper clippings and a trail of other evidence linking Sgt. Defenbum Kenkorry to war crimes against humanity while in his country of origin.

The officers unraveled the mysteries surrounding the solitary confinement of the fugitive's son to the log house. His reason for kidnapping and detaining the Sevensen girl also became clear to the investigating officers. Evidence found also solved the mystery of Tomas Brentkham's sibling, who'd been kept under surveillance in the refugee camp. The young female who'd identified herself as Caroleena Brentkham was, in fact, Graciena Kenkorry, offspring of Sgt. Defenbum Kenkorry, the wanted fugitive. The investigating officers collected the important documents and all other relevant evidence before setting fire to the structure.

It was an emotional moment when Savanna was being led down the mountain in the custody of the officers. Tears of grief flooded her eyes when she looked back at the thick smoke towering through the roof of the log house. All her dreams became a nightmare. The bright future she'd envisioned with Tom, her new lover, was going up in flames. Her tender heart grieved, not for leaving the log house and seeing it go up in flames but for her separation from Tom, the new love of her life.

A similar grief struck Tom's heart when he saw thick smoke towering through the roof of the log house. He watched in awe as his mountain sanctuary became engulfed in flames. As he stared at the inferno, Tom fought desperately to free himself from the strong hold of the officers. Did he have secret treasures hidden away in the house? Whatever items he may have hidden or the sentiments he'd had for his father's log house, were being consumed by the fire.

The sun was making its way toward the mid-sky as the officers made their way down the mountain. Their two captives were securely guarded by the keen K-9s. While Savanna was being led down the rugged mountain terrain to her freedom, Tomas had commenced his journey back to prison. In his heart, he knew there wouldn't be another lenient prison sentence. His heinous crimes of kidnapping and forcible confinement demanded punishment to the fullest extent of the law. As the officers escorted Savanna and her kidnapper down the mountain, the jubilant woodcutters took the lead. They rolled and tumbled ahead, bearing the news that Savanna had been found.

The officers carefully escorted Savanna and her kidnapper down the mountain and were making their way to the Sevensen home. The entire household shed tears of joy as the officers drew closer. In the minds of the elated folk, it was news that was too good to be true. Anxious folk joined with the Sevensen household to celebrate a resounding victory. The emotionally charged crowd converged on the Sevensen estate, drawn together by the sheer sense that the girl who'd once been presumed dead was alive and presumably well.

Even Spicer and Rex were barking their acclaim at the sight of the one they'd not seen and had missed for such a long time. When the officers placed Tomas in front of the Sevensen gate, there was a clash of emotions between Spicer and Rex and the vigilant K-9s. Spicer and Rex were securely locked away during the ensuing events. Tomas remained guarded by the side of the officers and the fierce K-9s. Meanwhile, his eagle eyes made constant piercing looks at those gathered before him.

The press of the crowd caused a frenzy amidst jubilation in front of the Sevensen gate. All eyes were focused on the kidnapper while he was securely held in the custody of the officers. He looked ferociously at the elated crowd. In a fit of anger, Tomas's face puffed up as if every ounce of blood had rushed to his head. Each time he made eye contact with the folk in the crowd, he cast a jeering smile. Some onlookers were amusingly smiling back, while others regarded him with disdain and vengeance in their hearts.

The sun had passed its midpoint in the sky. The anxious crowd awaited further details about Tomas Brentkham, the kidnapper. Melvia and Isaack as well as their elated offspring, maintained their constant stare at the villain who'd kidnapped Savanna. Savanna was quickly removed from the officers' vehicle, heavily guarded by the fierce K-9s. Great joy erupted as she was escorted toward Melvia and Isaack, her grandparents, and her jubilant siblings. All were exuberant with sounds of cheer and gleeful spirits.

Under the brilliant Wednesday afternoon sun, Savanna walked into the ecstatic crowd. It was a carnival-like atmosphere when she walked toward the gate leading to her home. She was once more reunited with her parents and her elated siblings. Their patience was wearing thin while they gathered in front of the gate to greet their once-lost sibling. Isaack and Melvia, Savanna's once-grieving parents, let out sighs of relief at the sight of their adorable daughter. Providence had answered the prayers and hopes of the Sevensen household. Savanna had been found alive.

Savanna's siblings reached forward and touched her face. They felt her hands to prove she was very much alive. Melvia and Isaack looked into her beautiful eyes. They'd hoped to see her beautiful smile, the way she'd smiled before her disappearance. The feeling of being released and coming back home, one would imagine, should have overwhelmed her heart. Her thought of coming back home should have ignited a sense of warm reunion with those she loved dearly, but her smile was not forthcoming.

There was no doubt that she'd lost that heartfelt yearning to reunite with her loved ones whom she'd left behind. Nonetheless, Melvia and

Isaack as well as the remaining offspring had clung to a thin ray of hope that someday, Savanna would return home alive and unscathed. Their dreams had finally become reality. Concerned folk stared at the girl who'd been missing for close to a year and had been presumed dead. Their sight of the once-lost girl hadn't quite tied in with reality. As Savanna stood before her parents and her overwhelmed siblings, the reality of her safe return had stricken hard.

Amidst cheers and songs of praise, the jubilant crowd thronged Savanna. Each waited to extend a welcome and a warm embrace. Anxious folk waited with wide-open arms for an opportunity to bestow upon her, their best wishes. The folk continually let out sighs of relief. Their vigilance, particularly the vigilance of the woodcutters, had paid off—the once lost girl had been found, safe and sound.

Harry had taken time from school to welcome his bride-to-be back home. At his first sight of Savanna, there were complacent smiles between them. Amidst the jubilation, Harry pressed against the thronging crowd to welcome Savanna with wide-open arms. To his dismay, she'd quickly shunned his embrace. Instead, she returned his welcome with a suppressed smile. As the celebration took on momentum, Harry remained on the sidelines.

Beneath the glow of the brilliant afternoon sun, the officers positioned themselves in front of the jubilant crowd. They stood poised to commence their briefing on the capture of the kidnapper and the release of his victim. Tomas Brentkham, the kidnapper, continually cast quick glances toward Savanna. He was no doubt, fully aware that he would soon sever ties with her. Meanwhile, Savanna repeatedly cast looks of love toward him as new tears trickled down her cheeks. She;d been making every effort to maintain a measure of composure while she regarded the elated crowd with mixed emotions.

At the commencement of the briefing session, one officer stepped forward to address the waiting folk. There was a sudden stillness never before seen or heard in Amerhurst. Even the autumn breeze had ceased from shuffling the leaves of the nearby trees. The atmosphere was suddenly hushed as the officer commenced his briefing to the overjoyed Sevensen family and the waiting crowd.

"We, the officers of the town of Bragerston, wish to inform Mr. Isaack and Mrs. Melvia Sevensen that Tomas Brentkham is the said Christopher Kenkorry, son of the fugitive Sgt. Defenbum Kenkorry."

The crowd remained hushed while the officer took a deep breath. Melvia clung firmly to Isaack's shoulders as she waited for further statements from the officer.

"On September 23, approximately three years prior, Christopher Kenkorry, who'd assumed the name Tomas Brentkham, was found guilty of the strangulation of his parents, whose names he'd given as Hornett and Kalister Brentkham. Christopher Kenkorry had also pled guilty to the attempted strangulation of his sibling, Caroleena Brentkham, whose legitimate name is Graciena Kenkorry, offspring of the deceased fugitive and his wife."

As the officer spoke, the crowd maintained total silence but stood with wide-open mouths. Isaack continually wiped the tears flowing down Melvia's cheeks. The Sevensen offspring remained dumbstruck as they looked at the face of Christopher Kenkorry with disdain. The name Caroleena resonated well in Savanna's mind, but she waited for further details of the young sibling Tom had repeatedly spoken of during his conversations.

Amidst mean gestures and frequent stares at Christopher, the officer continued to address the crowd. "I hereby further report that, it was the young sibling of Christopher Kenkorry who'd escaped with her life at the time of Christopher's heinous acts of strangling his parents. Graciena Kenkorryhad made her quick escape from the log house. She arrived in Bragerston in the early morning to report to the authorities, the tyranny that had taken place in the log house in the dead of night," the reporting officer further read. "May it be further known that, Hornett Brentkham is the long-sought fugitive, Sgt. Defenbum Kenkorry. Kenkorry was strangled along with his wife, Dafariena, by no other than his son, Christopher Kenkorry, the kidnapper standing before you."

Savanna looked at Christopher with tears in her eyes, not necessarily for his crimes that were being revealed but the realization that she would soon be separated from him.

Christopher maintained his innocence of any wrongdoing and therefore waited for the opportunity to once more express it. The officer's briefing session was promptly interrupted when Christopher yelled loudly to the astonished crowd, "I did not do it! I did not strangle my parents! I strangled animals, not humans! I strangled the wolves that attacked me, not my parents!" He wrestled to escape the strong hold of the officers but quickly maintained his stay when the four K-9s growled at his feet. Christopher was promptly quieted as the officer continued to address the now furious crowd.

At the officer's revelation, Melvia and Isaack sought comfort by weeping on each other's shoulders. The curious folk in the crowd remained hushed as the facts surrounding the kidnapping were being revealed. It appeared that the sun had withheld its brilliant glow from the skies of Amerhurst while the officers continued to read Christopher's crimes.

Meanwhile, Savanna appeared unfazed, portraying no element of surprise or fear, but glanced repeatedly at Christopher. Her glances were met with his amiable smiles and a demeanor that suggested that she'd been tricked. Savanna finally unraveled the secrets of the birth certificates. Christopher continued to toss glances of guilt that could only be interpreted as, "I should have told you."

Silence was once more resumed when the officer continued his briefing.

"I wish to further inform the family of the kidnapped young lady of the following important facts." The officer paused for a quick breath. "For their crimes committed against humanity, Sgt. Defenbum Kenkorry and his accomplices were being herded up in Korenith, their country of origin. The sergeant had escaped from the cutody of the authorities. He'd subsequently evaded recapture by fleeing from his country of origin. Sergeant Kenkorry's escape had resulted in a worldwide manhunt that, ironically, ended on Deadman's Mountain."

Isaack and Melvia wept persistently on each other's shoulders, while they clung to their beautiful daughter. Savanna's siblings surrounded their grieving parents to offer whatever support they could, while they too, shed tears of joy. Melvia and Isaack remained mindful of the fragile health of their parents. The older folk were therefore kept subdued and placed under close scrutiny for any signs of being stricken by their heart condition.

The officer continued to provide details necessary to justify the arrest and other actions taken to bring Christopher Kenkorry into custody. "We, the officers of the town of Bragerston, wish to further inform Mr. and Mrs. Sevensen of the following additional facts. Psychiatric examinations conducted by the town's health authorities revealed that, Christopher Kenkorry is an avid sleepwalker; one who drifts off into the outdoors in the dead of night, while he's asleep. Christopher is prone to commit heinous crimes while he sleeps, hence, his acts of strangling his parents while they slept and while he was walking in his sleep."

The officer made a brief pause when Christopher began to force his way toward the podium. He was promptly restrained by the swift K-9s.

"As a result of his prevailing condition, Christopher had received a lighter prison sentence for the strangulation of his parents and his attempted strangulation of his sibling, Graciena. Christopher Kenkorry does not only pose a threat to himself while he sleeps. He poses a dangerous threat to those around him."

At the officer's reading of this statement, Savanna once more stared into the eagle-like eyes of Christopher. They both quickly exchanged glances, amidst silent gestures of love, Christopher gazing at her with that freaky smile in his demeanor. Savanna had finally solved the mystery of Christopher's frequent scurrying throughout the house in the dead of night. She further discovered his reason for exiting the house through the rear door when he should have been sleeping. He'd been walking in his sleep.

After her thorough scrutiny of the contents of the canvas bag, Savanna had not connected Hornett Brentkham, Tom's father, to the real fugitive, Sgt. Defenbum Kenkorry. She was therefore unaware that she'd been held captive by the son of a notorious fugitive. Further, she'd been held captive by a sleepwalker who'd posed danger to her while she slept. Nonetheless, her ardent love for Christopher overshadowed all her fears and concerns. She perceived love and not the danger from being in a log house with an alleged murderer and a dangerous sleepwalker.

Christopher remained alert and fully attentive while the officer released further details of his fugitive father, Sgt. Defenbum Kenkorry. Christopher also listened attentively to the details provided by the officer about his endangerment to himself and others around him, as a result of his sleepwalking condition.

The officer continued his briefing to the Sevensen household as well as the astonished crowd. "For this cause, Mr. and Mrs. Sevensen, ladies and gentlemen, Christopher Kenkorry, previously living under the assumed name Tomas Brentkham, was sentenced to five years in the town's prison facilities. Notwithstanding the court's sentence of five years of imprisonment, Christopher Kenkorry was eligible for and had been granted parole after serving a bit shy of two years of his prison sentence. Be assured that for his crime of kidnapping and forcible confinement of Savanna Sevensen, Christopher will be imprisoned for a long time."

At the end of the officer's statement, Savanna's eyes were flooded with fresh tears.

"Furthermore," the officer continued, "the log house on the mountain was burnt to the ground, thus providing no further incentive for Christopher to return to his sanctuary. Mr. and Mrs. Sevensen, ladies and gentlemen, I've presented to you the facts of the mountain kidnapper and his parents, particularly his fugitive father. I now hereby end my report." The officer ended his briefing to the stunned crowd.

Before the officers made their departure, Savanna was asked to address the crowd, particularly Melvia and Isaack and her waiting siblings. It was pertinent that she related her version of the kidnapping ordeal. There was a sudden hush as Savanna stood before Melvia and Isaack and the anxious crowd to relate the details of her kidnapping. As she spoke, the officers noted her every detail.

There were tears of sadness as Savanna recalled the day she was forcibly removed from her quiet nook by the bank of the spring. She related the details of her capture and the life she'd lived while in captivity. In her heart, Savanna had given a plausible account of her kidnapping and subsequent confinement by her kidnapper, the then Tom Brentkham. When she related the details of falling in love with her kidnapper, her tears had quickly dissipated. As Savanna addressed the hushed crowd, she didn't show indelible scars from her alleged wrestles with her attacker as he had forced her up the rugged mountain. While she spoke, neither the officers nor the listening crowd detected signs of emotional trauma. The crowd listened with much skepticism and therefore remained with an element of doubt and suspicion.

Melvia and Isaack did not perceive their daughter's story as horrifying and overwhelming. The siblings had their doubts as to whether she had been kidnapped or she'd intentionally stowed away with a stranger. There was a fine line between being kidnapped and being in total consent. In the minds of the folk of Amerhurst, the question lingered—was Savanna running away from Harry? This was a topic the Sevensen household would certainly explore when the "runaway bride" debate would continue.

Christopher remained in the custody of the officers, surrounded by the fierce K-9s. He continually looked steadfastly at the fine lady who'd played a vital role in his young life. As Savanna spoke, he'd tried to reach out to her in every way he could but was continually restrained by the officers and further threatened by the surrounding K-9s.

Savanna's details of her capture and the long journey up the treacherous mountainside had created a changed atmosphere. As the facts of her disappearance were revealed, Harry listened with keen interest. He was no longer suspected as the jealous young man who'd allegedly lured his bride-to-be to her death and had carefully covered up the evidence. As the crowd looked into the eyes of the kidnapper, Harry was duly exonerated. The dark cloud of suspicion that hung over his head during the ordeal, had suddenly given way to a clear blue sky.

Melvia and Isaack, surrounded by their elated offspring, were more concerned about the safe return of Savanna, not about a fugitive or his son, who'd strangled him. They were privileged to stare at the face of the villain who'd taken their daughter away. Most of all, the Sevensens were in a gleeful spirit as they held Savanna in their firm grasp. The officers were making preparations for their journey back to the town of Bragerston. The K-9s were put in place to escort Christopher to the vehicle when a sudden uproar caught everyone by surprise.

Christopher suddenly shouted beyond the capacity of his lungs, *"Where is my sister, Graciena?"* He stared furiously at the officers and at the stunned crowd.

This prompted the officers to sort through their documents for more details, which were further read to the overwhelmed crowd.

"In the interest of Christopher Kenkorry, Graciena Kenkorry was taken to the refugee camp in Bragerston. She has been kept under close surveillance since the strangulation of her parents," one officer read. "Further, while the sibling of the accused had identified herself as Caroleena Brentkham, documents found in the log house have revealed her true identity. Graciena Kenkorry is, in fact, the other offspring of fugitive Sgt. Defenbum Kenkorry. Now that her identity has been revealed, the authorities will determine her fate."

Christopher's demeanor suggested that he was quite satisfied, knowing that Caroleena was still alive and had been securely held by the authorities. At the end of the officer's statement, Savanna gave a surprising stare at Christopher before uttering an audible sigh. She was relieved that the mystery of his missing sibling, Caroleena, was finally resolved. The officers completed their additional briefing to the crowd. They'd obtained the details of Savanna's kidnapping as she'd related to them. It was time to proceed to the waiting vehicle with Christopher. The officers soon discovered that he was not prepared to be led away without a fight.

"Please let me go!" Christopher shouted in defiance. "Savanna! I will not leave her here alone!"

Amidst his altercations with the officers and the pouncing K-9s, Christopher made quick glances behind himself as he was forcibly pulled along by the officers. Savanna returned his glances with her charming smiles. As she watched Christopher being led away, she took off running toward him. She glared as one in great fury. The officers as well as her worried parents, made every effort to restrain her, but she wrestled in defiance.

"Please let me go!" Savanna screamed. She tossed her slim body to the ground while clinging firmly to Christopher's chained feet. "Tom! Please don't leave me here alone!" she cried.

Amidst Savanna's pleas and cascading tears, Christopher was forcefully placed inside the waiting vehicle, hand-cuffed and bound at his ankles by a thick chain. Melvia and Isaack let out a series of deep sighs. The couple made a sigh of relief as they watched the kidnapper being placed into the waiting vehicle, the officers as well as the K-9s guarding his every move.

Savanna continually tossed herself to the ground as one in a drunken stupor. "Tom! Tom!" she cried. "Please don't leave me! Please, Officers, don't take my love away!" She wept bitter tears while pleading with the restraining officers.

In desperation, Savanna ran toward the locked vehicle but was forcefully apprehended by Isaack and Melvia as well as her concerned siblings. The curious onlookers watched in disbelief. Isaack and Melvia and the frightened siblings stood in awe as they pondered the behavior of Savanna. The girl who was allegedly kidnapped, had become inseparable from her kidnapper. The restraining hands of the officers kept the loud barking K-9s at bay as they stood guard around the locked vehicle with the kidnapper inside. Christopher peered through the meshed window as fresh tears flowed from his eyes.

Prior to commencing their journey to Bragerston, the chief officer presented documents to Isaack and Melvia. The documents contained protocols outlining Christopher Kenkorry's arrest and the requirement for Savanna to appear in court during his trial. After carefully reading the guidelines, Isaack and Melvia promptly signed on the dotted lines. The couple returned the documents to the waiting officer.

In front of the cheering crowd, the officers and their K-9s climbed aboard the waiting vehicle. Savanna consistently waved to Christopher. He frantically turned his head to see her as the vehicle moved slowly away from the Sevensen gate. At the vehicle's departure, Savanna wept profusely. She wrestled to free herself from the folk's restraining hold.

"Let me go," she said. "I must follow my lover. I cannot part with him."

Amidst her constant screams and struggles, Savanna was further restrained by Harry and Melvia, who'd maintained a firm grasp on her arms. Isaack joined the ensuing struggle to impede Savanna's attempt at following the vehicle.

"Savanna," Isaack said, "we've searched everywhere for you. Now that we've found you, please don't leave us again."

"We love you, Sav," Melvia and Isaack spoke in unison.

In their attempt at preventing her escape, Savanna's worried siblings formed a human fence around her. Savanna soon realized she could no longer resist the strong hold of those who'd been preventing her from making her getaway.

At the revelation of the facts surrounding fugitive Sgt. Defenbum Kenkorry, the crowd was left with mixed reactions. No one in Amerhurst had ever heard of Sgt. Defenbum Kenkorry, a fugitive who'd been the subject of a worldwide manhunt. Further, in the minds of the public, the circumstances surrounding the deaths of Sgt. Defenbum Kenkorry and his wife, Dafariena Kenkorry, had not been thoroughly investigated. The question therefore lingered in the minds of the folk as to whether the couple had been strangled by their son, Christopher, or by someone else on the mountain.

In all likelihood, Christopher may have committed the crimes he persistently denied; however, the folk perceived the injustice under which he was tried and convicted. His guilty verdict was based solely on evidence found in the house and evidence given by Graciena. Christopher had not been given the opportunity to be represented by a counsel, who would have acted in his defense. The crimes could have been committed by warriors living in the mountain peak. Some folk from Sergeant Kenkorry's country of Korenith could have learned of his whereabouts and may have climbed up the mountain to strangle him under the cover of darkness. Although Christopher had been found guilty of the strangulation of his parents and had served time for the crimes, the precise circumstances surrounding their deaths remained shrouded in mystery.

News of the strangulation of Sergeant Kenkorry and his wife was further met with mixed reactions. Did he deserve what he'd received, allegedly at the hands of his son, as a justification for his murderous acts? It all depended on the opinion of the folk. Some felt Sergeant

Kenkorry was innocent of his crimes against humanity until proven guilty. Therefore, without a trial to determine his guilt, the prison sentence that had been looming may not have been justified.

The majority of the folk felt strongly that, as a recompense for the civilians whose lives had been cut short at the hands of Sgt. Defenbum Kenkorry, justice was served at the hands of his son. His day of reckoning had finally come. At the officers' departure from Amerhurst, Savanna was thronged by the exuberant crowd of anxious folk pressing to be closest to her, each waiting to shower her with hugs and kisses. Melvia and Isaack remained tearful as they began to scrutinize their beloved daughter. In the eyes of her siblings, Savanna's eleven months in captivity had tarnished her appearance in more ways than one. She'd returned home wearing garments designed for an older woman, causing her to lose her once elegant looks and graceful charm.

Savanna became inundated with cheers from the thronging crowd, but she was held under close scrutiny and faced a barrage of questions. Curious minds among the crowd pondered the fact that she'd been kept in captivity with her male kidnapper and hadn't become pregnant. The crowd carefully scrutinized her from head to stomach. Everyone regarded her with the resonating question: Did she have a baby? The questions triggered a series of whispers and suspicious glances from the thronging crowd.

"There she is! The poor girl!" a voice rang out from the crowd.

"Did you have a baby?" another asked.

Savanna remained somewhat unperturbed by the questions triggered by curiosity.

Gorrana, one of Savanna's younger siblings, further ignited the flames of curiosity when she outrightly asked the question, "Savanna, did you have a baby? Are you pregnant?"

Savanna also remained under the close scrutiny of the curious crowd while the flames of curiosity were being fanned everywhere. News of Savanna's safe return home had finally reached Harry's parents. Upon hearing the good news, Addriana and Henry were on their way to Amerhurst. The "welcome home" celebration had been in full swing when the crowd was alerted to the sound of galloping horses heading toward the Sevensen home. Everyone remained on high alert. Individuals sought cover from a likely mishap.

The horses came galloping at high speed toward the Sevensen gate. The Lovethons arrived in their horse-drawn carriage. The horses had barely stopped when the couple jumped from the carriage, landing on their hands and feet. The two fatigued horses lay sprawled on their sides while the carriage tilted on one side. So fatigued were the horses upon their arrival that they were taken immediately to cool shade. The horses once more collapsed beneath the branches of a cluster of trees.

Henry and Addriana Lovethon, Harry's parents, quickly joined the celebration of the safe return of their future daughter-in-law. The couple, however, had much more on their mind. They'd come to express gratitude that their son had been finally cleared of the alleged crimes of kidnapping and murdering his future wife. Addriana remained vigilant in the crowd. She was bent on making her voice heard, also clearing her son's name.

"We knew our son, Harry, was innocent," Addriana said, her voice resounding among the cheering crowd. "My son, Harry, is not a murderer."

Henry stood by Addriana's side, letting out silent sighs of relief that Savanna had been found. He repeatedly nodded in attestation of his wife's words of assurance and her litany of words of gratitude that Harry had been cleared of all the accusations brought against him. Meanwhile, Harry stood at the rear of the crowd, letting out silent sighs of relief as well. Savanna's safe return home had finally cleared the air of suspicion and mounting allegations against him.

Addriana and Henry could once more sigh deeply in relief. The mystery of the missing Sevensen girl had been finally solved. Their son had been cleared of all the allegations against him. The couple once more proudly stood as the wealthy and noble folk whose son was about to marry the beautiful Sevensen daughter. Deep within their hearts, Addriana and Henry waited in great anticipation of their son marrying the beautiful Sevensen girl. Amidst deep thoughts and well wishes for their son, Addriana and Henry climbed into their carriage. The limping horses walked off, taking the couple back to their distant home.

The "welcome home" celebration continued into the late evening hours. The celebration was further heightened when the woodcutters were brought to the center of the crowd. For their bravery and their role in the discovery of Savanna, the men were showered with praises. To commemorate the return of Savanna, the folk around the mountain erected a monument at the Sevensen gate. The monument bore the name of the woodcutters and related their acts of bravery that led the officers to the log house in which Savanna had been held.

In the eyes and minds of the folk who'd gathered to celebrate Savanna's safe return, it became clear that Harry had not played a role in her disappearance. Harry was therefore deluged with apologies and kind words from folk in the crowd as well as Melvia and her gratified offspring. There were tons of apologies directed at Harry by the embarrassed Sevensen household, in whatever way their apologies could have been expressed. Amidst tears of joy, coupled with tears of embarrassment, Melvia stepped forward to greet Harry. She'd been reeling from the guilt of her persistent accusation of him being the one who'd kidnapped and murdered Savanna.

Isaack gracefully embraced Harry with that genuine look of "I didn't think you were guilty" in his demeanor. Without resonating or portraying their gestures of apology, Savanna's joyous siblings thronged her like a mob. Each expressed delight in having her back home. Most of all, they began to wait in earnest hope for Harry to reunite with Savanna so that the wedding could proceed.

As dusk approached, the jubilant folk returned home with a feeling of accomplishment. They'd all played a role in bringing Savanna home. Savanna's safe return became the talk around Amerhurst and neighboring places. Her return home was joyous news to Cecelia and Kladius, who'd been disadvantaged by their distance from home while the family searched for their lost sibling.

For the first time in eleven months, Savanna entered her home through the main door. Amidst her expressed love and warm embraces, she kissed Melvia and Isaack, who couldn't have imagined that she'd return home unscathed. One by one, she cuddled and kissed her siblings, who'd gathered around her. Her elated grandparents were overcome with joy to once more see her alive and well, as they'd perceived.

Savanna immediately perceived the difficulties she faced in returning to the realities of life. In the eyes of her parents and her overwhelmed siblings, she was incredibly resilient and could therefore resume her active life. She faced the difficult task of regaining the love and trust of her students. Her fellow teachers' hearts had been yearning to have her back at school.

Meanwhile, Harry had been waiting to embrace and shower his bride-to-be with kisses. Savanna, however, had difficulty portraying the image of the loving and romantic soul mate she once was. Instead of the warm embrace Harry had been waiting to receive from her, his love was met with disdain and resentment.

Would Savanna rekindle the love that had once welled up in her heart for Harry? Both families had placed considerable wealth on the table to finance their offspring's lavish wedding. They were therefore, showering heaven with ardent prayers that the wedding would proceed.

CHAPTER 23

The Kidnapper's Day in Court

A new day had dawned in the Sevensen household since Savanna returned home. Life was gradually returning to normal. The early autumn days buzzed with activities in Amerhurst, particularly around the Sevensen estate. The celebration of Savanna's safe return continued, amidst wide speculation about her reunion with Harry. The day of Christopher Kenkorry's court trial had arrived. Melvia and Isaack had no direct role to play in the trial; nonetheless, it was a legal requirement that they present Savanna to the court, she being the key witness to her own kidnapping and forcible confinement.

Under the warm October morning sun, Melvia and Isaack boarded the local bus to Bragerston. They were on their way to court, escorting the key witness. Many of the eager folk in Amerhurst made their way to Bragerston to be present during the court trial. Upon their arrival in Bragerston, Melvia and Isaack promptly presented Savanna to the court officials. The couple had never before entered a courtroom. They were therefore briefed on certain procedures while they waited for the trial to commence.

Eager folk made their way into the packed courtroom. They anxiously waited to once more look at the face of the kidnapper who'd taken the Sevensen girl. Most of all, the anxious folk waited to hear the verdict of the court and the sentence to be brought down by the judge. The court was momentarily brought to order by Justice Coronarer. Savanna was duly brought to the witness bench. Christopher Kenkorry was brought into the courtroom and placed in his holding cell, opposite the witness bench. All eyes popped wide open; ears perked up as those in attendance waited to hear the details of the kidnapping and Savanna's every moment spent in captivity with her alleged kidnapper, Christopher Kenkorry. Justice Coronarer, the presiding judge, waited to hear the horrors of the kidnapping, particularly the details of Savanna's confinement in the log house. He'd therefore commenced his interrogation of her, the key witness.

"Madam Sevensen," Justice Coronarer addressed Savanna, "please state your name and relate the details of your encounter with the accused, Christopher Kenkorry. Specifically, on the Sunday evening of October 4, a year prior, where were you, and how did you meet Mr. Christopher Kenkorry?" The justice waited for Savanna's response.

"Savanna Sevensen," she said. "Your Honor, sir, Tom Brentkham met me in my little nook by the spring while I waited for my then husband-to-be, Harry Lovethon." She stopped abruptly, staring at Christopher while tears flooded her eyes.

Melvia and Isaack sat among the curious crowd. Their ears were perked up like those of hunting foxes.

"Madam Sevensen, please state to the court what transpired on the day you were brutally abused and kidnapped by Christopher Kenkorry," the justice said.

Justice Coronarer waited as Savanna immediately lapsed into deep concentration. Savanna once more commenced relating the details of her encounter with Christopher, while she continually made eye contact with him.

"As I recall, sir . . ." She paused to take a deep breath. "I was seated in the nook while I waited for Harry to arrive. Tom met me in the nook while I waited for Harry." Savanna lapsed into silence, while making eye contact with Christopher.

The justice, along with the anxious audience, waited to hear the gruesome details of the kidnapping; however, Savanna kept her details clean and to the point. She did not provide details that would portray Christopher as the hostile kidnapper she'd previously described to the investigating officers. When Justice Coronarer failed to obtain Savanna's cooperation, he reverted to applying other tactics.

"Madam Sevensen, were you subjected to harsh treatment and physical and sexual abuse while in the confinement of your captor, Christopher Kenkorry?" Justice Coronarer asked.

Savanna once more lapsed into deep concentration. She appeared to have been searching for the right words to speak. "Your Honor," Savanna said, "I have a faint recollection of going up the mountain and entering a quaint log house. However, I have no recollection of physical abuse by Tom Brentkham."

While she spoke, Savanna glanced repeatedly at Tom, who was seated in his holding cell. Their eyes collided as they exchanged jovial smiles and glances of genuine love toward each other.

"Madam Sevensen, please refer to the accused by his legitimate name. His name is Christopher Kenkorry," the justice said. Savanna had not quite gotten comfortable with saying Tom's legitimate name. In the opinion of Justice Coronarer, the case of kidnapping and involuntary confinement could not be confirmed. As a last-ditch effort to continue with the trial of the accused, the justice further interrogated the key witness. "Madam Sevensen, on September 22, you were seen in the spring at the foot of Deadman's Mountain, you and Christopher Kenkorry. Were you in the waters of the spring with the accused?"

Savanna once more exchanged a gleeful smile with Christopher. "I don't recall being down the mountain or in the spring, Your Honor, sir. I also do not recall being with Tom Brentkham, Christopher Kenkorry," Savanna said as she made direct eye contact with Christopher.

In the opinion of Justice Coronarer, it was a futile effort obtaining the facts from a witness who'd been consciously and intentionally protecting the accused. The audience watched with mixed emotions as obvious questions went through their minds. Melvia and Isaack began to have further doubts as to whether Savanna had been taken forcefully by her kidnapper or she was in fact, a runaway bride-to-be.

Justice Coronarer ended his interrogation session with the key witness. It was time to question Christopher Kenkorry, the accused kidnapper.

Christopher stood in his holding cell, chained by his hands and feet. There was a brief stir in the courtroom when he began to wrestle with the guards. He'd been struggling to get close to Savanna while she remained in her witness box. Meanwhile, Savanna fought frantically with the guards as she tried to get closer to Christopher. She continually inched forward, hoping to embrace and kiss her lover, Tom. When all efforts had failed, the lovers exchanged glances of love and a display of deep passion. Christopher was finally subdued by the guards and reprimanded by the justice.

"Sir," Justice Coronarer said. "Please state your name."

Christopher looked in every direction as if he were reluctant to speak his legitimate name. He attempted to leave his holding cell but was restrained by the guards. Christopher adamantly cooperated with the justice's demand.

"My name is . . . Tomas Brentkham, sir," he blurted out to the justice who'd exercised much patience and understanding.

The justice responded in disgust, "Tomas Brentkham is not your legitimate name, sir. Please state your name."

Christopher had still remained faithful to his deceased parents and his sibling, Caroleena, to observe their pledge to secrecy. He'd therefore refused to reveal his true identity.

Justice Coronarer remained persistent as he waited for Christopher to comply with the court's requirement. "Sir, failure to state your legitimate name will result in a longer prison sentence," Justice Coronarer said.

With his hands locked in chains, Christopher held firmly to the sides of the witness stand. In a voice Savanna had never before heard, he blurted, "Christopher Kenkorry, sir!"

The justice sat with a straight face while the audience filled the courtroom with laughter and jeers. Savanna stood with mixed emotions as her lover unwillingly revealed his true identity. Christopher once more, cast a glance of guilt toward her. The tide of doubts and suspicions had quickly subsided. The justice accepted Christopher's blunt response as the trial proceeded.

"Mr. Kenkorry, as you've complied with the court's requirement, the trial will now proceed," the justice said. "The court has been presented with official documents taken from the crime scene on the mountain. The said documents reveal your true identity. While you've falsely identified yourself as Tomas Brentkham, you're no other than Christopher Kenkorry, son of the late Sgt. Defenbum Kenkorry. Christopher Kenkorry will now be tried before the court for kidnapping and forcible confinement."

Christopher stood in silence while he looked fiercely around the courtroom.

"Mr. Kenkorry, as you stand before the court, you're considered innocent until proven guilty of your crimes of kidnapping and the forcible confinement of Miss Savanna Sevensen," Justice Coronarer said.

Christopher took a quick glance across the room at the anxious audience, who kept their ears perked up like transmitting antennas. Christopher stared once more at Savanna with a display of love and passion. She stared directly at him. Their constant stares and exchanges of winks and smiles were no doubt, reminders of their pledge to secrecy.

Justice Coronarer proceeded with his interrogation of the accused. "Mr. Kenkorry, on Sunday afternoon, October 4, a year prior, where were you?" Justice Coronarer said.

Christopher turned his face toward the ceiling as if he needed a boost of his poor memory. He then turned his face toward Savanna, secretly tossing a deceptive smile. "I was down by the spring, sir," Christopher said in an abrupt manner. He had no desire to give due respects and honor to the justice, whether or not he knew how.

"Mr. Kenkorry, what was your intent when you left the log house on the mountain to be by the spring?" the justice asked.

Christopher once more looked toward the ceiling of the courtroom before casting a glance at Savanna. "I went fishing for shrimps, sir," he said.

"Did you see the young lady who is presently standing in the witness box?"

Christopher once more looked toward the witness box as he tossed another deceptive smile at his alleged victim. "I did see that fine young lady and took her home with me," Christopher said.

The audience sighed in disgust. Melvia and Isaack quickly changed their position, shuffling to the edge of their seats. Christopher's response was a far cry from the details Savanna had passionately given to the officers and to the waiting crowd. The officers who'd rescued Savanna from the log house, had presented details of her kidnapping to the court, just as she'd related to them. One of the officers therefore stood poised to present his findings before the court.

"I wish to present to you, Your Honor, the statements made by Miss Savanna Sevensen on the day she was rescued from the mountain," the chief officer said. "Contrary to the information given by the witness and the accused, these are the facts gathered, which I will graphically present to the court."

The audience shuffled themselves on the hardwood benches. The officer put on display before the justice a pictorial illustration of the ransacked nook from which Savanna had been forcefully taken. The officer further read verbatim the detailed account of the incidence of Savanna's kidnapping, as given by her to the four officers and before the welcoming crowd.

"Your Honor, contrary to the statements made in the court by the accused and his victim, evidence left in and around the nook from which Miss Sevensen was taken, suggested otherwise," the chief officer said. "Further, there were signs of a great struggle. Hence, a total ransacked nook was left behind. Christopher Kenkorry, the accused, had not left further clues as to the direction he'd taken when he made his escape with his victim, Miss Sevensen. By Miss Sevensen's own admission, she was, in fact, taken by great force and carried up the mountain by her captor, against her will. Your Honor, this is the end of my report." The officer promptly returned to his bench.

Justice Coronarer briefly left the courtroom to review the evidence presented by the officers. In the absence of the justice, the audience mocked and stared at Christopher while he remained in chains in his holding cell. There was no telling what the audience thought about Savanna as she continually exchanged glances and ludicrous smiles with Christopher.

The court was once more in session. Justice Coronarer had returned with his findings and a verdict. Melvia and Isaack anxiously waited at the edge of their seats. Savanna waited for what she was quite certain would be a "not guilty" verdict.

In his closing arguments and prior to bringing down his verdict, Justice Coronarer had given Christopher Kenkorry's first criminal offence serious consideration. "Mr. Kenkorry, you'd received a lighter sentence for the strangulation deaths of your parents, Defenbum and Dafariena Kenkorry, and your attempted strangulation of your sibling, Graciena Kenkorry," the justice said. "The light sentence you had received, came as a result of your confirmed sleepwalking disorder. In my opinion, Mr. Kenkorry, when you ventured down the mountain under the light of the sun, you were wide awake and in a sound frame of mind. For your crimes of kidnapping and forcible confinement, evidence confirmed that you'd wrestled with Savanna Sevensen in the nook before forcibly taking her up the mountain." Justice Coronarer paused while he shuffled a few pages of Christopher's court file.

As the justice gave his closing argument, Isaack and Melvia held firmly to each other's hands.

"Furthermore, Mr. Kenkorry," the justice continued, "you've collaborated with Miss Sevensen to withhold the truth that would have confirmed your acts of kidnapping and forcible confinement. Nonetheless, the evidence before the court confirmed that a kidnapping of Miss Sevensen had, in fact, occurred."

As Christopher Kenkorry anxiously awaited his fate, he continually bit his lips. His legs shook as one having a spell of convulsion. His eye contact with Savanna had quickly ceased. She'd been weeping buckets as she awaited the fate of her lover. Justice Coronarer had duly made his arguments. The audience once more stood to order as he commenced reading his verdict.

"By the powers vested in me, by the court of Bragerston, I declare you, Christopher Kenkorry, guilty of the crimes of kidnapping and forcible confinement of Miss Savanna Sevensen."

The courtroom was suddenly hushed. The audience stared at Christopher with disdain. At the reading of the verdict, Melvia slumped onto the hardwood bench with a loud thud. She was immediately overcome by a fit of convulsion. Isaack struggled to hold her upright as he wiped the cold sweat cascading down her cheeks. The audience cheerfully applauded the justice's verdict.

"You're a just judge, Justice Coronarer," Isaack said. He stared in the face of Christopher Kenkorry, the villain who'd kidnapped his daughter.

Melvia had been too shaken to speak and therefore remained slumped in her seat. Christopher Kenkorry stood without any sign of emotion after his guilty verdict had been read by Justice Coronarer. With his face held like a flint, he peered at the face of Savanna, his victim. Savanna wept bitter tears while she dropped her face into the palm of her hands. As she'd perceived, her days with Christopher had come to an abrupt end.

Before the sentencing of Christopher Kenkorry, he'd rejected an offer to apologize to the Sevensen family. Melvia had also withdrawn her offer to speak as she repeatedly lapsed into convulsion. The judgment had therefore rested with the justice to punish Christopher Kenkorry to the fullest extent of the law. The audience once more stood to attention as the justice read his sentencing of Christopher Kenkorry.

"Mr. Kenkorry, for your act of kidnapping and the forcible confinement of Miss Savanna Sevensen, you'll be held in the town's prison facilities for twenty years. There'll be no chance of parole during your twenty-year confinement. Mr. Kenkorry, do you have anything to say?" the justice said.

Christopher stood motionless. He looked fiercely across the courtroom, staring into the eyes of Savanna. Without prior warning, Christopher shouted, "No! I have nothing to say! Lock me up in your rotten dungeon!" He struggled to free himself from his shackles but was promptly impeded by the restraining guards.

At the reading of Christopher's sentencing, Melvia collapsed on the hardwood floor as perspiration oozed down her face. Isaack quickly propped her up on the bench to ensure she was alert to hear the full details of Christopher's sentencing. The justice proceeded to finalize his sentencing as Christopher and Savanna wept bitter tears.

"Furthermore, Mr. Kenkorry," the justice continued, "after serving your time in the prison facilities, you'll be sent back to your country of origin, where you'll reunite with your relations." Justice Coronarer had duly brought down his verdict and sentencing of Christopher Kenkorry and hence, rested his case.

Curious members of the audience remained in the courtroom to have a last stare at the kidnapper. Prior to the justice exiting the courtroom, Isaack and Melvia were summoned to a side table for a discussion of further matters. Melvia walked cautiously across the room, supported by Isaack, who'd maintained a small measure of his own dwindling strength. Savanna had also been summoned and brought to the justice's side table for the short session.

Justice Coronarer commenced the session with the matter of the reward for the capture of Sgt. Defenbum Kenkorry, the fugitive. The saga of the mountain fugitive and his son—who'd committed the crimes of murder, attempted murder, and kidnapping—had finally ended, but what of the reward of a million dollars offered to the one who led the authorities to the capture of the fugitive, Sgt. Defenbum Kenkorry?

In the opinion of Justice Coronarer, Christopher Kenkorry had kidnapped Savanna Sevensen and held her in the mountain. Had he not kidnapped her, the secrets hidden in the log house would not have been uncovered. The true identity of the fugitive, Sgt. Defenbum Kenkorry, and his wife, Dafariena Kenkorry, as well as their offspring, Graciena and Christopher Kenkorry, would not have been determined. Christopher's act of kidnapping resulted in the authorities stumbling upon the documents in the log house once occupied by the fugitive. The documents and artifacts revealed the whereabouts of Sgt. Defenbum Kenkorry, the fugitive, bringing an end to the worldwide manhunt. Furthermore, had Savanna not been kidnapped and subsequently made her way down the mountain with her kidnapper, the woodcutters and the officers would not have followed their trail up the mountain to the secret log house.

The justice had thoroughly reviewed and discussed the circumstances leading the authorities to the discovery of the fugitive, Sgt. Defenbum Kenkorry. Justice Coronarer therefore made his decision to apportion the reward of a million dollars equally to Savanna and the woodcutters. The justice further justified his denial of a portion of the reward money to the hikers. Had the hikers reported seeing a girl and a young man escaping into the woods, they would have been entitled to receive a portion of the reward. By reporting their sighting of two mermaids in the spring, the hikers had not set the searchers on the trail to find the girl and her kidnapper. The hikers therefore were not entitled to a share of the reward. With this decision made, the justice rested his case. The reward was therefore apportioned between Savanna and the woodcutters.

The briefing session was officially adjourned. Melvia and Isaack smiled cheerfully as they led Savanna away from the justice's side table. The anxious audience had no doubt that the family had received good news. Christopher Kenkorry was removed from his holding cell and led away, shackled by his hands and his wobbly feet. More fuel was further added to the flames of his mounting grief when Christopher realized that he was on his way back to prison. He knew he would have no chance at freedom anytime soon. His chances of reuniting with the damsel he'd kidnapped and with whom he'd fallen in love, were likely filtered to zilch.

As Christopher was led out of the courtroom, a member in the audience shouted on behalf of the remaining folk, "Justice has come to Amerhurst! Christopher Kenkorry is a prowler, seeking his victims in our community! He's a murderer and a kidnapper! He must rot in jail! There will be no door to the exit while you're asleep! You'll sleepwalk in your prison cell!"

As Justice Coronarer exited the courtroom, the audience rose with a resounding "Amen!"

They left the courtroom feeling that justice had been served to the vicious kidnapper. Melvia and Isaack let out a sigh of relief as they watched the chained convict being led away to prison. Knowing that his next destination would be Korenith, his place of origin, the couple left the court in a most gleeful spirit.

Savanna was overcome by grief. She stormed frantically out of the courtroom in tears, Isaack making every effort to restrain her. Isaack joyously exited the courtroom, holding Melvia and Savanna in his firm grip. In his heart, his family had been compensated for their mounting grief. They were taking home their once lost daughter and a decent reward of half a million dollars.

In the minds of Isaack and Melvia as well as the concerned folk in attendance at the trial, justice had been served. Christopher would never again return to the mountain, unless a twist of faith overturned his guilty verdict. Nor would he return anytime soon to resume his love and courtship of Savanna, his kidnapped victim. In the minds of the elated couple, Savanna's waiting years for Christopher Kenkorry had just begun. In the minds of the officers, Christopher's imprisonment and Savanna's release, were testaments to their commitment to serving civilians. The saga of the discovery of the fugitive, the capture of the kidnapper, and the safe return of the kidnapped victim had ended well.

Meanwhile, in the town of Bragerston, the remains of Sgt. Defenbum Kenkorry and his wife, Dafariena, were buried in the town's public space as Hornett Brentkham and Kalister Brentkham. Their remains were exhumed for positive authentication that would bring closure to the justice system. A positive identification would also bring closure to the thousands of families who'd waited for justice for the loss of their loved ones at the hands of Sgt. Defenbum Kenkorry.

The folk of Grecko Bay, Korenith, felt that the authorities had failed to find the fugitive, Sgt. Defenbum Kenkorry, and bring him to justice. His discovery was made much too late for his trial for crimes against humanity. Nonetheless, in the opinion of the survivors of his victims, upon learning of the sergeant's dilemma on Deadman's Mountain, they felt that justice had been served at the hands of his son, Christopher Kenkorry.

The folk of Amerhurst strongly believed that the authorities had failed to monitor the movements of Christopher when he was released from prison for his crime of strangulation. As a result, Christopher returned to his mountain sanctuary, where he reoffended by kidnapping an innocent resident. Knowledge of Christopher's imprisonment therefore, came as a great relief to the folk of the communities surrounding the mountain. Since the kidnapping ordeal, Deadman's Mountain has gained added notoriety. It resonated as the mountain of startling discoveries, horror stories, and kidnapping that drastically changed the folk's perception of the mountain wilderness.

CHAPTER 24

The Love Saga Continues

The saga of kidnapping and falling in love in the mountain log house, ended in a court trial that sent Christopher Kenkorry back to prison and subsequently, back to Korenith, his place of origin. Melvia and Isaack returned from the court in Bragerston, proudly bringing Savanna back home. Savanna was regarded by the folk around the mountain as the girl who had been freed from her kidnapping ordeal, also the recipient of a half-a-million-dollar reward.

Savanna had spent eleven months adapting to a jungle lifestyle. She'd been removed from her structured mountain living and had to resume her normal way of life back home. As she remained traumatized by her kidnapping ordeal, her parents had the mindset that she'd been profoundly resilient and could once more resume her normal way of life. The household had been mindful of the strong support of her elated grandparents. They'd pledged to continue where they'd left off, giving their sound words of wisdom.

As her siblings keenly observed, Savanna became haunted by visions and thoughts of her ordeal—her kidnapping and the strange life she'd lived in her mountain confinement. The siblings feared her life had been forever changed by an event so diabolic. However, they'd remained hopeful that she could reinvent herself and continue her life of hopes and dreams—certainly not hopes and dreams for her former soul mate and husband-to-be, Harry Lovethon.

As the days came and went, Savanna cried consistently. She continued to dream of someday becoming the loving wife of her kidnapper and lover, Tom Brentkham, but would she ever realize that dream? In the town of Bragerston, Christopher Kenkorry had commenced serving his twenty-year prison sentence. Each day, Savanna waited in unfading hope that he would be freed. She couldn't imagine herself loving anyone else but Christopher. As he waited in earnest hope, Harry couldn't perceive loving anyone else but Savanna.

The love saga therefore continued as Savanna waited for Christopher, while Harry clung to a thin ray of hope that she would rekindle her love for him. Harry remained hopeful that their love would once more reignite and culminate in marriage. He soon, however, realized that Savanna's love remained wedged between the embrace of two lovers: Christopher, the kidnapper from whom she'd been rescued, and Harry, her husband-to-be, with whom she must now reunite.

The big question therefore lingered in the minds of the anxious folk—would Savanna wed Harry Lovethon, son of a noble and wealthy farm lord, or wait in earnest hope for Christopher Kenkorry, a convicted murderer, a kidnapper, the avid sleepwalker who is prone to commit acts of violence in his sleep?

Meanwhile, Addriana and Henry, Harry's parents, had a lot of convincing to do to sway the stagnant mind of their son. True love comes to those who wait, but it seemed that Harry would be waiting in vain. Savanna's love for him had long dissipated in a quiet log house on the mountain.

In the minds of Melvia and Isaack, their offspring, and the grandparents of sound wisdom, Savanna's waiting years for Christopher Kenkorry had just begun. In the eyes of Harry, upon Savanna's return from captivity, she looked more beautiful than he'd ever seen her. Nonetheless, while Harry waited for that first kiss of reunion, he soon realized that he had a difficult task of clearing Savanna's twisted mind and regaining the love lost to Christopher Kenkorry, her kidnapper.

Lightning Source UK Ltd.
Milton Keynes UK
UKHW011852301120
374378UK00012B/1409/J